Praise for
Prev...

D0640194

LONG TIME GONE

"Yes, he's my brother, but [*Long Time Gone*] is a fierce, truthful novel about the way the '60s came to Brooklyn, the wounds inflicted, the scars that never went away. Sometimes appalling, but full of deep human pity."

—Pete Hamill, *Daily News*

"[An] engaging tale . . . compellingly well paced and laced with a moderate dose of sex and violence, as well as threads of psychological probings and revelations that go well beyond the scope of routine whodunit fare."

—*The Boston Globe*

"[A] vivid picture of the sixties . . . hazily remembered."

—*New York* magazine

"[A]s true as an overdose: the sex, the slice-and-dice of Brooklyn street rap, indelible characters. . . . Imagine Scorsese on a Stratocaster and you'll be close. Read the book, and you'll be immersed."

—Peter Coyote, author of *Sleeping Where I Fall*

FORK IN THE ROAD

"When you follow the career of Denis Hamill in his journalism and novels, you see the development of a powerful talent. As far as I know, this is the first time an American writer has dared grapple with an Irish inner city. No one has done it better."

—Frank McCourt, author of *Angela's Ashes* and *'Tis*

"Hamill is a writer of many talents; his characters get up and strut off the page. They are in turn pugnacious, highly sexed, pathetic, mixed up, but never, never at a loss for words."

—*Boston Herald*

"There is never a dull moment in this charming story . . . Hamill has perfectly captured the trill of an Irish brogue, and he loads the plot with remarkable twists, keeping readers in suspense until the final page of this lively, sad, humorous tale."

—*Publishers Weekly*

THROWING 7'S

"No one does New York better than Denis Hamill."

—Robert B. Parker

"It's a sure bet you'll go missing for at least a day after. . . . [you] read the first chapter."

—*Denver Rocky Mountain News*

3 QUARTERS

"3 *Quarters* supplies a full measure of first-rate thrills."

—*People*

"A terrific read—smart and gritty, tough as a Brooklyn cop bar."

—*New York Post*

"Denis Hamill gives New York the justice it deserves. *Three Quarters* is a page-turning life on the dark side of this city as only Denis Hamill can portray it."

—Winstom Groom, author of *Forrest Gump*

HOUSE ON FIRE

"A carefully plotted thriller."

—*Booklist*

Also by Denis Hamill

EMPTY STOCKINGS

A Brooklyn Christmas Tale

DENIS HAMILL

POCKET STAR BOOKS

New York London Toronto Sydney Singapore

This book is a work of fiction. Names, characters, places and inci-
dents are products of the author's imagination or are used ficti-
tiously. Any resemblance to actual events or locales or persons living
or dead is entirely coincidental.

An *Original* Publication of POCKET BOOKS

A Pocket Star Book published by
POCKET BOOKS, a division of Simon & Schuster, Inc.
1230 Avenue of the Americas, New York, NY 10020

Copyright © 2003 by Denis Hamill

All rights reserved, including the right to reproduce
this book or portions thereof in any form whatsoever.
For information address Pocket Books, 1230 Avenue
of the Americas, New York, NY 10020

ISBN: 0-7434-7706-5

First Pocket Books paperback edition November 2003

10 9 8 7 6 5 4 3 2 1

POCKET STAR BOOKS and colophon are trademarks of Simon
& Schuster, Inc.

Cover design by Min Choi; front cover illustration by Ben Perini

Manufactured in the United States of America

For information regarding special discounts for bulk purchases,
please contact Simon & Schuster Special Sales at 1-800-456-6798
or business@simonandschuster.com.

With love to my beautiful sister, Kathleen—
no six brothers ever had a better one.

CONTENTS

ACKNOWLEDGMENTS

I'd like to thank Ben Hammer, Executive Director of the Battle of the North Atlantic Historical Society for his great help on the plight of the U.S. Merchant Marine World War II veterans and for his very helpful notes on an early draft of this novel.

I'd also like to credit the excellent book *Heroes in Dungarees* by John Bunker (Naval Institute Press), chronicling the large and heroic part the merchant marine played in World War II. His information and insights were invaluable to portions of this novel.

And to Warner Bros. for the home video version of the rousing propaganda film *Action in the North Atlantic*, starring Humphrey Bogart, with a screenplay by John Howard Lawson and additional dialogue by A.J. Bezzerides and W.R. Burnett, based on a story by Guy Gilpatric and directed by Lloyd Bacon, the best movie ever made about the merchant marine during WWII.

And thanks to the late, great Jimmy Cannon, one of the best newspaper columnists ever, and for the precious collection of his columns *Nobody Asked Me, But . . . the World of Jimmy Cannon* (Holt, Rinehart Winston, edited by Jack Cannon & Tom Cannon).

I'd also like to thank my daughters, Katie and Nell, who read early drafts and gave their valuable ideas.

And special thanks to my brothers Pete and Joe for their careful notes and ideas.

And for my editor, Mitchell Ivers of Pocket Books, who wanted a Christmas yarn set Brooklyn in 1963 from first mention.

And, as always, thanks to my agent, Esther Newberg, who made it happen.

—DH

PROLOGUE
Election Night, 1960

Tuesday, November 5, 1960

Rory Maguire helped get Jack Kennedy elected president.

The Chairman said so.

On Election Night Rory stood on line with the other young volunteers outside the local John Fitzgerald Kennedy campaign headquarters on Seventh Avenue in Brooklyn, waiting to shake Charlie "the Chairman" Pergola's hand.

The gruff, blocky pol waved his big cigar, buttoned his cashmere coat over his double-breasted, pinstriped suit, and gave a personal thanks to each kid for putting up the final blitz of JFK/LBJ posters and handing out the crucial campaign palm cards. He pressed his trademark Liberty silver dollar into each of their palms as he shook hands.

Charlie Pergola was the boss of the Brooklyn Democratic machine, a fixer who could solve any problem. He fixed everything from traffic tickets to a bank-fraud court case. He marched local kids into West Point or Annapolis, handed out summer jobs like lollypops, and got forever-indebted candidates elected to various offices. Over the years, dozens of politicians—councilmen, state representatives, mayors, governors, congressmen, and U.S. senators—owed him their jobs. Pergola also stocked the local courts and the bureaucracy with loyal Democrats. He ruled over his Brooklyn domain from his brownstone headquarters in the Benjamin Franklin Club on Union Street near Prospect Park.

The Chairman was the most powerful politician in Brooklyn, and today he was in charge of delivering Kings County, the second largest Democratic county in the USA, to John Fitzgerald Kennedy.

And Rory Maguire helped him do it.

Just as the Chairman reached eleven-year-old Rory on line, Rory saw his father, Harry Maguire, strolling along Seventh Avenue in the dim night light of the candy-cane-shaped iron lampposts that boasted the JFK/LBJ posters. He wore his old merchant marine watch cap and knock-around peacoat on his way to the subway. Rory knew his father would be taking a D train to the taxi dispatch office in lower Manhattan to push a Checker cab through the busy election night.

"Hey, big guy," Harry said, stopping and kissing the top of Rory's head.

Rory said hello to his father and introduced him to Charlie Pergola.

"Nice to meet you, Maguire," the Chairman said, staring at the pin on Harry's watch cap, the one with the initials USMM, for United States Merchant Marine.

"My son speaks highly of you," Harry said.

"That's nice. Vote yet?"

"Nah," Harry said.

"On your way to the polls now, then?" the Chairman asked, attempting to pin a JFK/LBJ button on Harry's peacoat. Harry smiled and stopped him.

"No offense," Harry said. "But no thanks."

"You're not a *Republican?*" the Brooklyn boss asked, making it sound like a rare disease.

"No."

The Chairman tried to hand him a voting palm card and said, "Then take this with you to the poll and vote the straight Democratic ticket. . . ."

Again Harry declined.

"Actually, I don't vote," Harry said and Rory felt dread scald through him like a gulp of ammonia. "It only encourages the bums. Besides, if I don't vote no one will ever let me down or break my heart."

"You don't like *JFK?*"

"I like that he served his country," Harry said. "I like the way he tosses a football. But neither one makes me want to vote for him for president. Or the other guy."

Rory saw the Chairman's cobalt eyes fix on the USMM pin on his father's hat.

"Whatever floats your boat," said the Chairman. "*Comrade.*"

Harry leaned close to the Chairman and said just loud enough for Rory to look up and hear, "Give my regards to your son, Charles. We were *comrades* on the same Liberty ship during the war."

Harry zippered Rory's coat to his neck, kissed the top of his head, and kept walking for the subway. Rory would never forget the Chairman's enraged eyes as he watched Harry Maguire walk away. Rory took his Liberty silver dollar and hurried home before the Chairman could say anything more to him.

Smoke drifted on the night wind as bonfires raged on every other block of the predominantly Irish parish of St. Stanislaus.

As Rory approached his tenement he was drawn like a moth to the flames of the giant bonfire on Twelfth Street, where sparks danced loud and bright into the black Brooklyn sky. A brilliant orange glow lit up Seventh Avenue. *It's like the Batlight beaming across Gotham,* Rory thought.

Rory stood on the corner of Seventh Avenue, watching the raging bonfire that was built smack in the middle of the gutter on Twelfth Street, located between two closed-for-the-night garages. No traffic dared come up the block.

"The polls just closed," someone shouted and a cheer rose from the crowd of hundreds while a team of young guys tossed wood and furniture off the roof of the gray garage and their pals on the street built the bonfire higher and broader. They heaved on stripped old sofas, painted wooden doors, forklift pallets, packing crates, broken tables and chairs, dilapidated cribs, bureaus, bassinets, high chairs, newsstands from three local candy stores, Borden's wooden milk boxes, and stacks of old discarded furniture and magazines foraged from the storage wood bins of the tenement cellars.

Rory's eyes opened wide, focusing on the old Red Devil enamel paint blistering and peeling from an old wooden door ripped off the hinges of a tenement. He watched the hungry fire find bundles of scrap lumber that leapt to flame, saw a coffee table sizzle with its three legs in the air like a dying animal. As the fire swirled and climbed the wind shifted and smoke blew down Twelfth Street, clouding Rory's wide eyes.

The acrid smoke stung, but Rory felt like there was something else in the air. Something exciting. Something thrilling. Something special. Something that Rory Maguire was a part of. Something that had never happened before. People on the TV news kept saying this election might be history in the making. He felt like there was something big—bigger than his whole neighborhood—in the wind. The flames seemed to shout this to the whole wide world. There was something scary, powerful, and important about this year's annual rite of Election Night bonfires that Rory never understood until his father explained it to him that morning.

"It's a demonstration of unity," Harry Maguire said.

His father explained that Election Night bonfires were political statements, citizens sending smoke signals to the powerful politicians of Manhattan. Telling them that they had better listen to the little people. Or face their fiery wrath. And so, in Brooklyn, voters saved inflammable bulk trash all year long and gave it to the local street kids on Election Day for the traditional bonfires that Rory's father said were lit to let the powerful people in City Hall across the harbor know that Brooklyn had voted. And when the count was finished Brooklyn and its three million common citizens better get what was coming to them from the city fathers or else they'd remember the snub come next Election Day.

It bothered Rory that his father wasn't here celebrating with the rest of the neighborhood. It bothered him that Harry Maguire didn't vote. Especially for Jack Kennedy. And it bothered him most that the Chairman knew it.

Rory watched the flames reach the second story of the tenements and now the sirens of the fire engines screamed from the nearby Eleventh Street firehouse. The firemen stretched their hoses from the johnny pumps, shooting big arcs of freezing water through the November night while others searched the rooftops for possible flames.

The fire was soon extinguished. The night grew dark and colder. And as the firemen departed a song rose from the hundreds of citizens who had gathered to watch their symbolic bonfire: *"We hate to see you go/ We hate to see you go/ We hope to hell you never come back/ We hate to see you go. . . ."*

And as soon as the firemen were gone a second bonfire ignited on Twelfth Street on the other side of Seventh Avenue. And another on Eleventh Street. Then one on Thirteenth Street. As the firemen ran to extinguish those bonfires, a new one was always built, doused with kerosene and torched on the smoldering remains of the first fire on Twelfth Street, the flames so intense this time that a four-foot-deep crater was always melted into the tar covered street and would require a morning road crew from the Department of Transportation to refill the hole in the gutter.

Then Rory watched the Election Night saloons open. Citizens carried out cardboard containers of tap beer, cheering the flames that once again lit up the Brooklyn night. Rory had never seen the bonfires burn as bright or in such abundance as they did on this Election Night when the Brooklyn Irish voted for John Fitzgerald Kennedy.

Our Jack. One of their own.

At home in his tenement flat Rory's mother, Tara Donovan Maguire, bottle-fed Rory's infant sister, Bridget, as his other sister and two brothers slept. Tara had emigrated from Belfast when she was orphaned at sixteen. And now she sat in front of the black-and-white TV waiting for election results.

"If our Jack wins it'll be like having Finn McCool himself in the White House," she said.

"He's gonna win," Rory said. "God can't ignore the prayers of all us Catholics."

Tara laughed, blessed herself, and said, "Your dinner's in the oven, *grà*."

Rory ate lukewarm beef stew, kissed his mother good night, and climbed into the chilly top rack of the bunk bed he shared with his kid brother Dermot, staring at the cracked plaster of the ceiling. Before he drifted to sleep, Rory heard Walter Cronkite say that the final tally would not come until the next day. Rory listened to his mother mumbling a rosary, asking God to help make John Fitzgerald Kennedy the first Catholic president of the United States of America. If that happened it would also mean that Charlie Pergola would be more powerful than ever before.

But as his mother prayed into the night, all Rory thought about was the Chairman glaring at his father. . . .

PART I

The Day the President Was Shot

1

Friday, *November 22, 1963*

The President Is Dead. School Dismissed.

Rory Maguire thought this must be what it was like to have a death in the family. The only other time he'd ever felt this kind of hollow, awful feeling in his gut was the day last May when his father fell from the Prospect Expressway at work and got hurt bad.

But this was different.

Worse.

He knew for sure that his mother was home crying her eyes out.

Miss Seltzer had been so distraught in typing class after Mr. Sears, the principal of Manual Training High, called her out of class into the hallway to whisper to her that when she came back in she couldn't get any words out of her little, always-pursed lips. So she'd grabbed an eraser, wiped off *The quick brown fox jumped over the lazy dog,* and chose a brand-new piece of chalk from a box, as if an old stub wouldn't be respectful, and wrote those words on the blackboard in big horrible letters.

Then she'd flopped in her chair—the same one where nutso Lulu McNab once hid a whoopee cushion under her pillow—dropped her small graying head in her arms, and began to sob. That started a chain reaction with all the other girls in class, even the ones Rory knew had Republican parents.

"Oh, my God," said one girl in the first row, her hand going to her mouth as she wept. "Oh, my God . . ."

Rory hurried down the school stairs holding back his own tears in front of the girls who passed each other hankies and Kleenex to wipe their runny noses and mascara.

Rory was the only guy in the typing class. So he had to be strong. When he'd asked Mr. Sears for permission to take typing Rory explained he needed to learn how to type to become a sportswriter.

An amused Mr. Sears had said, "Typing is for girls."

"Clark Kent types," Rory said. "Jimmy Cannon of the *Journal-American* types. Dick Young of the *Daily News* types. I read in a biography of Samuel Clemens that Mark Twain handed in the first typed manuscript in America. None of them're girls."

Mr. Sears laughed and said okay, he could take typing instead of a wood-shop class, but that he didn't want any fistfights in the hall if other guys called Rory a sissy. Or else he'd transfer him out and have him suspended.

A lot of the Manual High football jocks did bust Rory's chops. They called him a *quiff* for taking typing. Or they'd yell, "Maguire, take a letter!" "Exactly what *type* of homo are you, Maguire," asked one flabby lineman named Minogue.

"Someday you'll take it back when you read my interviews with Y.A. Tittle and Johnny Unitas in the *Daily News*," Rory said.

"*Daily News?*" Minogue said, standing amid his taunting football teammates. "My old man says your old man reads *The Daily Worker*. Like all the other draft-dodgin' merchant marines during the big war."

The jocks had a good laugh.

In school, Rory often took these rank-outs on the chin. In his freshman year the jocks were bigger and older than him and they stuck together like a lynch mob. Now that he was a sophomore, he'd grown to five foot nine, and weighed 165 pounds, with hard muscles from working his buns off in the butcher shop, pedaling his big bike about twenty miles a day, eating steak sandwiches and sausage-and-pepper heroes. Only the week before, Noonz, one of the butchers where he worked, said, "Mingya, kid, but you're gettin' huge like Charles Atlas."

Rory laughed and said, "You never know when I might have to punch one of these crew-cut football clowns right in the fat face."

Especially Minogue, Rory thought.

But Mr. Sears had warned him that if he got in any fights in school he'd take him out of typing and suspend him. That would go on his record and hurt his chances of staying on the honor roll, which was important if he wanted to get a scholarship to a good college. He needed a scholarship, because no way could Rory's parents afford to pay his way through college. His father didn't even have a job, couldn't work if he wanted to. The old man was still on crutches or parked in a wheelchair, fighting to get workmen's comp and disability insurance.

Besides, Rory'd learned to live with certain stuff. He spent half his childhood rolling in the gutters, having fistfights with big-mouthed kids, sticking up for his father who'd served in the merchant marines instead of the regular marines during World War II.

Rory's mother once told him, "Your father was a hero during the war. He sailed the treacherous North Atlantic on Liberty cargo ships that supplied the war effort, all the while being attacked by bombs, shells, sea mines, and torpedoes from Hitler's U-boats, the Luftwaffe, and Surface Raiders. Not to mention watching mates die from the cold and the sharks and the sea."

But as far as he knew, his father had no medals besides a Victory Medal and Atlantic Service Bars to prove it. And the old man would never even talk about his time in the war. Never. Ever. In fact, the only time his father ever lost his temper with Rory was when he pestered him for details for a school essay about his time in the merchant marines in World War II.

"Off-limits, damn it!" the old man had barked. "Case closed."

To make matters worse, his old man wasn't even a registered Democrat. And in that working-class Irish Catholic parish of St. Stanislaus (he was a Polish saint but it was an Irish neighborhood) not being a Democrat, loyal to "the Chairman" was like being a secret Protestant and snubbing the Pope. Because Harry Maguire didn't vote at all, people whispered that maybe he was a secret commie.

But all that seemed so stupid right now as Rory joined the stampede out of Manual after President John F. Kennedy was shot in Dallas. The girls from typing were still weeping as Rory joined them and blended in with other classes on the second-floor stairway, all heading toward the Brooklyn street.

As he descended Rory spotted Carol Sturgis a few heads in front of him. His heart jumped. At fifteen Carol was a junior and a full year older than Rory. Even from the back, he could pick Carol out of the rush hour crowd. She had hair like the gorgeous girls in the Prell commercials on TV, long and blond and bouncy with lots of that shiny stuff they called lanolin. She was so blue-eyed and pretty and

walked with such shoulders-back confidence that she terrified Rory. She had posture, poise, *class*. She made his
mouth dry and his palms sweat.

This was Carol's first term in Manual. She'd moved
from the City, which is what Brooklynites called Manhattan. Her father, who was some kind of lawyer, bought a
fancy brownstone with a backyard and a peach tree on
Tenth Street. The house must've gone for at least fifteen
or twenty grand. Instead of work boots and dungarees like
most of the local fathers, Mr. Sturgis wore snazzy suits to
work in the morning, like the father in *Ozzie and Harriet*.
Instead of taking the subway, he drove his shiny Chevy to
work somewhere in Downtown Brooklyn. Carol's mother
was almost as pretty as Carol. She looked a little like that
hot tamale Stella Stevens, and wore the kinds of clothes
Rory never saw his mother wear. Clothes like ladies wore in
movies about rich people from Manhattan.

They were different than other neighborhood families.
Since they moved into the neighborhood in July, Rory had
seen Carol and her parents in Freedom Meats, where he
worked. Every Friday night, like clockwork, the Sturgis
family came in around 5:30 to order their weekly meat
order. *That was weird all by itself*, Rory thought. He
couldn't think of any other family that shopped together.
Most local wives shopped alone while their husbands went
to the bars. Plus they ate meat on meatless Fridays and
he'd heard Mrs. Sturgis tell Sal that they had a big deep
freezer in the finished basement. So they ordered lots of
special freezer-wrapped porterhouse steaks, ground round
instead of chuck chop, center cut pork chops instead of
shoulder, the $1.69-a-pound veal cutlets, and the best
chicken cutlets and eye round roasts. Top-shelf. Nothing
that was on sale. The same grade meat his boss Sal Russo

ate. The only steak Rory had ever eaten before he worked at Freedom Meats was chuck steak. When Sal cooked him his first sirloin on the electric skillet in the back room of the butcher shop, slapped between two pieces of seeded Italian bread from Robestelli's bakery, it was so delicious that Rory felt like he was committing a mortal sin. He checked to make sure it wasn't a meatless Friday.

Every time Carol came into the store with her parents Rory hurried into the back room, ducked into the bathroom, and checked to make sure his hair looked good. It was getting longer every week, like those guys from Liverpool, the Beatles. He was convinced they were going to be a big huge hit when they first came to America and went on *Ed Sullivan* in February. Everyone was starting to grow mop tops, but Rory was ahead of them all, ahead of the Fab Four fad.

But right now everybody he met in school and the neighborhood busted his chops about his long hair. His parents, classmates, teachers, his boss, even his friends told Rory he needed a haircut.

"You look like Moe from the Three Stooges," said Timmy, one of his stickball pals from Eleventh Street.

The football jocks told him he looked more like a quiff than ever. Bad enough he was the only guy in typing. Now he was growing his hair long. But he'd seen a *Daily News* centerfold spread and all kinds of TV news footage about young chicks going ape over the Beatles so he hoped his hair might attract a sophisticated older girl like Carol Sturgis from Manhattan.

He'd been watching Carol now for four months, since she moved into the neighborhood, checking her out as he passed her on the street pedaling his big industrial delivery bike, the basket loaded with meat orders. Stealing glances at her in the butcher shop mirrors as he carried sides of beef or scraped the big butcher blocks or unloaded meat from the wholesale trucks. Or when he passed her in the hallways of Manual. A few times, he'd rushed ahead of her to hold open the lunchroom doors for Carol, just to be able to hear her smoky little Lauren Bacall–ish voice say "Thanks."

He'd always just nod and stare in those blue eyes. And his heart would do a Gene Krupa drumroll in his chest.

Even if a delivery took him in the opposite direction, when Rory was out on his bike from Freedom Meats, which was on the corner of Eighth Street and Seventh Avenue, he always went out of his way to pedal up Tenth Street, hoping he'd see Carol going into or coming out of her house. He saw her a few times in the summer in white short-shorts and almost crashed the bike. What a shape! Like Annette Funicello in *Beach Party*. Just looking at her made him want to run to confession. Thank God temptation wasn't sin, because every time he laid eyes on Carol Sturgis he had temptations worse than Jesus had in the desert.

And now here she was, a few feet in front of him, wrecked by the news about John Fitzgerald Kennedy, blotting tears and mascara from those gorgeous blue eyes. The way he knew his mother was probably doing at home right then.

"Why couldn't this nigga-lover get killed on a Mondee 'stead of a Fridee so we coulda got a whole week off," shouted a familiar voice from behind him on the stairs.

Rory saw a white blur in front of his eyes, like someone had just popped a flashcube in his face. He turned and there was Minogue. Trotting down the school stairs, wearing his football jacket, flanked by a few crew-cut teammates. His big round head reminded Rory of the pig heads he had to trim in Freedom Meats, pink and flabby and his hair cut into a Detroit-style one-inch flattop with a square back.

Rory dropped his books, which were bound with an elastic strap, climbed three steps, and all the insults Minogue ever threw at him about being a quiff and his father being a commie coward and a welfare artist just roared out of him like a Jules Verne volcano. He punched Minogue flush in the mouth. The big jock's head bounced back against the steel-plated wall. A few girls screamed as blood lashed from Minogue's mouth. Then Rory grabbed his lapels and slammed Minogue against the wall of the stairway because now this big fat pig was ranking on Jack Kennedy, who'd just been assassinated!

"Take it back!" Rory shouted. "Take it back, you fat son of a bitch, or I'll friggin' kill *you!*"

A shocked Minogue, blood leaking from a split lower lip, gaped in a dazed way at Rory. And then his eyes shifted to his teammates, who also wore Manual High football jackets. They seemed as outraged by Minogue's remark as everyone else. So did Mr. Sears, who appeared at the top of the stairs peering down, his silence an eerie approval of Rory's reaction.

"I take it back," Minogue whined in a half-crying way.

Rory let go of Minogue and turned to go down the stairs. Carol Sturgis stood in front of him now, her damp muddied eyes staring up into his dark eyes.

"Hi," she said.

"Oh . . . hi . . . um, sorry. Sorry I cursed in front of you like that. . . ."

"It's okay," she whispered. "He's a real asshole."

They shared a small pained laugh and descended side by side. His mouth went dry and his palms dampened.

"I'm Carol, by the way," she said.

"I know," Rory said, handing her a clean tissue from his ski-jacket pocket. "Everyone knows who *you* are."

"*Can* it, Maguire," Mr. Sears said. "Take it out onto the street."

2

As they stepped out onto chilly Seventh Avenue, Carol said, "My dad worked in JFK's campaign in 1960."

"So did I," Rory said.

She smiled, looked Rory in the eyes, and said, "*You* worked for the president's campaign?"

"Well, I put up JFK/LBJ posters on every lamppost from Flatbush Avenue to Prospect Avenue right here along Seventh Avenue," Rory said, grinning. "You took two cardboard posters and wrapped them around the pole, high enough so kids couldn't rip them down, and you'd staple them together. There are a hundred and four lampposts from end to end. No Parking signs are too skinny. The Chairman organized all the neighborhood kids."

"Who's the Chairman?"

"Charlie Pergola, he's the local Democratic boss," Rory said. "Like the Casey Stengel of the Democratic party in Brooklyn."

She forced a laugh and said, "Imagine crazy old Casey in politics? I'm surprised you got involved so young."

"Well, my mom, she's Irish from the other side and we're Catholic, too, and so she loves . . . *loved* . . . how weird is that? . . . Jack Kennedy . . ." he said. "It just rubbed off. I mean, I was only eleven. . . ."

He knew as soon as he mentioned how old he'd been that he'd made a doofus out of himself.

"So, you're what, *fourteen*, now?" she said.

"Well . . . yeah, but I *work* and I'll be fifteen next month, on the thirteenth, and—"

"You're a *sophomore*, then."

"Yeah, but honor roll—and I'm gonna be a sportswriter and—"

Before he could finish the sentence a gleaming red 1963 Buick Riviera slid up to the No Parking zone in front of the school, springy curb finders grating, the passenger window gliding down with that new power-window contraption the TV car commercials bragged about. Other students turned to admire the car, saying it was "boss." One guy sang along with Dale and Grace doing "I'm Leaving It Up to You" on the car radio. Rory thought how odd it was that life just went on after the president was murdered.

Sal "Babe" Russo sat behind the leopard-skin-covered steering wheel of the Riviera that matched the seat covers. Large yellow sponge dice with black dots hung from the rearview mirror. A Roger Maris bobblehead doll bounced from the vibrations of the speaker under the rear-window ledge of the car. *They belong in a playpen,* Rory thought.

Babe turned down the music and leaned across the front seat.

"Eh, champ," Babe said, calling Rory what he'd nick-named him the year before when Rory won second prize in an essay contest in the *World-Telegram* on what the arrival of the New York Mets expansion team meant to old Brooklyn Dodger fans. "The old man says for me ta say ta you ta come in early ta work if you got outta school early on account the assass-im-ya-call-it over in Dallas, there. Jesus-H-You-know-who, but how sad's alla that? Makes you wanna weep. No? The radio keeps playing that 'My daddy is president, what does your daddy do' song. Breaks your stinkin' heart."

Babe turned seventeen in October, went to ritzy and private Poly Prep High (after flunking out of Xavieran), and wore his hair in a perfect Fabian pompadour, heavy on the Brill Cream. His father bought him the Riviera as a birthday gift to go with his driver's license and he looked like he belonged behind the wheel. He had one of those handsome Italian faces with heavy eyebrows like the bad guys on *The Untouchables*, but Rory didn't think Babe was a bad guy at all. As Babe's Uncle Noonz always said, "Nice kid, Babe, but don't expect no cure for cancer outta him, neither."

Even though Babe was an only child who had everything, Rory felt kind of sorry for him. First off, his mother died when he was fourteen. That ate a real big one. Plus, Rory knew Babe wanted to follow his father's footsteps, become a butcher, dress in an immaculate starched apron, and laugh and joke with the customers on a Saturday afternoon while tying a perfect eye-round pot roast or filleting wafer-thin veal cutlets and filling the silver registers with crisp payday cash. Rory thought Babe had the perfect personality for the job—handsome, a little flirty but never dirty with the housewives, making them feel special by saying they looked beautiful and youthful, telling dopey jokes, giving little kids slices of baloney or American cheese, patient with fussy old ladies.

Babe argued with Sal all the time about letting him become a butcher and taking over Freedom Meats when his old man retired. But Rory'd heard Sal bellow at Babe, "Sal Russo's son will never go home with blood and sawdust on his shoes! Unnerstand? Never! I busted my hump twenny-seven years building this business so you wouldn't

have to bust *yours*. You're going to college! To be a lawyer.
Maybe work down Wall Street. Class! Now you go home
and study till your eyes crack because Sal Russo's son will
never go home with blood and sawdust on his shoes!"

Rory knew something else. Sal didn't want his kid taking
over a sinking ship. He told friends all the time that the end
of the mom-and-pop shop was coming fast. Sal had started
out with a mom-and-pop shop in the 1940s, expanded to a
chain of six Freedom Meats stores in the boom years after
World War II, and in the last seven years every one but this
one, his first, his flagship, had been closed in different
Brooklyn neighborhoods because of the arrival of supermarkets. He was back to one mom-and-pop shop.

And last month a Bohack supermarket opened just two
blocks away from Freedom Meats, on Sixth Street and Seventh Avenue. And Rory had heard Sal talking to his quiet
brother and one-third partner, Tony, that they were in for the
fight of their lives. "We can't compete with Bohack's *quan-
tity*," Sal said. "So the only thing we can do is give the customer the *quality* a supermarket can never give. And pray."

"Tell your father I'll be in as soon as I go home and
change," Rory told Babe.

"Ya want, I can tell him I never seen ya, too," Babe said.
"It's like a bad day for the Irish, no?"

Rory shrugged and said, "I could use the OT for the holidays."

"You have to work on a day like this?" Carol asked.

"Thanksgiving rush," Rory said. "Gotta unload like five-
hundred turkeys . . ."

"He's a good kid, the Champ, irregardless what everyone
says about him," Babe said, echoing his old man, and talking like he was somehow much older. Rory didn't think
Babe meant to be patronizing. Babe just adored his father

so much that he aped all of Sal's speech patterns and man-
nerisms. The good ones and the bad. It didn't help matters,
though, for him to be calling Rory "kid" in front of Carol,
who'd just learned he was a fourteen-year-old sophomore.

"You need a ride home, sweetie?" Babe asked Carol.

"No, I'm okay, thanks," she said, shivering and glancing
at Rory, her eyes still radish-red and smudged from tears
shed for the dead president.

Rory's palms began to sweat again. He thought of asking
her if he could walk her home, but she was older than him
and he was afraid his nervous voice would come out high-
pitched and that she would reject him and then Babe
would break his balls about it until the end of time.

Babe threw the car into park in an elaborate flourish and
opened the heavy door and walked around the car to the
sidewalk, fastening his camel-hair coat. Just like Frank
Nitti. All he was missing was a white ascot. Instead, Babe
wore a V-neck mohair sweater underneath so you could see
the black chest hair and the little gold chain with the cruci-
fix that Rory knew his mother had given him before she
died of the big casino from chain-smoking Hit Parade cigarettes. Rory knew that Babe bought all his *vines* from Belmont's down on Fifth Avenue. Sometimes Sal ordered
stuff for him, too, from Mr. Levitsky, the little Jewish door-
to-door tailor who came around Freedom Meats with catalogues, samples, and a measuring tape. Top-shelf stuff, too,
Banlons, knits, tweeds, wools, mohairs, blends, silks. All
imports.

The horseshoe taps on Babe's Florsheim Featherweights clacked on the pebbled-cement sidewalk as he
approached Carol. He was six inches taller than Carol and
smiled a perfect row of white teeth that Rory always
thought looked like Liberace's keyboard.

He opened the passenger door of the Riviera. Sir Walter Raleigh, circa 1963, Rory thought.

"C'mon, hon, I won't bite if you don't," he said. "It's a cold, sad day. Lemme take you home to clean yourself up nice."

Carol looked at Rory, as if expecting him to offer an alternative. He looked at older Carol and then at Babe, handsome, older, who already shaved and had chest hair and wore Belmont's clothes, Florsheims, and drove a brand-new Riviera, and lived in a big fancy house while his father had a new one built in Staten Island from the ground up. Rory felt self-conscious of the peach fuzz on his face, his un-*boss* Mr. Gutter thick-soled Boy Scout–style shoes, the John's Bargain Store sweater, and the old ski jacket.

There was nothing to say. He nodded.

Carol shivered and shrugged, looked at Rory.

"See ya," she said.

Rory said, "Bye."

"I know your last name is Maguire," she said. "What's your first name, anyway?"

"Rory . . . Rory Maguire."

"As in Rory Calhoun, the movie star?"

He nodded and said, "I was Rory before anyone ever heard of Rory Calhoun. Like I said, my mom's Irish, from the other side."

"I like that," Carol said. "*Rory*. It's different. I like different."

He wanted to tell her he liked her, too. Liked her so much she kept him awake nights trying to find her face in the cracked plaster of the ceiling.

"Thanks. I like your name, too."

"Bye, Rory."

"Bye."

Carol kept looking at him as she climbed into the front seat of the Riviera. Babe shut the door. Her face was obscured by the frosted window. As Babe walked to the driver's door Carol wiped a little patch of the frost from the window and looked out at Rory. Bewildered.

As the car pulled away down Seventh Avenue, Rory smacked his own face. The president was dead and on the same day he blew a chance of walking home the girl of his dreams.

"Goddamnit!" Rory said, and walked with great reluctance toward home.

3

"It'll be a miserable Christmas," someone said. Everywhere Rory looked, women cried.

He knew his mother would be weeping so he was in no hurry to see her. He loved her too much to see her so sad. In a doorway on Sixth Street he saw two women embracing, heads on one another's shoulders, weeping. He recognized them as mother and daughter. Four women stood with full shopping carts in the doorway of Bohack supermarket, under the red, white, and blue bunting and flapping pennants of the grand opening, sharing Kleenex.

"It musta been the commies," said one.

"Aye, maybe, but I never trusted that LBJ fella," said another with a Dublin accent. "Something about them Dumbo-y ears."

"We'll never see another Catholic in the White House in our lifetime, sure," said a third, blessing herself and kissing a pewter medal of the Sacred Heart of Jesus she wore around her neck. "I bet it was a Protestant SOB shot him. Mark my words. No Catholic would kill our Jack."

"Will yiz all be at the special mass tonight, sure yiz will?" asked and answered the fourth, her Irish accent thick and more like his mother's friends from Belfast.

The others said of course and kept wiping tears, and Rory kept hearing "Our Jack, Our Jack."

"Did everyone get their turkey coup-ins?" asked the northern Irish woman. "Buy thirty-five dollars of messages and get a free turkey, Butterball like on the telly, no less, come Thanksgiving. All right, wha'?"

"Aye," said one of the others. "But that'll be the only thing to give thanks for this durty oul year after what they done to our Jack. It'll hardly be Christmas at all."

Rory stared through the window into the packed store. Nothing, not even an assassination, could keep the women out of the new supermarket with their coupons clipped from the *Daily News*. Even men stood on line, stacking cases of on-sale Piels beer, as if preparing to drown the sorrow of the dark day late into the Friday night. Rory swallowed hard. He knew the more crowded Bohack was, the grumpier Sal Russo would be at work in Freedom Meats.

He hurried along Seventh Avenue, passing saloons with names like Fitzgerald's, Rafferty's, Quigley's, Gallagher's, the frosted windows all shining with muted green neon shamrock beer signs advertising Rheingold, Schaefer, Budweiser, Ruppert's, Piels. Rory peeked through each window where all the men gazed at television sets carrying coverage of John Fitzgerald Kennedy's murder.

A beat cop named Coyle stared into the window of Benson's TV store, watching a somber Walter Cronkite mouth words as footage of John Fitzgerald Kennedy's inauguration played on the TV. Rory could lip-read the words he already knew by heart: "*Ask not what your country can do for you, but what you can do for your country.*" Coyle the cop's eyes were wide and lost and wet. Rory stopped for a moment. The cop glanced at him. "Get a haircut, Maguire," he said, and looked back at the TV like a man at a private wake. Rory said nothing.

He kept walking toward his tenement between Eleventh

and Twelfth Streets, but dreaded seeing his mother. She already lived with so much disappointment that Rory hated the idea of seeing her also grieving for JFK. She thought of him as family and the beacon of better days ahead. *Our Jack.* Now he was dead.

They killed a part of her, too, Rory thought.

Then he thought about Carol, about what a stooge he'd been standing there like the wooden Indian in front of U-Need-a-Cigar on Ninth and Fifth. *Was she hinting she wanted me to walk her home?* he wondered. *Why couldn't I get those stupid words out of my mouth? How can I expect to be a sportswriter and do interviews with Mickey Mantle and Sonny Liston and Sandy Koufax if I'm afraid to ask a fifteen-year-old girl if I can walk her home from school? I wasn't afraid of punching fat Minogue in the face but I was afraid of asking Carol if I could carry her books. What a boob, what a doofus, what a* quiff.

He stopped in front of Freedom Meats on the corner of Eighth Street. Sal and his brothers Tony and Nunzio (whom everyone called Noonz) stood behind the gleaming showcase. Two customers stood in the sawdust facing the counter. *Everyone else is either home crying or in Bohack,* Rory thought. *Or getting loaded in the saloons.*

Rory popped his head in the door. The butchers looked up. The radio was giving updates on the assassination.

"I'm just going home to change, Sal," Rory said. "Be right back."

Sal waved him over to the end of the showcase, near the window where an artist's hand-lettered signs boasted chickens for 33¢ a pound and leg cut veal cutlets for $1.39 and homemade Italian sausage for 89¢ a pound. He held his favorite black-handled Stanley slicing knife down along the leg of his blood-spattered white apron.

"You okay, kid?"

"Just sad."

"The whole world's sad. I know your mom loved him."

Rory nodded.

"Tell her I send my condolences."

Rory nodded again.

"You pass Bohack, kid?"

"Yeah," Rory said. "Dead."

Sal's eyes widened, searching for good news. "Yeah?"

Rory nodded. It was a good lie. *The truth wasn't gonna change anything anyway*, he thought. *Just make everybody sadder.* Sal ruffled Rory's mop top in an affectionate way and play-slapped his cheek. "Hurry back, the turkey truck's coming. And get a freakin' haircut."

Over Sal's shoulder he saw Noonz wink and make a half-measured sign with his two hands, which he knew meant he wanted Rory to stop into the German deli three doors away on the way back and get him a can of Rheingold. Behind Sal's back, Noonz and Karl the Kraut had worked out a deal where Noonz sent Rory over with bags of cold cut ends every Friday night, which Karl would grind together into a meat mash and roll into balls and coat with bread crumbs and pan fry into "German meatballs" that he sold over the counter for fifteen cents apiece. In exchange Karl sent Noonz over two cans of beer a day with Rory. Rory would hide the cans behind the tubs of preground chuck chop in the walk-in icebox. Whenever Noonz went into the box to bone sides of beef or grind chuck chop, he'd down the beers. Then Rory would have to get rid of the empties. Sal didn't allow Noonz to drink on the job.

Rory nodded to Noonz and headed home.

At Ninth Street, workers sent home early because of the assassination were now pouring from the subway, many of them women with muddy eyes and cracked faces, holding each other up as they wobbled on high heels. The men walked in lost and saddened knots, discussing politics and conspiracy theories and heading for the bars before going home.

"Castro hadda be behind it," said one guy carrying a hard hat.

"Yeah, that bearded spic and Khrushchev," said another guy carrying a longshoreman's hook. "Payback for the missiles. . . ."

"Hoffa was no fan, either," said a guy in a suit and tie, carrying a briefcase. "Jack's brother Bobby double-crossed a lot of people. Mobsters, union people, dagos."

Rory had read about some of that stuff in Murray Kempton's column in the *Post*. His father had told him to read Kempton but his columns were like trigonometry equations, so hard to read you almost needed a slide rule to figure them out. But Rory read them anyway, even when he didn't understand them. He found Walter Lippmann in the *Herald Tribune* easier to read.

Pausing, walking, listening, Rory thought that in Brooklyn everybody had a theory, as if it were part of a big game of *I've Got a Secret*, and Bill Cullen or Kitty Carlisle would guess the answer to the assassination by the end of the night.

He fingered the lone nickel in his pants pocket and popped into Mr. B's candy store, where Mr. B sat in gloomy silence, as he always did, listening to the radio. Rory grabbed five hard caramels from one of the fifty boxes of penny candies that lined a long shelf of the store. He handed Mr. B the nickel that vanished into an ink-soiled *World-Telegram* apron pocket. The gloomy man had a copy of *The Sporting News* on his lap, opened to a story about the winter trades.

"Any Mets trades I should know about, Mr. B?"

"Forget the Mets," he said. "The only time you'll ever see them in first place is if you turn the goddamned newspaper upside down. And shut up. I'm listening to the news about JFK. Who cares about the Mets today?"

Rory took a small brown paper bag off the counter, put the hard caramels in it, and left. He knew he should go right home. But he was hesitating, unable to face what might be there. His mother in a pile of tears. Hope gone as the holidays approached, with no money in the house.

Then he thought about little Caroline and John-John Kennedy, who would never again see their father.

Right now, no matter how broke and broken up he was, more than anything or anyone else, Rory needed to see his own father.

4

Rory peeked through the window of Ryan's Tavern on Eleventh Street.

Sitting on a stool closest to the men's room was Harry Maguire, watch cap on his head with his USMM button pinned to the fold. His wooden crutches leaned against the bar. His wheelchair, which he called his "living hearse," was parked by a small service bar near the window. Harry was wearing his knock-around peacoat. He kept an identical prized dress peacoat—one that he'd worn to sea and now wore only on special occasions—wrapped in S&S French Dry Cleaner paper, safe in a padlocked tin armoire in the tiny back room of their railroad apartment.

Every Friday morning, before he left for school, Rory would carry the wheelchair down the three flights of tenement steps for his father. Harry Maguire would swing himself down the stairs two steps at a time, using his crutches and the banister for support, just to get out of the apartment. Harry said he got cabin fever after sitting home all week. One reason was that Harry didn't much like TV. And he'd already read almost every single book in the four overflowing bookcases in the apartment. Rory got him two books a week out of the library. And on Friday mornings, Rory would wheel his father over to Ryan's. The tavern opened at eight A.M. and Harry'd sip coffee and club soda, read the papers, and shoot the breeze with the local guys, maybe watch a ball game. Rory's mother would usually meet Harry at the back door to give him a sandwich at lunch, and in the late afternoon, when the local men came in on payday, he'd have a few beers.

Isn't much of a life, Rory thought. And felt a pang thinking of the whole life.

Rory was about to enter the bar when his father pushed himself up off the stool, grabbed his crutches, and jockeyed through the smoky crowd and into the men's room.

Rory waited out on the sidewalk and took an eight and a half by eleven–inch manila envelope from his loose-leaf binder containing a typed letter he'd written to President Kennedy about his father. Clipped to the letter was a half-finished essay about his father.

All of Harry Maguire's problems started during World War II.

Rory's mother had told Rory that in a vague, blurry way Harry Maguire never knew his own father. Harry was raised alone by his single mother. In 1941, at seventeen, while dating Tara, he tried to join the United States Marines but was rejected for being deaf in one ear, the result of getting hit by a line drive while pitching for Manual.

She'd filled him in on lots of small details like that. And at his mother's urging, Rory had been writing the letter and essay to President Kennedy to explain his father's predicament. To ask Our Jack for some help. Rory wrote it in the second person, in the style of Jimmy Cannon, his father's—and Rory's—favorite sports columnist. Harry had clipped and saved some of his Cannon favorites over the years and shown them to Rory. Like the one Cannon wrote in 1951 called "You're Joe Louis":

"You're Joe Louis, aged thirty-seven, a main event heavy-weight. You were the greatest champion of your time. But now you're trapped by the fight racket which you conquered. You're absolutely through but you can't declare yourself. You're still making money the only way you know . . ."

Rory loved the way Cannon crawled inside another man's life and wrote about him, what his father called "writing from the inside out." And for the last year he had been writing his essay about his father, using Cannon's second-person technique. To try to break into that complicated head that stored a treasure of stories about Harry Maguire's life. Especially tales about his time in the merchant marine, in the North Atlantic during World War II.

Harry Maguire wouldn't share those stories with anyone. He kept them sealed in his brain as if it were Fort Knox. But his mother told Rory sketchy pieces of Harry's life. And so Rory kept writing the essay, always trying to pick his father's brain, scratching for details, and preparing the cover letter.

Now Jack Kennedy would never get to read it.

He glanced down at the cover letter that he'd kept short and sweet because he knew Jack Kennedy was a busy man, dealing with things like missiles in Cuba, the Soviet Union, Red China, the teamsters' union, problems in some place called Vietnam, cutting taxes, and reelection.

Dear President Kennedy:

My family needs your help. In 1960, when I was 11, I worked for your campaign here in Brooklyn. My mother, Tara Donnelly Maguire, who is from Belfast, Northern Ireland, voted for you. She's so proud that we have an Irish Catholic president like you. My father, Harry

Maguire, was a Merchant Marine in World War II and got badly wounded and now he has sirens in his head and he gets dizzy spells. He fell off an overpass last May and broke his back and ankles. I know that you always had problems with your back, so you might understand what he's going through. You were also a Navy officer, so you might identify with my father getting hurt in a big sea battle. All the details of my father's situation are listed in my essay called "You're Harry Maguire."

Anyway, my father gave me your great book to read and now here's my own profile of courage about my father. He's getting railroaded and it just isn't right and we really need your help.

Thanks so much for taking the time to read this.

Sincerely,
Rory Maguire

Rory hadn't yet sent the letter because the attached essay was still incomplete. There were a lot of blanks he needed to fill in about his father's past. But now it didn't matter. Jack Kennedy, Our Jack, was dead. And by comparison, the murder of Jack Kennedy made his father's problems seem small and insignificant.

Rory looked through the bar window again and the men's-room door was still closed and his father's bar stool was empty.

He glanced at the essay underneath the letter. He would finish it anyhow, as soon as he had enough of the blanks filled in about his father's life. He would send it to someone else. But somehow he just didn't think Lyndon Johnson, a Protestant from Texas, would care a whole lot about an Irish-Catholic family in Brooklyn.

As he waited for his father to come out of the men's room, Rory reread the unfinished essay about his father that he held in his hands, always looking for places to revise and make it better.

"You're Harry Maguire, aged thirty-nine, a loyal husband and loving father to five kids. You live in a Brooklyn tenement and you cannot work because you got hurt real bad in a fall on a city job.

After Pearl Harbor you tried to join the service but the Air Force, Navy, Marines and Army all rejected you for the same reason—deaf in the left ear. You were seventeen, and the Brooklyn Dodgers scouts saw you pitch for Manual Training High and made you an offer to play on a farm team. But you said, "Don't you know there's a war on?" You said you couldn't play baseball while other guys your age were fighting and dying in Europe and the Pacific. You said that first you had to do some kind of war service for your country.

So, you joined the United States Merchant Marine at Sheepshead Bay which took people of every race, nationality and religion, even those who had physical ailments like blindness in one eye or deafness in one ear, and shipped them out on Liberty Ships into the North Atlantic carrying tanks, weapons, bombs, airplanes, food and medical supplies, and oil and gasoline for the war effort. The Merchant Marines ran into wolf packs of Hitler's U-Boats that sunk hundreds of Liberty Ships and killed thousands of Merchant Marines.

Your wife, Tara Maguire, says you got wounded in some big sea battle. You were on a Liberty Ship called the _____ sailing from _____ to _____ on _____ and then you got attacked by a U-boat [or ship] called the _____. In that battle ___ men died and you wound up on a raft with ____ other men and you drifted for ____ days before you and ____ other shipmates were rescued by a ship called the _____, and taken to _____, where you were treated in _____ Hospital for ___ days before being shipped home.

While you were away, your mother died of cervical cancer, which sent you into deeper depression when you got home.

Ever since the war, you've suffered dizzy spells, nightmares, and noises in your head from the battle that you refuse to ever talk about. After you came home, you tried out for the Dodgers again. But your equilibrium was so bad that you could no longer pitch.

Whenever your son Rory asks you about all of this, you say, "Let's talk about the Mets."

But your wife, Tara, says that before the war you always made everyone laugh like Jack Benny. You could dance like Gene Kelly. She says the war took away the laughter and the dancing. And then when you came home from the war, you couldn't play baseball anymore. Your wife says, "More than anything else—more than being found half-dead, more than the headaches, the nightmares, the sirens in his head, even more than the neighborhood whispers about him being a draft dodger or worse—not being able to play baseball anymore changed my Harry."

Your wife says it was like a piece of you that died in the war.

Your wife also says that you haven't danced with her once since you came home from that war.

You wanted to get medical help but because you were a Merchant Marine you couldn't go to a military hospital. Because you were a Merchant Marine, you couldn't go to college on the GI Bill, either. You also didn't qualify for a GI homeowner's loan. You couldn't join a VFW Post and the government never gave you any real medals, because Merchant Marines rarely got medals even when they were heroes. When you looked for work all the veterans from the other services got priority hiring in all the government jobs. You believed they should get preferential treatment over civilians who didn't serve in the war. But you thought Merchant Marines who served in the war deserved the same privilege.

So you drove a cab, you worked in factories, and you loaded trucks. Finally, after years of waiting you got a provisional city job filling potholes and putting up fences for the Department of Transportation. Then, back in May, when you were working on the Prospect Expressway overpass, you got one of your dizzy spells. And you fell. And you broke your back and your ankles.

But your foreman, Chuck Vermillier, who wanted to give your job to a buddy, claims you were drinking at the time. Which was a lie. But the people in power believed him over you. You were denied both state workmen's compensation and federal disability.

And because you were a Merchant Marine and not in the regular military service, you can't get treatment in a good military hospital. The US Public Health System officer will not grant you a waiver. And so now you don't have the medical coverage for the delicate spinal fusion operation you need on your spinal column. Which you need to have performed in order to get back to work. But your operation is too risky to have at a city hospital, which you say is "like the ASPCA for human beings." And now your unemployment is almost finished. And so what are you supposed to do now?

There were so many blanks in the essay that he'd never gotten to send it to Jack Kennedy. Rory didn't know where his father's ship was coming from or where it was going. He didn't know the cargo on board. He didn't know if the ship was attacked by a German sub or a destroyer. He didn't know if his father fought back against the jerries or if he got wounded in a fall or out on the raft. He didn't know the names of any of the men who served with him. He didn't know where he was taken when he was rescued or how long he was in the hospital.

And Harry Maguire wouldn't tell him. Wouldn't even talk about it to his own wife. Wouldn't talk about it to anyone. It was like a private cargo of despair that he carried locked in his noisy head.

Through the tavern window Rory saw his father pump his crutches out of the men's room. Just watching him in a roomful of men made Rory's heart thump. Rory stuffed the letter to Jack Kennedy and the unfinished essay about his father back into the envelope, as people passed him on Seventh Avenue, talking about the assassination. The neighborhood was like one big outdoor wake. He stared at his father with another kind of sadness as Harry picked through the crowd to get to his stool.

Harry was appealing both decisions by the federal disability and state workmen's compensation boards. He was convinced that a red flag rose next to his name because he had no political affiliation and because he was a merchant marine in World War II.

Rory wasn't sure about that. But he knew the drinking charge was a lie, because it was a Saturday, his father was working overtime, and his mother had sent Rory to bring his father a hot thermos of soup and a grilled cheese sandwich to the job site on Sixth Avenue an hour before he fell. His father had been cold sober. Besides, Harry Maguire never drank on the job. Never drank at home, except at parties. The only place he ever drank was in a bar, only on Fridays. Payday. It was like a strict rule in his life.

Then on that sunny spring day in May, as Harry stepped to the edge of the overpass to fasten a new length of hurricane fencing, he swooned. Coworkers said his eyes rolled, he let out a growl, and he cupped his ears. Before anyone could catch him, Harry Maguire stumbled backward off the overpass. He landed feetfirst on the expressway, cars and trucks swerving around him, the impact breaking both legs and crushing five disks in his spinal column.

But at the workmen's compensation hearing the state believed his boss, Chuck Vermillier, who said Harry Maguire had been drunk.

Harry said Chuck Vermillier wanted the slot for a political crony who paid his dues to the Chairman's Ben Franklin Club. Rory also knew it didn't help that his father had snubbed the Chairman that time, on Election Night in 1960.

Rory delivered meat to the Chairman's club every week, always received the Liberty silver dollar tip from one of his cronies, but he never got to speak with him again since the night Jack Kennedy was elected.

Harry hired a local Republican lawyer named Rico Esposito because none of the Democratic lawyers would take his case. Especially on consignment. And so, unable to work, Harry received forty-four dollars a week in unemployment checks to support his family. But the checks were ready to run out just in time for the holidays.

Now, with Harry Maguire back on his bar stool staring up at the images of Jack Kennedy's assassination on the TV, Rory entered Ryan's.

His father saw him coming in the reflection of the back-bar mirror, shifted on the bar stool to face him, pain still contorting his features like a character being punched in a Marvel comic.

"I'm so sorry, big guy," his father whispered in the crowded bar where men stared at the TV in stunned reverential silence. "It's a filthy, rotten day for the country. I didn't vote for him, but Jack Kennedy was my president, too."

"How's mom?"

"A wreck."

"Just wanted to say hi before I go to work. Any news from Esposito?"

Harry just shook his head. Rory held out his hand to shake. His father grasped his son's hand and Rory pressed the silver-dollar tip he got every week from delivering homemade Italian sausage to the Chairman's club into his father's hand. Since he got hurt Rory always saved that dollar just for his father, so that he could have something to put up on the bar on Friday afternoon in Ryan's. He didn't even tell his mother about it.

"Buy yourself a beer," Rory whispered to his father.

"Thanks, big guy. I wish I could buy you one, too."

"Don't worry, Pop, we're gonna win these appeals," Rory said.

"That's what you always say about them Mets."

"I'm gonna try to talk to the Chairman about your case," Rory said.

"Easier recruiting the Pope," his father said, zipping Rory's jacket to the neck, gently headlocking him, and kissing the top of his son's head, as he always did.

"Go comfort your mother before you go to work," Harry Maguire said. Rory looked his father in the eyes and nodded and hurried out of Ryan's and across the street to the three-story tenement to see his mother.

5

Rory scrambled up the three flights of metal-edged stairs to the apartment on the top floor right and pushed open the never-locked door. The black-and-white Philco TV played with the sound down low in the living room, like the background drone of history in the making. His mother was at the stove ladling Campbell's chicken noodle soup into bowls for three of his four siblings. Caitlin, a precocious ten-year-old who liked to dress in her mother's clothes, and Connor, a third-grader who talked too fast for his still-growing second teeth, had been sent home from school. Bridget was only three. She was the only one in the room unaffected by the news of John Fitzgerald Kennedy. They all wore heavy Irish wool sweaters in the cold apartment. Rory's just-turned-thirteen-year-old brother Dermot was missing from the table.

The oven door was open, battling to heat the railroad flat that only got steam heat three hours a day. His mother, a compact redhead who never worked hard on her natural beauty as she approached forty, didn't even have to turn around for Rory to know she was weeping. If she wasn't singing or humming or whistling, it meant Tara Donovan Maguire was weeping. Silent as prayer. Without show. Which made it even sadder.

Caitlin looked at Rory, wiped her nose with her sleeve, and nodded toward her mother and sobbed. Connor sniffed back a tear, and bit his lower lip, trying to be strong. Bridget shouted, "No cry, Mommy."

"Make Mommy stop, Rory," whispered Caitlin.

Rory said, "Mom . . ."

"That bullet that killed Jack Kennedy pierced my own heart, Rory," she said, wiping her eyes with her apron and turning and handing out the bowls of soup to the kids and a pile of grilled cheese sandwiches. Rory helped her pass out the food.

"I know, Mom."

"Our Jack was hope itself, son."

"Don't cry, Mom, please," Rory said, looking at his siblings, who cried because their mother was crying. "Stop, please, for them."

"If I don't cry my head'll bleedin' explode, Rory," she said.

Rory passed the triptych of framed pictures of Pope John XXIII, Jesus Christ, and President Kennedy on the wall near the bathroom and crossed to his mother. He hugged her.

"Please don't say it'll be all right because it won't be," she said. "Please don't say it could be worse, because it couldn't be."

"Yes, it could," Rory said. "It could be one of us."

She seemed to stop crying all at once. Swallowed a muffled sob and nodded.

"Aye," she said. "It could be one of my beautiful wee uns."

Rory felt like crying himself. But he couldn't do that in front of the kids.

Tara tapped Rory's cheek and dried her eyes with her apron. She wore no makeup. She didn't need any. She was as pretty as anyone on TV without mascara and lipstick and all that other gunk. People always made remarks about Rory's mother's thick red hair and beautiful big green eyes. She didn't dress like anyone on TV but she always looked good. Like right now, as she fed the kids before going to work in

Mayflower Laundry, where she washed and folded the laundry of strangers for $1.35 an hour.

She knocked a cockroach off the side of the sink onto the worn linoleum floor with the edge of a soup can and stepped on it, crackling it under her plain flat shoes bought in a two-pairs-for-one sale down in National Shoes. The kids giggled through a slurping contest with their soup.

"No slurping," Tara said. "This isn't China . . . yet. Oh, God, poor Jackie and her kids. Rose must be in agony, wha? Suffering Mother of Jesus on the Cross, why?"

She threw the soup cans into the soiled brown paper bag under the sink where mousetraps were cocked for ambush near the edge of the stove. Steel wool poked from the crevices where the wall failed to meet the floor under the stand-up cast-iron sink. Slices of raw potato smeared with J-O roach paste were placed around and under the sink, the area his father called the Grand Central Terminal for roaches. The November wind rattled the windows in their loose frames, still porous despite the rags stuffed between them to stave off the drafts. The counterweight chains reminded Rory of the clanging of Scrooge's Ghost of Christmas Past.

"I have to get to work," Tara said. "Riley the foreman, who thinks he's God's gift, will be yapping if I'm a minute late. Two minutes past and he docks a half hour. It's the busy season."

"I gotta get to work, too," Rory said. He placed a hard caramel in front of each kid and hurried through his parents' bedroom off the kitchen, through the floral-patterned curtain and into the second windowless bedroom of the railroad flat. He heard his siblings yelling thanks to him and his mother telling them they couldn't touch the candies until they finished their lunch.

Rory stripped off his good school clothes, placed them

under his top mattress of the bunk beds that he shared with Dermot. He preferred the top bunk so he could stare into the cracked plaster of the ceiling at night, surplus army blanket pulled tight to the neck, imagining faces. In particular, the face of Carol Sturgis.

He shivered in the cold room, removed a faded hooded sweatshirt and old dungarees from under the mattress, and a pair of heavy steel-toed work boots from under the lower bunk. His uniform for Freedom Meats. He grabbed a ski mask with holes cut out for the eyes, nose, and mouth from his top drawer. They were the rage this winter. He pulled it on and rolled it from the bottom into a watch cap.

From the other side of the flowery curtain his mother asked if he was decent. He said he was and Tara pulled the curtain aside and entered.

"Speaking of something happening to one of our own," she said, "I need you to have a few choice words with your brother Dermot."

"What the he—heck did he do now?" Rory asked, sitting on the "big bed" that the two girls shared in the same room. He began tying his laces as his mother leaned against Connor's folding cot that was opened only at bedtime.

"Gallivanting and running amok with that cleft-hoofed Lefty Hallahan and that gang of blackguards he calls the Shamrocks, God help us all," she said. "Swearing and smoking cigarettes and I could have sworn I smelled drink off him yesterday. He'll be getting a juvenile delinquent card, sure, or worse. Jail, or the undertaker."

"I'll talk to him, Mom."

"Ever since your father got hurt, Dermot pays him no mind," she said. "And he laughs at my threats. He needs talking to, so he does, before he needs praying over."

"Promise, Mom."

"I think he's up on the roof sneaking a smoke behind Lipinsky's pigeon coop."

"You're gonna be late for work, Mom. Go. Mr. Riley'll dock you, give you a hard time. Stop crying and fretting and go to work."

"Your father's on his way up," she said. "I'll see you at the special mass for Our Ja—for the president?"

"I'll be there, Mom."

She nodded, took a deep breath, and turned to the kitchen and the door.

Rory crunched across the pebbles toward the pigeon coop and found Dermot sitting on Lipinsky's folding chair, curling a twenty-five-pound dumbbell, a Marlboro dangling from his lips. His ski jacket was zipped to the neck, hood up. The roof had one of the best views of the Manhattan skyline, rising just across the Brooklyn Bridge like a stone-and-steel Oz, the place where all the big-city newspapers were printed before being distributed across the five boroughs.

"Throw that cigarette away before I make you eat it," Rory said.

Dermot took a dramatic drag, blew two obnoxious smoke rings that tore in the wind, switched hands with the dumbbell, and flicked the half-smoked butt off the roof.

"Whadda you supposed to be?" Rory said. "Hot stuff?"

"What? I'm supposed to sit downstairs bawling over a dead politician?"

Rory took out the little candy bag, gave a caramel to Dermot, and popped the last one in his own mouth. Dermot took it without saying thanks.

"What's this about Lefty and the Shamrocks? Collection of a-holes."

"Like to see you say that to Lefty's face," Dermot said.

"No problem, one on one. But he's always with his boys. Alone, he's a punk."

"He's doing better'n you are busting your balls on the bike."

"I have an honest job," Rory said. "I put money in this house."

"So did the old man," said Dermot. "Look how they took care of him. Lefty don't wait for the world to give him nothin'. He takes it. I'll put money in the house soon, too."

"This your idea of, 'Top of the world, Ma?' Cagney in *White Heat*, sneaking a smoke next to Lipinsky's coop? Thinking of pulling scores with punks like Lefty?"

"He ain't a punk."

Rory grabbed Dermot by the front of his shirt, dragged him off the folding chair, and pointed toward the Brooklyn House of Detention, a white eight-story brick fortress a few miles down on Atlantic Avenue. "Hang out with that clown and you'll end up in the House of D having your pants pulled down by a six-foot-six monster," Rory said. He spun Dermot around and pointed toward the meandering meadows of GreenWood Cemetery dotted with the stone tablets of the dead. "Or there in the GreenWood pushing up daisies. Then he pointed to the dazzling skyline. "Me, I'm going there."

"Yeah, on your bike," Dermot said. "As an order boy."

Rory smacked his kid brother off the back of his head. "Mom's already got enough problems with Dad being hurt, fighting the disability, workmen's comp, unemployment running out, no hospital coverage for Dad's operations, now Kennedy dead. She don't need you getting in trouble with Lefty Hallahan, understand? I hear the fish store needs an order boy. You work Thursdays and Fridays and—"

"You deliver your meat," Dermot said, pulling free. "I have my own plans."

Dermot pulled the hard caramel out of his mouth, threw it into the pebbles, and ran across the rooftops that connected the six tenements, jumped across a six-foot air shaft, and descended through the open door of another tenement, to the street.

Rory stood by Lipinsky's coop and stared at the Manhattan skyline that always seemed to pull him like a giant electromagnet. He felt like having a good cry before unloading a few hundred turkeys. For his father, for his mother, for John Fitzgerald Kennedy, for blowing a chance to walk Carol Sturgis home. And for Dermot. He stood staring at the skyline, listening to the chilly birds nestle together.

But after two minutes of staring at the skyline, nothing came out of his eyes. The clock on the Williamsburg Bank building told him it was almost three o'clock. He walked to the edge of the roof and peered down Seventh Avenue and saw a big white Rabinowitz Poultry truck pull up in front of Freedom Meats three blocks away.

And Rory ran down the stairs to work.

6

Rory hefted the fifth wooden crate of turkeys onto the hand-cart and rolled it to the sidewalk and yanked it up the curb. Over to the side, a light-skinned black man was paste-waxing Sal's gold Cadillac El Dorado, polishing every square inch with cheesecloth, using toothbrushes and Q-tips on the hub-caps. This job usually took him four solid hours and paid him fifteen dollars, which was five bucks more than Rory was paid for a whole week.

Sweating and grunting, Rory noticed another guy wearing shades like masks, sitting in a Plymouth that was parked at a hydrant across the street. He kept looking down as if writing something, then looking back up. He looked like he could be a detective, but Rory knew the names and faces of almost all the bulls in the 72nd Precinct. *Maybe the guy was casing the joint,* he thought. Whatever the reason, he sure was eye-tapping Freedom Meats. Maybe he was a health inspector. Or from weights and measures. Or the United States Department of Agriculture. They'd busted a big chain called Merkel Meats the year before for selling hot dogs made out of kangaroo meat. Big scandal. Sal was always worried about people like that and that's why he tortured Rory about cleanliness. Made him "imm-ac-u-late this joint from top to bottom every day." Rory had never heard *immaculate* used as a verb before.

Rory pushed the handcart past a half-dozen customers, all of them whispering and sighing about John Fitzgerald Kennedy, the melting ice dripping into the fresh sawdust. He passed Sal, who sat on one of the customers' waiting chairs, looking at new fabrics and shirts that Mr. Levitsky the tailor had brought in. Sal shifted in his chair, moaning about his sciatica, which Rory first thought was just another one of Sal's Italian relatives.

"Did you know you didn't have to be Jewish to love Levitsky?" Sal said, making a joke out of the Levy's rye bread commercial.

Levitsky said. "Only the best for Salvatore Russo."

"*Sal.* Get it straight. *Salvatore* was my father's name. He was from the other side. I'm a Ramerican. My name is Sal."

"Sorry, Sal. So how much do you love my knit shirts?"

"Gimme one in every flavor," Sal said, waving his hand, grimacing in pain.

Rory paused, leaned next to Sal's ear, and told him there was a guy parked at the Johnny pump across the street who kept watching the store. Sal glanced past him.

"Good eyes, kid," Sal said. "You're okay, irregardless of what everyone says."

Rory pushed the cart toward the back of the store, turning the handcart right at the end of the thirty-foot showcase. The store buzzed with Thanksgiving activity. A guy from the Toledo Scale Company balanced the five scales. A one-eyed knife grinder who wore a black eye patch sharpened the cutlery on a portable grindstone in the back room. A linen supply guy carried in bundles of towels, rags, and aprons. Two other deliverymen hauled in burlap bags of sawdust. The fat and bone collectors hauled out three large barrels of trimmings and suet that would be boiled down and used to make soap, lipstick, and makeup. He loved telling stuck-up girls that when they smeared on lipstick and makeup they were wearing dead pig grease.

"Hadda be about the arrogant brother Bobby," Rory heard the sawdust guy say to the fat collector. "You don't convict fifty-eight teamsters and expect a merry Christmas in Hyannisport."

Rory made the turn around the end of the showcase, pulled open the heavy wooden door to the walk-in icebox, and yanked the handcart up the six-inch step and inside where his breath was frostier than it was on the street.

"I hope somebody chokes on a friggin' wing bone," Noonz said, stacking the 100-plus-pound boxes with Rory into the corner of the big box. "I hate these big dirty boids. Hate 'em almost as much as I hate that fat slob of a brudda a mine."

Noonz was dressed in an overcoat, watch cap, and work gloves.

Rory reached into his ski jacket pocket and pulled out the can of Rheingold. Noonz grabbed it and gazed through the six-inch spy window cut in the wall that looked out on the store to make sure Sal wasn't coming. On the outside wall the small window was covered by a one-way mirror like the cops used in station houses. Noonz took out his key ring and flicked to a can opener. He punctured one hole on one side and three connecting holes on the other side of the can, lit a Pall Mall with a Ronson lighter, took a big drag, and then downed the whole twelve-ounce can in one long Adam's-apple-jumping guzzle.

He took another two drags on his smoke and handed Rory the empty can. He belched into his fist and motioned for the second can.

"Karl only gave me one."

"Stingy Kraut!"

Rory grabbed a box of birds with Noonz, dodged around a dozen sides of beef and several slaughtered pigs that hung from overhead hooks and stacked it on top of the other turkey boxes in the far corner of the twelve-by-twelve-foot icebox. The wooden slat shelves were piled with loins of pork, racks of steaks, and tubs of preground chuck chop that was given a fake bright red coloring with bottled beef blood. The chop meat came out a brilliant scarlet when sent through the grinding machine a second time and then oxidized in the cold air before being presented to the customer.

Oxidized is a good word, Rory thought. *I can use it describing a badly cut fighter.*

Noonz snarled and said, "I thought we won the friggin' war! That goose-stepping war criminal's another hump. He makes over forty clams a month on them poison meatballs and he gives me back, what, tops eight bucks wortha Rheingold? What's my name, *Goldberg* to him? That Nazi cockknocker's on my radar screen, now, too."

Rory didn't say anything, just put the empty beer can in his coat pocket.

"You okay, kid?"

Rory shrugged and nodded and the two of them lifted another box of turkeys together and stacked it in the corner.

"Sorry to hear about what they did to Kennedy, kid."

"Me, too."

"Hound face with the jug ears from Texas, talks like he's on goofballs, he takes over right away anyways, right?"

"Vice President Johnson is president right now," Rory said.

"No offense, but it's the same difference. Just another politician. The Kennedys got their problems and I feel bad for 'em. But I got my own problems in my own family. Holidays coming and all. My fat swine brudda woiks me like a song-singin' slave in the cotton fields six days a week, ten hours a day, and pays me a hun'rid and a quarter. The colored guy that waxes his car makes more by the hour than me. I got five kids home, the oldest rabbit is twelve, ready to start high school next year. She did the math for me. My own brudda pays me two-oh-eight an hour and he pays the car wash dinge three-seventy-five! And I'm his brudda! His flesh and blood! He spends more on a pair of ginzo alligator shoes that he wears once and throws away when he gets blood and sawdust on 'em. His kid, Babe, who thinks IQ means I'm Queer, he drives a brand day newsky Riv-I-era. Me, I take the B-67 bus to woik every mornin', rain, shine, or snow, or earthquake. Meanwhile, back at the ranch, Sal's havin' a brand-day-new mansion built from scratch over Staten Island, braggin' to everybody he meets he's payin' fifty grand cash. Before his wife died, God rest her miserable, greedy soul, he draped her in Tiff'ny jewels, furs, the fancy clothes, a maid, streamline phones, a gardener, her own Caddy. Meanwhile, I'm livin' in the same roach-trap rent-controlled apartment our parents moved into when they got married off the boat from Palermo forty-eight years ago. But I got news for this fat slob brudda a mine. He don't give me a decent bonus this year, I'll go to the Bohack. I'll steal customers away from this fat slob, following me like the Pied Piper."

"That'd kill Sal," Rory said, lifting another box of turkeys with him.

"Hey, kid, between me, you, and them dead boids, I got torpedoes haunting me, puttin' the hairy arm on me for bad bets, overdue paper. To pay the bets I hadda take money on the street from Frankie No Toes, with eighteen percent vig. Now I got new zips, siggies with no necks, putting the arm on me. I'm in deep, kid. *Deep.* I went to Sal, to my fat slob brudda, for a loan. He says to me, to *me*, brudda to brudda, 'Drop dead.' Which is the same as telling me to tell my wife and five rabbits to *die*, too. He says to me he heard our parents say once that I was a mistake on a hot summer night when the old man had too much wine. Nice, right? Really *nice* he says this to me, that I spilled outta a gallon of cheap Guinea red? Okay, we'll see who's the *mistake*. I swear on the eyes of my five rabbits, this here year it's either a big bonus or the Bohack."

Rory thought about the guy with the shades outside the store. But he said nothing. He didn't want to get involved in that Russo family business. Noonz was right in a lot of ways. Sal treated Noonz like the black sheep, never invited him over to his house for dinner or holidays, and paid him leash money. But it wasn't Sal's fault that Noonz drank like a fish and gambled like a lunatic. But he thought a guy with five kids should be making more than two bucks an hour from his own brother. Even Rory's father made two-fifty an hour filling potholes before he fell. Minimum wage was a dollar fifteen. Rory didn't even make that. His job was off the books but when he added in the tips he made about a buck and a quarter an hour. He was just happy to have the job. If Rory quit today there'd be a line around the block to get his job tomorrow, so you took what Sal gave you.

Rory stepped out of the icebox, shivering, and saw Babe by the band saw talking to the sawdust guy, legs apart, jingling his car keys like altar bells.

"I drove home this tomata a little while ago, and madon, but she's a knockout," Babe said. "She makes out like a French maid. . . ."

Rory felt a burn of loss in his gut that added to the President Kennedy loss. Then out of nowhere, Sal lurched past them toward the back room. He pushed aside the sawdust guy and the fat collector, and startled the knife grinder. And Babe, too.

"Hey, Pop, what's wrong?" Babe said.

"Get back here, Babe," Sal said. "You, too, kid."

His brother Tony stared at Sal in mild concern from behind the showcase up front, stealing glances in the mirror at a customer. Rory recognized the customer; the man with the sunglasses he'd seen sitting in the parked Plymouth Fury across the street. The guy was pacing, watching everything, chewing a piece of gum. Rory noticed that the Plymouth was now double-parked in front of the store, flashers blinking. He felt a small ripple of fear.

Rory eased into the back room where Sal stretched toward a high linen shelf over the long butcher block that was heaped with ground pork and salted pig-gut casings bound for the manual Italian sausage machine mounted on the end of the table. Sal leaned against the table and reached for the shelf but stopped and cringed. He moaned in pain. He took two steps sideways, like a cowboy who'd just been shot. Babe caught his father in his arms before he could fall.

"You okay, Pop?"

"Goddamned sciatica," Sal said, clutching Babe and his lower back at the same time for support.

Babe said, "I'll call an ambulance. . . ."

"No!" Sal said, looking at Rory. "Kid, get me my gun from under the aprons. Quick! Careful, it's loaded! I don't like the look of this hump with the sunglasses you pointed out to me. This guy has a bulge like a gun under his sweater."

Rory climbed up on a chair and reached for the holstered pearl-handled .38 Smith and Wesson. It weighed about as much as a pound of Boar's Head ham. He blinked, looking at it, the first time he'd ever touched a real-life gun. It made him feel funny holding a gun on the day someone shot John Fitzgerald Kennedy.

"C'mon, that ain't no cap gun, kid," Sal said.

Rory handed the gun to Sal.

"What's a matta?" Noonz asked, stepping out of the icebox and into the back-room commotion, seeing Sal pull the pistol from the holster that he then dropped to the floor.

"Guy up front's packing," Sal said. "Your goddamned leg breakers looking for you in my freakin' store?"

"You blamin' *me* on a guy casing the joint? Go ahead, Sal. Blame *me*. You blame me for everything else around here, including snowstorms and taxes already, so blame *me* for this, too."

"Everybody stay put," Sal said, checking the cylinder to make sure the gun was loaded. It was. He limped back out to the front of the store with the gun pressed at his side, cupped in his hand, hidden by his right leg. Babe stood with the workmen. Rory inched up the aisle leading from the crowded back room and used the back counter mirrors to search for the suspicious guy.

He was gone.

Sal hobbled into the back room, clutching his lower back. Rory handed him the holster. Sal fitted the gun in the holster and handed it to Rory and told him to put it back on the high shelf. As Rory placed the gun back, he noticed Sal glare at Noonz.

Sal talked about how doing a stickup on the day the president was killed was pretty cagey. Because everybody was a little off guard and distracted. The workmen didn't believe a word he was saying. Sal cursed out his sciatica as Rory hopped down from the sausage counter.

"Thanks, kid," Sal said. "Now go get them orders delivered. The Chairman's people called twice, waiting for his sausage and chopped veal, pork, and sirloin for his meatballs. Make sure you don't forget his pork bones this time. He must be a wreck over the president. Probably having their own big strategy meeting at the Ben Franklin Club tonight before he flies down for the funeral."

Rory felt kind of honored that he'd be delivering meat to a man who would be at the John Fitzgerald Kennedy funeral.

With that Brooklyn connection to this major event, an almost historic mission, Rory loaded up his big bike and pushed off into his neighborhood, which always made him feel like Huck Finn on his raft on the mighty Mississippi.

7

Rory fitted his transistor radio in the special compartment he'd made in the bike basket so that he could listen to ball games in the summer and Murray the K, the WINS disc jockey who always talked about the Beatles. Rory's father had won the transistor radio at the St. Stanislaus church bazaar two years ago and given it to Rory for Christmas. He cherished it. As he pedaled through Brooklyn, stray dogs always trailing him to lick up the dripping blood, the rock and roll mixed with the wind and the horns and the traffic. And as Rory's legs pumped faster and faster—and they got bigger and stronger and rock hard with muscles—something magical also happened in his head. Words, phrases, whole sentences formed, new ideas popped into his mind like little explosions. Or like thought balloons in a comic book.

Sometimes Rory whispered his own rock and roll lyrics, and poems to lonely old ladies. Or he'd imagine how he'd write the first paragraphs about the ball game he'd just listened to. Or describe the home run differently than the way Mel Allen or Red Barber just described it on the radio. He came up with his own "Nobody Asked Me, But . . ." oneliners, like the brilliant Jimmy Cannon wrote in his *Journal-American* column, keen observations about sports and life and politics and women and the world.

When he got out of Freedom Meats on the bike, racing through snarled traffic, running through red lights, zooming up and down tree-lined brownstone streets, past smoke-belching factories, along crumbling, tenement-jammed avenues, or across shopping strips like Seventh and Fifth avenues, checking out the pretty girls in their new fashions, waving at friends hanging on corners, pitching pennies or playing stickball or touch football or off the point or street hockey, or zooming past the cops on the beat or the Con Ed guys and Ma Bell workers digging holes in the gutter or climbing poles, Rory felt privileged.

He was a kid with a j-o-b.

And a job was where you learned about money and responsibility and business and was the first step toward manhood. People relied on Rory, depended on him. What he did was important. He provided a valuable service. His father explained that there was nobility and pride in any honest work. And that was more important than the money itself.

Having a job that people relied on you for meant you mattered in your little patch of the world. Work gave your life meaning, Harry Maguire always said. That was something you couldn't learn in a classroom. It was also why not working made Harry Maguire hurt more inside, in his soul, than from the physical pain.

And so, when Rory Maguire was on his bike, like Huck on the raft, he couldn't believe that he was getting paid for it. This wasn't work; this was adventure. For a future writer, this was research. *Experience.* This job brought him into people's lives, gave him a peek behind closed doors, showed him how different people of different religions and different nationalities and different salaries lived. He smelled cooking he never would have smelled before. Heard music he never knew existed. It gave him ideas about people and places and things to write about. He delivered to guys he'd heard Sal say were real-life mafia gangsters, but who were quiet and generous, giving one-dollar tips and saying almost nothing except, "Thanks, kid." He remembered how they dressed, how they moved, whether or not they shaved. He wanted to remember how things looked and smelled and sounded in case he ever wrote a story about a gangster.

He delivered to the Chairman. He also delivered to another guy on Carroll Street who was nice but acted kind of swishy, and he had big framed posters from Broadway plays all over the walls, and bookcases from floor to ceiling stuffed with more books than Rory'd ever seen one man have at home before. The guy said he danced on Broadway in shows like *The Sound of Music* and *Oliver*. Rory delivered to nuns who sometimes took off their habits in the convent and old ladies who lived all alone in apartments that smelled like decaying fat in the bottom of the barrels. He delivered to a Protestant minister at the Episcopalian church on Eighth Street, who had little kids, which meant he must have had sex, and a wife that he slept with at night, which Rory thought was kinda boss. You could dedicate your life to Jesus and still sleep with a woman. He didn't seem like the kind of guy who would go to hell or limbo when he died for not being Catholic. What were Protestants doing right? Who the hell would be a priest when you could be a minister and have sex and a wife and kids?

He delivered to saloons where they cooked burgers in the small kitchens in the rear and listened to men curse and swear and tell stories about sex with women. He loved going in the kitchen of Fitzgerald's because the cook, a bald guy whom Noonz called Mr. Clean, had a nudie calendar on the wall of women from around the world, chicks so hot they were tattooed on Rory's brain. Whenever Mr. Clean left Rory in his kitchen and went up front to get the money for the meat out of the register Rory would flip through the calendar. He fell half in love, or lust, with Miss May, who was Hawaiian and like a gorgeous creature from another galaxy, a zillion miles from Krypton. Rory sometimes searched for and found Miss May in the chipped plaster of the ceiling at night, too.

He delivered to one place where a woman about his mother's age always answered the door in a see-through slip and behind her there were always three or four younger ladies also in slips, most of them Puerto Rican, watching TV and smoking cigarettes and talking in Spanish and giggling. Everyone said it was a who-wah house. But at first Rory didn't believe it because he saw Coyle the cop coming out of it a few times. Noonz said later his guess was that Coyle was taking "some in trade." The woman, Betty, who always looked sleepy, tipped fifty cents, too.

He knew he would never forget this day, November twenty-second, nineteen hundred and sixty-three, not for the rest of his life. He made sure to remember details—the weather and the things people said and the way they looked when they said them, the crumpled faces, and the way tears made adults look like helpless children, and how grief made tough guys stutter and slouch. He knew this was a day his kids and grandchildren would ask about, and he wanted to be able to tell them. He knew school kids until the end of time would study about this day the way he had studied about the day Abraham Lincoln was murdered, and so he felt like an eyewitness to history. He would also remember it was the day he first got to talk to Carol Sturgis and the look on his mother's face and that his father said he wished he could buy him a beer.

"Blowin' in the Wind," by Peter, Paul, and Mary, came on the radio. He listened to the song as he sped two blocks out of his way to Tenth Street, the cold wind scouring his face, made a left, and slowed as he pedaled up Carol's block. Hoping he would see her.

Pay dirt!

Halfway up the block, Carol stood in front of her brownstone, Scotch-taping Thanksgiving turkey decorations on the window of her stoop door. She didn't look like she was in a holiday mood. Her father was adjusting an American flag to half-staff above the door, chipping old paint out of the flag pole bracket with a screwdriver.

To get Carol's attention Rory turned the transistor up as high as it would go and slowed down as he approached. She turned and saw Rory pushing the big bike uphill toward Eighth Avenue. She smiled. He showed her how strong he was by not having to stand up to pedal the loaded bike uphill.

He glanced at her, his own mop top blowing in the wind as the song played, and his heart did the same leap it always did, whenever she looked at him. She was dressed in black stretch pants that had stirrups that went under her feet and a tight turtleneck sweater that showed off her curves. Even as the sun went down her big blue eyes stood out.

Nobody asked me, but Carol Sturgis's eyes are so blue they look like little patches of the morning sky . . .

He thought he should write that phrase down in his notebook that he always carried in his back pocket. He might use it in a story someday.

Then he thought of Babe saying that Carol made out like a French maid and it made him sick, like the first time he ever drank one of Noonz's beers. He didn't believe she even kissed Babe. Not after one measly ride home. She couldn't be that much of a who-wah. He figured Babe was just talking big to impress the sawdust guy.

Carol's father followed his daughter's smiling gaze to Rory on the bike. He had one of those never-smiling faces like the suit-and-tie clerks he'd met when he wheeled his father into the workmen's comp and disability offices. People who looked at you like you were after something you didn't deserve, that you weren't good enough for, like you were a chiseler, or on the make.

Mr. Sturgis looks at me like I'm not good enough for his daughter, Rory thought. *The dirty order boy. Just wait'll he spends Sunday mornings reading my interviews with Weeb Ewbank and Jim Brown. Or when he learns about the new Mets winter trades in my column. Then let's see if I'm good enough for his precious daughter.*

"Hey, knucklehead!" Mr. Sturgis yelled. "Careful of my car!"

Rory realized that as he gaped at Carol his mind drifted and with it so did his bike. He slammed on the foot brake just inches from Carol's father's Chevy. The basket whipped right for the rear fin. Rory swung the basket hard to the left, causing all the weight of the orders to sway with it. The bike tottered and toppled and he had to hop off the seat and balance it with his feet, the bar digging into his groin, the pain shooting to the top of his head like a hammer-and-bell game down Coney Island. Two bags of meat flew out of the basket into the gutter. The dogs galloped for it. Rory let the bike drop and stamped his feet and flailed his arms and chased the growling barking dogs away. The radio played the end of the song and moved to a commercial for a rock and roll show with Little Stevie Wonder at the Paramount Theater.

But thank God I didn't hit Mr. Sturgis's Chevy, he thought.

"Who listens to goddamned music like that the day the president is killed," Mr. Sturgis said, shaking his head, adjusting the half-staff flag.

Rory was so embarrassed he could feel his face roasting like a chicken on a spit. "You okay?" Carol asked, trotting from the stoop to the gutter. She was smiling.

"It's okay," he said. "Man, I'm a doofus."

"Let me help," she said, bending beside him, her beautiful hands with the painted nails collecting packages of meat from the gutter. Rory smelled her expensive, rosy perfume. Her sparkling hair smelled clean and fresh and her breath was spearminty and this time, up close, her blue eyes reminded him of two mini–swimming pools. Little puffs of frosty breath came out of her small nose and soft lips. *Nobody asked me, but Carol's the kind of girl people write hit songs about.*

"Your father hates me," he said.

"Ah, don't mind him, he makes his living hating people," she said. "He's a prosecutor. The president just got murdered and he's worrying about his car."

"You mean he's like a D.A.?"

"Assistant district attorney," she said, stuffing a pound of chuck chop, a pound of bacon, and a whole chicken back into a bag. "That's why we moved to Brooklyn, for the job. He thinks everyone in Brooklyn is guilty until proven innocent. Especially around me. If he only knew what was going on in my head he'd sentence me to life."

They laughed as "He's So Fine" by the Chiffons came on the radio while he stuffed six pounds of Italian sausage and the special meatball mix into a bag marked THE CHAIRMAN in dark pencil. At the same time he wondered if her words meant she did kiss Babe like a floozy French maid. Then: *What exactly is a French maid? And what does she kiss like?*

"You deliver to this Chairman guy?" she asked.

"Yeah, I mean, he never comes to the door or anything. I just deal with the Chairman's flunkies. I never meet him, but he makes meatballs and sausage for his club every week and I deliver the raw materials. People come from all over for Freedom Meats' handmade sausage alone."

"Since we moved to Brooklyn, my parents don't shop anywhere else."

"I know. . . ."

"After you told me about the Chairman I asked my father about him and he said he got his own job through the Chairman's club," Carol said. "My father's boss—the D.A. himself—belongs to the Chairman's club. Small world."

"That's the way it works in Brooklyn. Maybe everywhere. He's the boss, the Chairman. He runs everything. He was friends with JFK, for crying out loud. Helped get him elected . . ."

Rory stood up and straightened the bike. He stacked the packages in careful order in the basket. None had broken open. The Chiffons song faded out on the transistor.

"I *love* that song," she said, smiling those perfect teeth at him.

"Yeah, it's boss," Rory said, wondering if she was trying to tell him something. *Am I so fine, to her?* He saw Carol's father glaring at him from the stoop, the flag flapping behind him.

"You all set now?" she asked.

"Yeah, except for my pride. I never fall on the bike. But when I looked at you I just went, I dunno, sorta, um, blank. Good thing I wasn't driving a truck."

She laughed and said, "I guess I'll take that as a compliment . . . *Rory.*"

"Carol, get up here," her father shouted.

"I better go take my daily plea bargain," she said and they laughed together.

"Thanks," Rory said, aching to ask her to go to the special St. Stanislaus mass with him later. He swallowed, moved his lips, clutched the hand grips of the bike, and he said, "Bye, Carol."

"Bye, Rory."

He pedaled up Tenth Street, thinking, *You blew two chances in one day. You are a waste.*

* * *

Rory delivered an order on Prospect Avenue and as he pedaled past Mayflower Laundry he noticed his frantic mother
dashing into work from her lunch break. He figured she'd just
lit a candle in front of St. Anthony's statue in Holy Name
church, and was trying to beat the clock. As usual. A short
red-haired man in a pressed khaki uniform stood with a clipboard, tapping his watch and shaking a finger at her. He
seemed to reprimand Rory's mother as she passed. Rory
made him for Riley, who thought he was God's gift. *Who
cared if Jack Kennedy was dead?* Rory imagined him saying.
Those shirts need starch.

Rory was stopped for a light now, straddling his bike,
watching his mother enter the complex. He saw the red-
haired man and a fat truck driver ogling her as she hurried
off. They made comments to each other. And laughed. The
red-haired guy did most of the talking, pantomiming in an
almost obscene way, and laughing some more. The way Rory
and his pals sometimes did when they saw a hot teenage
chick pass. A chick like Carol Sturgis. He'd never seen anyone look at his mother that way before. It made Rory want to
go punch this red-haired grown-up hard in the mouth.

He couldn't stop thinking about it as he zoomed on his
bike to the far side of the neighborhood, dropping off four
orders along the way. His last stop would be to the Chairman.

8

When he passed the corner of Ninth Street and Eighth Avenue, Rory spotted Lefty Hallahan standing with a few of the Shamrocks outside of Bennie's candy store, which they used as their headquarters. Two of them wore ski masks—with sinister-looking holes cut out for the eyes, nose, and mouth—which came in handy if you were a thug. Dermot wasn't with them. Rory pedaled straight over to Lefty and braked with a skid at the curb. Cool.

"Lefty, we gotta talk," Rory said.

Lefty was sixteen and wore a real leather motorcycle jacket with steel zippers like Marlon Brando wore in *The Wild One*. The four other Shamrocks wore similar jackets, but imitation vinyl. They passed around a single Marlboro and a pint of Twister wine. Lefty was tall, skinny, moving his hands and legs all the time when he talked, like a guy trying to stay warm. He looked light in the ass to Rory. But people said he was good with a blade and a car antenna and he wasn't afraid to use a rod.

"Just the quiff I was lookin' for," said Lefty.

"You have me confused with your flunkies," Rory said.

A few of the Shamrocks made a move toward Rory. Lefty held up one finger and they stopped.

"Tell me what you want first, then I'll tell you what you are gonna do for me, homo," Lefty said.

"I want you to leave my kid brother Dermot alone."

"*Me* leave *him* alone? Kid follows me around like Sweet Pea follows Popeye. He quiff too? Run in the family? Like your old man quiffed outta the draft in World War II."

"Someday, big mouth, how about you and me alone? Name the schoolyard."

"Sure, and I get arrested for beatin' up a butcher boy? Who takes the meat in the back way? But tell you what, Rory. I'll give your punk kid brother a hop in the hole and tell him to scram after you do something for me."

"I'm listening."

"We got us a rumble comin' up with the Roman Emperors in two weeks, soon as Pee Wee Carbo gets out of Rikers."

"Yeah, and?"

"These dagos pack heat," Lefty said, making an imaginary pistol with his right hand and firing.

"Yeah? And so what's that got to do with me?"

They fell silent as Rory noticed a Plymouth Fury passing by with a big, tall antenna sprouting from the back, the tell-tale sign of a detective car. Without straining his eyes Rory knew it was Detective Anthony "Ankles" Tufano, head of the Youth Squad at the 72nd Precinct. Everyone knew he was looking to make a few big busts so he could get promoted to a different squad. Like narcotics, where he could go after the junkies and pushers who brought smack to the neighborhood.

Ankles slowed to a prowl and watched Rory talking to Lefty as the Shamrocks looked on, all freckle-faced and runny-nosed from passing cigarettes and sharing beers and wine. If one Shamrock had a cold, all of them always had it. None of them worked. Most were constant truants, and all of them had records of time spent in Lincoln Hall or the Youth House. They pulled burglaries, sold fireworks, dealt in hot jewelry and boosted clothes, rigged token turnstiles, robbed subway candy machines, shoplifted, extorted lunch money from rich kids, stole pocketbooks, did muggings, and pulled other scores to make money. Rory even heard Lefty sold marijuana, Mary Jane, to make money.

Lefty pantomimed a pistol again and said, "Here's what it got to do with you. It's simple. I hear the fat wop you work for packs."

"Who told you that?"

"Nevermind."

"Dermot's full of it."

"I know what I know," Lefty said. "We got a rumble with the Emperors who will be packin' real heat, not no little zip guns. They get them from the Mafia wops down in the Gallo's Boys social club. I need a real rod for this rumble. And you're gonna boost it for me from your wop boss. That's called poetic justice."

"If you can spell either word it's a miracle," Rory said. "But maybe you can spell this: n-o. As in no way."

"Okay, then I can't be held responsible if your kid brother leads the Shamrock charge into the middle of the Emperors. See ya at his funeral."

"Stay away from Dermot or the only funeral you'll be going to is yours."

Three of the Shamrocks made a move toward Rory. One yanked a heavy chain from his pocket. Rory also heard the metallic *ka-ching* of a switchblade unfolding. Lefty smiled, snapped his fingers like a bad guy in a B movie, and they all stopped. Rory believed that a lot of the bad guys in Brooklyn used B movies as training films, imitating the bad guys the way other kids imitated sports stars.

"Cool it, fellas," Lefty said. "We need Rory. Rory here's gonna think it over. First of all, he's a mick, like us, and he don't wanna see the dagos rule our turf, mess with our broads. Second, he'll do what he's told because he don't wanna see his Ma's heart broken no more. She already married a crippled commie coward who's ready for the home relief. Rory won't want his Ma seeing his kid brother comin' home DOA."

"At least my mother isn't doing time for killin' my father, like yours."

Rory regretted saying it as soon as it came out of his mouth, and could see the hurt in Lefty's eyes. Lefty's animated arms and legs froze like a toy with a battery that just went dead. He stared at Rory and sniffled, wiped his nose with the back of his hand. The Shamrocks gaped at him waiting for his reaction. Lefty motioned for his boys to go stand by the candy store, out of earshot.

"Who told you that?" Lefty asked, unable to look Rory in the eye.

"I read it in an old newspaper in the library. On what you call a microfiche machine. I was looking up something else and saw your name. Eddie Hallahan. Only it was your father's name. It said your mom killed him in his drunken sleep because he beat her and you all the time. Ten years ago . . ."

"She gets out next year, ya know," Lefty said, his voice thin and soft. "They didn't even let her go to my grandmother's funeral."

"Look, I'm sorry I brought it up. I hate mother and father ranking. I take it back. But I'd appreciate it if you stopped ranking on my old man."

Lefty blinked a few times. He swallowed, looked at the sky, rolled his jaws, and shrugged. He said, "I need the gun by next Thursday."

"I take back what I said about your mother and father," Rory said. "I don't take back anything else. Leave my kid brother alone and forget about me boosting any gun."

"By next Thursday," Lefty said, firing the imaginary pistol and leading the Shamrocks into the candy store.

Rory raced to Sixth Street, squealed a left toward Seventh Avenue, already running late on his orders. *Too much talking,* he told himself. *Too much getting in the way. This is a day historians will write about for centuries. And I'm here to see and hear and smell and touch and feel. Here to remember. I have to sponge up the mood, the images; the things people say and do. So that later when I write about* The Day Jack Kennedy Died, *it will pour out of me, like it was yesterday. I need to hurry with these other damned orders. I have to get to the Chairman, who knows Jack Kennedy, who helped get him elected. He is part of the story. And I am the kid that brings him his meat for the dinner at which the Brooklyn machine will all plan the future without John Fitzgerald Kennedy. I'm a fly on the wall of history . . .*

He delivered an order to Mrs. Collier, who always gave him a quarter. She said she'd give him an extra quarter if he came in and moved a couch from one side of the room to the other. Rory hesitated, then said sure, and finished the job within three minutes, eager to get to the Chairman. He had a special use for that extra quarter.

As he left the areaway and climbed on his bike Ankles pulled up in his detective car. The six-foot-four cop with the famous size-14 shoes—which he used to kick kids in the ankles until he got confessions, earning him his nickname—climbed out of the car with a big White Owl cigar smoldering in his thick lips. He pulled his collar up to the November cold, yanked the stingy brim of his fedora over his left eye and scowled.

"All right, no bullcrap, what did that lowlife Hallahan want before?"

"We were talking about the Mets," Rory said

"I seen him make a pistol outta his hand."

"Oh, yeah, the assassination. We talked JFK."

"Only reason I don't break your ankles this second is because I know your mother needs the few coins you put on the table," Ankles said. "But you know that I know that you're full of crapola, Maguire. I know there's a gang war in the works between the Shamrocks and the Roman Emperors. Those savages use guns. Lefty's a two-bit thief, in way over his head. Someone's gonna get hurt. Bad. Maybe die. Which wouldn't bother me at all except it's on my watch. I also worry because I see your little brother—what's he, thirteen?—running after Lefty like a lapdog puppy. Now tell me what's goin' on, numb nuts, or I'll haunt ya."

"I have no idea what you're talking about," Rory said, believing that the only thing lower than a guy like Lefty was a rat.

"I know your old man, kid," Ankles said, flicking Rory's cold red ear with a big heavy finger, stinging him. "Good man. Takes a bum rap from a lot of people. I think he's gettin' jobbed now on the disability. I rode by the day he fell. I didn't smell no liquor on him. And I got a good nose. I also think your mother's a good, decent hardworking woman. She tried raising you kids right. I think your kid brother's on a collision course with disaster. You can help him by helping me get this Lefty Hallahan off the street and into a cage where he belongs. Now, what did he say about a gun?"

"I have no love for Lefty Hallahan, but I don't know anything."

"You just live by the dumb-ass code of the street," Ankles said, straightening the brown bag in Rory's basket and snooping the Chairman's penciled name.

"When was the last time a cop ratted on another crooked cop?" Rory asked.

Ankles took a deep puff on his cigar and nodded his head. "Great. A *smart* dumb ass."

"I work for a living," Rory said. "I'm trying to do my job right now. I'm sorry Detective Tufano, but I can't help you."

"Can't help me help your own kid brother? For your mother's sake?"

"I'll take care of Dermot."

"I know your boss, Sal Russo, ya know," Ankles said. "Good guy. I wouldn't want to have to put a bad word in on you."

Rory looked at him, his heart racing, and looked past him where he saw Lefty Hallahan and the Shamrocks walking along Eighth Avenue, pausing to watch Rory talking to Ankles. Then he saw Dermot hurry to catch up to them. He saw Lefty drape his arm over Dermot's shoulders.

"I'm sorry," Rory said, pedaling away from Ankles, giving him the finger for the edification of Lefty Hallahan. "Really, I am . . ."

Ankles looked at Lefty and the Shamrocks and Dermot and nodded as Rory sped toward the Chairman's.

9

He was in a rush to get to the Chairman's. But he had to make one more stop on the way. With the extra quarter from moving Mrs. Collier's couch he raced down to Krauss's New and Used Business Machines on Sixth Avenue near Flatbush Avenue. He put the kickstand down on the bike and rushed to the dusty window and peered at the twenty-five-dollar used Royal manual typewriter that sat there like a black stallion.

Nobody asked me, but . . . a good typewriter is like a thoroughbred that you can ride into the winner's circle of life.

He loved looking at the SOLD sticker across the price tag. He knew it meant the machine was sold to Rory Maguire on the Lay-a-Way. Rory galloped down the three steps into the crowded old shop that smelled like machine oil and ink.

All the local shopkeepers and businesses, including Sal Russo and the Chairman, had their cash registers and typewriters and adding machines serviced and repaired here at Krauss's.

"Aha, it's Ernest Hemingway of Brooklyn," said Mr. Krauss. "How are you, Maguire? You have another quarter for me? So you can write about home runs and touchdowns and knockouts?"

Rory handed old man Krauss a quarter. Krauss took out a marble-faced copybook, turned the dog-eared pages, found

Rory Maguire's name and made the twenty-five-cent entry that brought the balance down to an even twelve bucks. The original deal was that Rory would pay off fifty cents a week starting in January, totaling twenty-five dollars by Christmas. But after his father fell in May, Rory had to cut back to a quarter a week because he couldn't afford to splurge a half a buck a week on himself when his mother needed money so bad. A quarter a week was a buck a month and that buck would buy five pounds of potatoes and a quart of milk and some spinach or a pound of chuck chop to feed the kids. His mother always told him to pay for the typewriter. And his father tried to make him keep the silver dollar he gave him each week. But it was important to Rory that his father had his dollar and that his mother got an extra buck a month, too.

A buck was a buck.

He was fourteen so if he had to wait another year to get the typewriter, he'd wait. But whenever he got an extra quarter he hadn't planned on getting, he flew down to Krauss's before he was tempted to buy another transistor radio battery or a bag of chips, a Spider-Man comic about a newspaper photographer from Queens, and a Coke.

More than a car like Babe's, a leather coat from Belmont's, or a pair of Florsheim featherweight shoes with horseshoe taps, Rory dreamed of owning that Royal typewriter. Every time Rory came in, Krauss took it out of the window for him, placed it on a typing table, let him wind a sheet of typing paper on the black roll, listening to the clean gears clicking and then he typed: *Now is the time for all good men to come to the aid of the party. The quick brown fox jumped over the lazy dog.*

He felt the magical give in the smooth brass-rimmed keys, little detonations of power like the handle you plunged down on an explosive, heard the powerful staccato clatter of the keys striking the paper that sounded like Sammy Davis Jr. tap dancing, leaving the little symbols that made words that added up to sentences that would give him a life in a newspaper cityroom across the great Brooklyn Bridge.

When the carriage reached the end he heard the bell ring like the gong of the first round of a championship fight. Then he grabbed the smooth chrome handle of the carriage return and sailed it back on its cable and started to type a third sentence. Krauss stood and smiled, his sad wrinkled old face etched with memories of life as a Jew under the Nazis, looking now at this dreamy-eyed young Irish kid banging out sentences on the beautiful Royal.

"She's a beautiful little darlink, no?" Krauss said.

"It's the best typewriter in the world," Rory said.

Rory traced his fingers across the gleaming ebony and brass-rimmed keyboard and got up and walked for the door.

"Gotta run, Mr. Krauss. Thanks."

Krauss yanked the paper out of the roller.

"What this means?" Krauss asked, reading what Rory had typed. "What means 'Nobody asked me, but . . . she had eyes like little patches of the morning sky.'?"

Rory shrugged as he pulled open the door, a little embarrassed.

"Nothing," he said.

"This sounds good to me but what do I know from English?" Krauss said. "Two things I can tell you. Your typing improves every week. No errors this time."

"Thanks," Rory said. "What's the second thing?"

"You're a nice kid," he said. "So, okay, you think you're in love but don't let some young goil break your heart, Maguire."

Rory laughed and said, "It's just typing, Mr. Krauss."

And then Rory left as Krauss put the gleaming baked black enamel Royal with the brass-edged keys back in the dusty window.

10

Without Carol Sturgis around to impress, and his cargo much lighter, Rory pumped up Union Street, standing up on the pedals to go faster. He felt the calf and thigh muscles bulge inside his suety-slick dungarees, leaned his strong arms and back into the ride as he outraced the B-69 bus as it roared toward Grand Army Plaza. The transistor played "Surfin' USA" by the Beach Boys, and he thought the tune was a bad choice on the day the president was shot.

As he neared the Benjamin Franklin Club in its three-story brownstone, the Chairman's battered meat order bouncing in the basket, he wondered how the old politician was feeling. Since that night in 1960 when Rory's father and the Chairman exchanged testy words on the sidewalk in front of the John Fitzgerald Kennedy storefront campaign office, the Chairman had become even more powerful because the president of the United States owed him big-time for delivering Brooklyn, which meant the state of New York. It said so in the *Daily News* and the *Post*. Jack Kennedy won by 100,000 votes, and a ton of them were from Brooklyn.

But Rory had heard his mother and father discussing politics a few times, like the time she swooned over Jack Kennedy, which made his father laugh. She would tell Harry Maguire to go see the Chairman and tell him that his wife voted for John Fitzgerald Kennedy and that therefore the Chairman should help Harry out with his workmen's comp.

Harry said he and the Chairman had already had words once and he wasn't the kind of politician to ever forget a slight. "He's a grievance collector," Harry said. "He collects grievances and favors and takes care of those who scratch his back. I didn't scratch his back or vote for his candidates so he'll never do me any favors."

"Then I'll ask," Tara said.

"You will not," Harry said. "Not on my behalf. I won't ask for handouts from home relief or a machine boss. And I won't have my wife do any genuflecting or begging for me. I'll fight for what I'm entitled to. I got hurt in the war and I got hurt on the job and all I'm asking is fair compensation for that like any other working man."

"You can't ignore a man like Charlie the Chairman," his mother had said. "The Chairman has power."

"Not for much longer," Harry said. "Walter Lippmann and James Reston and Murray Kempton are all saying it in the newspaper columns. The day of the machine boss is dying. This is the last hurrah. After 1960 all elections will be fought on TV, they say. There'll be no need for these old mummies giving out their turkeys and their summer jobs and their favors. That's what they say. Candidates will be sold to the American people like boxes of soap."

But here it was three years after the John Fitzgerald Kennedy election and the Chairman still had all the power. More power than ever. Even his father admitted that the Chairman still stocked the bureaucracy and the courts with loyal, indebted Democrats. The Chairman was still the fixer who could finesse everything from a parking ticket to a zoning variance to a felony charge.

"The Chairman is the only one who can cut through your father's red tape," said Esposito the lawyer, whenever Rory stopped by his Seventh Avenue office to ask for updates. "I keep telling him he needs to talk to the Chairman."

Rory wedged the bike between two parked cars, grabbed the shopping bag with the Chairman's order, and climbed the stone stoop to the upstairs entrance. He thought again of his father telling the Chairman to say hello to his son Charles Jr., *"We were comrades on the same Liberty ship during the war."* Which Rory learned later on was meant as some kind of a put-down because the Chairman and his son had had a big public falling out a few years before and the son moved away somewhere and he and the Chairman didn't talk anymore. Or so the story went. Rory didn't know all the details.

For years after getting the job at Freedom Meats, Rory prayed that he wouldn't meet the Chairman. He didn't want the Brooklyn boss to remember that incident with his father and call Sal and put in a bad word that might get him fired. Bosses were like that. But ever since his father got hurt and was turned down for the workmen's comp and disability Rory had changed his view; he hoped now he would run into the Chairman so he could make a case about Harry. Maybe that letter he was writing to John Fitzgerald Kennedy should go to the Chairman.

Rory rang the bell and squinted through the smoked glass in the oak doors trying to spot the unmistakable silhouette of the Chairman. His whole speech was all worked out in his head. He'd tell him about how his father needed help and how the Chairman was the only one who could help him now, and how Rory worked for the John Fitzgerald Kennedy campaign, and how his mother voted for John Fitzgerald Kennedy, and how his father was wounded in the war and had five kids and that he didn't drink the day he fell and he was getting shafted. And the reason Harry said those things to the Chairman about his son that day in 1960 was because he heard voices and sirens in his head from war wounds.

He'd rehearsed it a zillion times while riding his bike to deliver the meat to the Chairman. But he never did get to see him. And that's why Rory started writing the *You're Harry Maguire* letter to Jack Kennedy. But Rory could never get all the crucial war details from his father he knew he needed in his story. Details a naval hero like Jack Kennedy might relate to and understand.

This time, standing on the stoop with the late-afternoon light shading to the charcoal gray just before night, Rory didn't see the Chairman either. Instead he saw two familiar figures move his way, the same two guys who always answered the door. One of them was tall and skinny and wore a fedora and always kept his hand inside his jacket like Napoleon. Rory figured the guy either had constant heartburn or a gun. The other guy was short, fat and bald and he was the one who always paid for the meat and gave Rory the Liberty-silver-dollar tip from the Chairman. Both of them looked as if they'd been crying.

"Come in outta the cold, kid," said the short bald guy. Rory carried the shopping bag and followed the tall guy with his hand in his jacket down the long high-ceilinged hallway with the oak borders, gleaming oak stairs, parquet oak floors, and Persian rugs. A chandelier dangled from the curlicued ceiling. A gold-framed oil painting of John Fitzgerald Kennedy hung on a wall, surrounded by photos of JFK chummy as hell with the Chairman. Somewhere, three different TV sets were playing.

They entered a large kitchen, bigger than Rory's living room and two bedrooms put together, with bare brick walls and gleaming copper-bottomed pots hanging from overhead racks. Sal told Rory that the Chairman was a great chef, a gourmet, and he always cooked for people. He cooked for mayors and governors and the last four presidents, including Republicans. Even Harry Truman. For foreign leaders. For movie stars. For Frank Sinatra. He cooked for John Fitzgerald Kennedy when he was still a congressman right here in this room! And even once when he was president. Rory sometimes bragged to people that he delivered the meat that John Fitzgerald Kennedy ate.

All the countertops were made out of the same butcher-block Rory scraped every night in Freedom Meats. In the adjoining room, there was a huge dining table with a dozen chairs around it and big stained-glass lamps hanging over it. Rory always imagined the Chairman sitting at it like Jesus at the Last Supper talking to the Apostles, dishing out heaping bowls of spaghetti topped with the meatballs and sausage that Rory delivered.

Tonight's dinner is gonna be as sad as the Last Supper, Rory thought.

The short bald flunky looked at the price on the shopping bag: $22. He paid Rory from a thick, crisp green wad and then reached in his left pocket that clunked with the sounds of a dozen Liberty silver dollars. He pulled one out and handed it to Rory.

"That's from the Chairman, kid," the bald guy said.

"Thanks," Rory said and hesitated.

"So long," said the tall guy. "C'mon. Bad night."

"Can I see the Chairman?"

The bald guy smiled and nudged Rory down the hall. "C'mon kid, that's not possible."

"I need to see him about my father."

"What about your father? What's his name?"

"Harry Maguire."

The two guys looked at each other, the name unfamiliar. "What's the problem?" asked the tall guy.

"Workmen's comp, disability . . ."

"The Chairman's too busy for that there, a night like this. The president . . . but tell your old man to see his Democratic district leader, go through party channels . . ."

"Well, he isn't a Democrat."

The tall guy laughed, and said, "Then tell him to hold his nose and see the Republican leader."

"He isn't a Republican either," Rory said.

"Then tell your old man to see a priest," the short bald guy said, ushering Rory into the vestibule. "For Chrissakes, kid, the president is dead. You hear the news yet? Jack Kennedy is dead and you wanna talk about your old man's workmen's comp case? Scram. Get outta here!"

Just as they stepped into the vestibule, Rory looked past them into the house and saw two big oak doors slide open and the Chairman strode out of the living room and entered the kitchen, dressed in a long silk robe, big cigar in his mouth. He began taking the meat out of the shopping bag, lost in a swirl of blue smoke.

"Chairman Pergola," Rory shouted. "Please I need to talk to you . . ."

The Chairman turned and squinted down the long hallway in Rory's direction. Through the soft light and the smoke Rory thought his cobalt eyes looked like they'd been crying.

The tall guy nudged Rory through the outside door of the vestibule. "Not tonight, kid. Now am-scray, before I call your boss."

The bald guy closed and locked the doors and Rory stood on the stoop as night swallowed the cold city.

11

Rory raced to Freedom Meats, angry, slightly ashamed of himself. He had another eleven orders waiting for him that he delivered in record speed, collecting quarter tips from all but one, the guy named Joe Eighteenth Street, a gambler who always told Rory, "Bad day on the nags, sonny boy, catch you next time." Once he hit a horse and he gave Rory two bucks but didn't tip him again for three months.

A few minutes past six Rory hosed out the showcase after stacking all the white enamel platters in the walk-in icebox for the night. He'd hand washed the platters that were empty in the backroom sink. Now, stripped down to his undershirt to wash out the showcase, he heard the automatic bell ring over the front door.

He looked through the double-glass front panel of the showcase and saw the woolen tights and knee-high leather boots of Carol Sturgis, flanked by her father who wore khaki chinos and lame tan Hush Puppies, and her mother, who wore pleated black pants and stylish low heels. Rory froze. He was afraid to confront Mr. Sturgis.

"Too late to order?" asked Mrs. Sturgis.

"Not at all," said Sal, leaning against the butcher block by the window. "Never too late for our best customers."

They ordered porterhouse steaks, baby lamp chops, chicken cutlets, veal cutlets, an eye round roast beef, and a loin of pork. Plus cold cuts—ham, provolone, salami, Swiss.

Nothing but Boar's Head. And a fresh-killed turkey. It was enough for a week.

Rory kept hosing out the showcase, long after all the soap was rinsed away.

Then he saw her face. Carol dropped a quarter and bent to pick it up out of the sawdust and smiled at him through the steamy showcase glass. He smiled back, then blasted the glass with the hose, her smiling face distorting in the spray. She wore a black capelike coat with a wool hood that pushed her long hair up from the back.

"Hey, kid, you watering a lawn in there or what?" Sal asked. Rory straightened from the showcase. Sal handed him a piece of butcher paper where he'd written the Sturgis order. "Tell Noonz I need this, top-shelf, and then cut me the cold cuts. Take this side of beef inside the box with ya on the way. And scrape the last block and sweep out the store and we're finished. C'mon. Let's move like a needle in a groove, kid."

Rory turned off the hose. Mr. Sturgis glanced coldly at him and looked away with what Rory thought was mild contempt. Mrs. Sturgis smiled at him in an amused way. Rory caught a glimpse of himself in the mirrors behind the counter, muscles jumping in his arms and shoulders, his mop top hair thick on his head, as he took the list from Sal. He yanked on a white butcher jacket and hoisted an eighty-pound side of beef on his shoulder, and carried it toward the walk-in icebox.

Inside, Rory gave Noonz the list. Noonz peered through the little window that looked out onto the store as he gathered the steaks, lamb chops, roast beef, and the rest of the order for Sal.

Noonz said, "That little tomata can't take her eyes offa you, kid. You know what to do with a cutie pie like that?"

Rory gaped through the window at Carol, who freshened her lipstick in a hand mirror. He wondered why the whole family shopped together. *Weird*, he thought.

"I don't really even know her," Rory said.

"I got some hot books I could lend ya, the readin' kind, you could learn. But I need 'em back. Nothin' worse than not knowin' what you're doin' when the time comes. But Jesus Christ, be careful, you don't need no rabbits at your age. I had my foist at seventeen. Been broke every day since."

"I only talked to her the first time today," Rory said, staring out at Carol, who did a little dance in the sawdust, practicing moves. Rory wondered if she was a dancer.

"Hey, it's the Pepsi generation, no?" Noonz said, stacking the whole order in a beautiful display on a long, rectangular, sparkling white enamel platter.

Rory laughed and went back outside carrying the platter to Sal.

" . . . between crazy assassins and supermarkets, telling you, the whole country's going in the toilet," Sal said.

"Manhattan's even worse," said Mrs. Sturgis. "Supermarkets opening everywhere. Mom-and-pop shops closing one after the other for chain stores and department stores."

"Can't stop the future," said Mr. Sturgis.

"Yeah, but it goes against the American way," Sal said. "It tears the stars offa the flag and encourages nuts like this banana who shot the president. Supermarkets kill small business, which is the heart and soul of America. Assassins kill the president. Hand in hand. Nothing surprises me anymore."

Rory handed Sal the platter of meat. Sal trimmed each steak and cutlet, dumping the fat and trims into the fat barrels under the butcher block, and placed the meat onto separate sections of heavy butcher paper. Rory stole a glance at Carol in the mirror. She caught his eye, rolled hers as she nodded toward Sal and her parents. Rory grinned.

Sal handed Rory the cold cut list and said to Mr. Sturgis, "Five of my other stores went under because of supermarkets. I'll go down with this one because it's my flagship."

"You'll survive," Mrs. Sturgis said. "Some people will try the supermarkets for the novelty and the loss-leader prices and the S&H Green Stamps. But then they'll come back for the quality. You'll see . . ."

At the far end of the showcase, near the walk-in icebox, Rory slapped the head of provolone cheese onto the electric slicer, adjusted the spacer to a one-sixteenth of an inch measurement, and began to cut, arranging the slices in an attractive layered pagoda on wax paper for easy separation the way Sal taught him.

After six slices he saw Carol's elegant hand enter his line of sight, palm up. He cut a slice and laid it on her hand, his fingers brushing hers. He looked into the blue eyes as she nibbled. Her rosy perfume clashed with the strong gamey smell of his clothes. He glanced down to the other end of the showcase, where Sal gabbed with her parents.

"I hope you're right," Sal said in the background.

"I know women," Mrs. Sturgis said.

"Thanks, Rory," Carol said.

He wasn't going to let a third opportunity pass him by in one day, so Rory took a deep breath, looked her in the blue eyes and said, "So, um, you going to the eight o'clock mass tonight at St. Stans for the president?"

"There's a saint named Stan?"

"Stanislaus," he said, laughing. "Polish."

She smiled, looking him deep in the eyes. He cut her another slice of provolone and put the big cheese back in the showcase and took out the ham and jammed it into the slicer carriage.

"You going?" she asked.

Before Rory could answer the front door of Freedom Meats burst open, the loud overhead bell clanging, the door reverberating and cold air blowing in. Rory thought it was like a commercial right in the middle of the dramatic good part of a *Million Dollar Movie.* Mr. Sturgis became startled. Mr. Sturgis spun, as if ready for combat.

"Easy, Babe," Sal shouted.

"Gettin' cold out there, Daddy-o," Babe shouted, rubbing his hands together, pulling up the collar of his three-quarters length leather coat with the removable fleece lining, the coat everyone in the neighborhood drooled over in Belmont's window, the one with the one-hundred-and-thirty-nine-dollar price tag. Babe seemed to pick the bare spots in the sawdust-covered linoleum tile floor just to make sure his Featherweight horseshoe taps clacked. Rory smirked but admitted to himself that he'd do the same thing if he had those shoes.

Rory looked from Babe to Carol and saw that she was watching Babe from the end of the showcase, her face obscured to him by the scale where Rory heaped the Boar's Head ham. Carol kept watching Babe as she nibbled her rolled up slice of provolone. Rory's heart tightened in his chest as he took out the Swiss cheese and sliced. Carol hadn't answered him about going to the mass.

"Hey, Dad, what can I do to help?" Babe asked. "You have any damsels in distress that need rescued? Santa Claus call looking for directions? Hollywood call looking for me? You need me to balance the books? Name it, your one and only, ever lovin' son is front and center and accounted for, sir!"

"Be serious for a minute, Babe," Sal said, smiling and waving him over with his slicing knife. "I want you to meet Mr. and Mrs. Sturgis. This is my son Ba . . . Sal Junior. We call him Babe."

"Babe is short for junior," Babe said, and laughed at his own joke.

Rory watched Carol lean against the wall at the end of the showcase, expensive boots crossed, eating her cheese, watching Babe. Rory loved the casual, confident way she looked in boots and wool tights, the hood hanging down her back like Joan of Arc.

"Pleased to meet you, ma'am, sir," Babe said, nodding and shaking hands.

"Sal's in Poly Prep," said Sal. "He's gonna go to law school. Maybe someday he'll work for you when you go into private practice."

"Always looking for new blood," Mr. Sturgis said.

"I've heard a lot about Poly Prep," said Mrs. Sturgis.

"Hear they have a great sports program," said Mr. Sturgis.

"He's too busy studying for sports," Sal said, answering for his son. "He gonna be a lawyer."

"I would love either baseball or football," Babe said. "But my dad is paying so much tuition I figured I owed it to him to dedicate myself to academic touchdowns and home runs."

Sal beamed. Carol nodded, as if surprised to hear those words coming out of Babe's mouth. Rory bit his lower lip and smiled because he remembered standing alone in the back room one day making Italian sausage when he overheard Babe and Sal rehearsing that very line in Sal's small office in the cellar directly below. You could hear everything Sal said in the office through the loose floorboards. He knew the truth was that Babe had tried out for and failed to make any of the Poly Prep teams.

"No flies on my kid," Sal said.

"Carol," Mrs. Sturgis called, looking around for her daughter. "Carol, I'd like you to meet someone."

"See you at the mass," Carol whispered to Rory and walked across the shop, that confident shoulders-back, long-striding Manhattan walk of hers. Rory watched her go with a shortness of breath. *She's gonna meet me—me—at mass,* he thought.

He grew so excited he thought he would leave his skin, leave orbit. *This must be what John Glenn felt like in outer space,* he thought.

"Hurry up with them cold cuts kid," Sal said. "These people don't have all night."

Rory speed-wrapped the Swiss and sliced the Genoa salami and used the mirrors to watch Mrs. Sturgis introduce Babe to Carol, afraid that a monkey wrench was being tossed into his unofficial date with Carol.

"We've already had the pleasure," Babe said.

"He gave me a ride home from school," Carol said.

Mr. Sturgis nodded, and smiled. "What kind of law you thinking of pursuing, Babe?" Mr. Sturgis asked.

"I figure since I grew up in Brooklyn I might as well go after criminal," he said. "Never run out of work."

"I know what you mean," Mr. Sturgis said.

"But I might look at corporate to help out my dad," he said. "Look at the wholesale end of the meat business."

Mr. Sturgis nodded, impressed. "Good, keep your options open. Good luck, son."

He shook Babe's hand.

Babe has nothing but luck, Rory thought. *Horseshoe taps on his Featherweights and a horseshoe up his ass for luck. Carol's father thinks I'm a dunce and that Babe is a genius. The kind of guy he'd love his daughter to date.*

Rory finished wrapping all the cold cuts and brought them down to Sal, who stuffed them into the paper bag and tallied the tab on one of Mr. Krauss's adding machines. Mr. Sturgis paid Sal and grabbed the bag of meat.

"Sure you don't want my order boy to carry that home for you?" Sal asked.

Mr. Sturgis glanced at Rory and said, "No, thanks."

Carol and Babe said a polite good night and then Carol nodded to Rory, holding his stare as she pulled up her wool hood and left with her parents.

Nobody asked me, but . . . the light from her big blue eyes lingered like the afterglow of a flashcube. . . .

12

After scraping the rest of the butcher blocks with the heavy steel brush, washing out the fat bins with ammonia and sweeping the sidewalk and the sawdust from the front and back of the showcase, Rory laid a fresh blanket of sawdust on the floor of the customers' side of the showcase as Sal sat on one of the customers' chairs with his overcoat and hat on, smoking a Pall Mall.

"Go home to your mother, kid," Sal said.

On the way along Seventh Avenue, Rory spotted the same Plymouth as earlier, with the same man behind the wheel, parked a half block up and across the street. He turned, thinking of rushing back to warn Sal, but saw him and Tony and Noonz leave Freedom Meats. Sal and Tony climbed into Sal's gleaming Cadillac.

Noonz walked alone to the bus stop.

On the corner of Ninth Street, Rory saw Rico Esposito the lawyer closing up his storefront office, fastening a big padlock on the front door.

"Hi, Mr. Esposito," Rory said.

"Oh, hi, Rowdy."

"Rory."

"Sorry, I can never get those funny Irish names straight. "

"Any news on my father's case?"

"Still waiting for the appeal I filed," Esposito said.

"What are his chances?"

"Politics, son," Esposito said with a sigh, walking to his Ford. "It has a lot to do with who you know. Problem is, your father doesn't know anybody and doesn't want to. But I have my fingers crossed, Rowdy."

"Rory. Me, too. When do you think we'll hear?"

"I'm hoping any day before Christmas."

"Thanks, Mr. Esposito."

Rory stood in the two inches of hot water giving himself what his mother always called a two-shakes-of-a-lamb's-tail stand-up sponge bath. No one in the tenement ever got more than two inches of hot tub water before it turned cold. Especially on the top floor, where the water often went cold in the steel risers. Most times the Maguires dumped boiling potato pots of water into the chilly tub water until there was a half-full bath of lukewarm water. Rory always started by washing his hair first so he could pour pots full of clean water over his head to wash out the lather he made with the bar of lye-based Borax Oxagon soap, a big brown bar that his mother said "could wash freckles off a Kerryman."

Rory stepped out of the bath, teeth chattering in the cramped L-shaped bathroom, dried himself, pulled on clean underpants and black Banlon socks, and dressed in a clean pair of high-water black chinos and his Mr. Gutter's shoes that were round and ugly like the shoes cops wore, even uglier than the brown Wall Streeter cordovans. The right shoe had a crack near the little toe that grew a little more each time he wore them. He needed new shoes but he was putting it off to see if his father got his settlement because he ached for a pair of Featherweights. Or a pair of Floaters with the thick rubber soles. Rory knew that if he asked for new shoes now his mother would take him to Mr. Gutter's because it was the only shoe store around that sold shoes on credit, paying Mr. Gutter off a dime or a quarter a week.

Standing at the bathroom sink, he scooped some of his mother's Arrid deodorant from a little round jar and smeared it under his armpits that had just grown hair in the last year. He took his father's double-edged blue-steel Gillette razor from the top of the medicine cabinet and dry-shaved the peach fuzz off his face, hoping the constant shaving would promote a beard. He made sure he gave himself a little nick. This way if Carol asked what happened Rory could say he cut himself *shaving*. The way Babe shaved. He blotted the droplet of blood, then dabbed it with his father's styptic pencil like a war wound of early manhood. Then he splashed on a dose of his father's Old Spice and donned a white shirt and the John's Bargain Store sweater.

He ran his mother's big comb through his hair and let it dry without hair goop, like John Lennon, his favorite Beatle.

He opened the small bathroom door, carrying out his greasy Freedom Meats jeans that he would wear again tomorrow on the busy Saturday.

His mother and father sat at the kitchen table reading afternoon editions of the *Post* and the *Journal-American*, sipping tea, while the three younger kids slurped hot Bosco. Dermot was not home. Again.

"I kept your dinner warm on the stove," his mother said.

"Not hungry, Mom," Rory said, looking at the owl wall clock that said it was 7:25 P.M. "Maybe later. After mass."

Rory dug into his pants pocket and pulled out his tips and piled the quarters on the table. All except for the Chairman's Liberty silver dollar that he would save until next Friday for his father.

As he counted out the change he gave two pennies to each of his three younger siblings.

"Get candy in Mrs. Sanew's on the way home from mass," he said.

"You're the best, Rory," said Connor.

"Yeah," said Caitlin. "I'm getting two packs of Kits because they have five pieces in each."

"We could pool it all and buy a nickel Bit-O-Honey and one pack of Kits, or a box of Good & Plenty and divvy it all up," said Connor.

"Maybe," said Caitlin. "Depends on my mood."

"You're always in a bad mood," said Connor.

"Who wouldn't be, with you as a brother."

"Stop it!" Tara Maguire said. "I'll not have my children bickering on the day the Kennedy children lost their father. Be thankful you have each other and a father and mother and a big brother as good as Rory. Just stop it!"

"Easy, Ta," Harry said. "They're just kids."

She nodded, took a breath and blessed herself and told the kids they could run down to the candy store now but that they weren't to eat the candy until after mass because she wanted them to receive communion. The three kids grabbed their coats and stampeded out the door and down the stairs in what always sounded like a building collapse.

Rory's mother counted the tips in short whispery intakes of breath. The total came to $8.75.

She glanced at Harry. Ever since he fell, Rory knew Harry was uncomfortable at the ritual of his son forking over his tips for the household. He was also abashed—Rory learned that word reading Murray Kempton—taking an allowance from his son instead of the other way around.

The TV bulletin in the living room gave details about the presidential memorial service scheduled for the next day and said that an assassin named Oswald had been arrested in some movie house.

"I'm gonna watch Cronkite," Harry said, pushing himself up from the table, fitting his crutches under his arms.

"I'll see you later, Pop."

"Thanks," Harry said, glancing at the tip money on the Formica table. Then he swung through the curtain leading into the other rooms. The kitchen fell so silent that the ticking of the clock on the wall sounded like a time bomb.

"It's a tough time for him," Tara said. "The unemployment is ready to run out. He's in constant pain. Esposito says he can't work at any job because it'll hurt his case. And Christmas is only around the corner. As proud as he is of you, Rory, it hurts your father to see his teenage son become the man of the house."

"Pop'll always be the man of this house," Rory said.

"Make him feel that way."

"How?"

"Go ask your father for a few pointers on how to behave on this date you're going on tonight," she said, pushing four quarters from the tip money toward Rory. "Take whoever the lucky girl is for pizza after mass."

Rory blushed. "How'd you know, Mom?"

"You're bloody bleedin' for her, for God's sake!"

He touched his shaving cut. They laughed. "I don't need a whole dollar, Mom."

Tara smiled at him and said, "Put a dime in the collection at church. Put a dime in for the girl as well."

"I talked to Dermot," Rory said. "And I talked to Lefty Hallahan. I'm sorting it out, Mom. I'm sorting it out."

"Careful with that Hallahan," she said. "He's the devil's postman."

"Don't worry, Mom," Rory said, scooping up the four quarters.

* * *

Rory sat on the edge of the couch telling his father all about Carol, who was older, who came from Manhattan, who lived in a brownstone, whose father was a lawyer and a D.A. He told him about almost hitting his new Chevy with his butcher bike and how Babe drove Carol home in his new Riviera and how Babe might go to law school and how Carol's parents seemed to be impressed by that and he thought they'd rather see Carol go out with him than Rory and that he thought Carol's father looked down his nose at him.

Harry Maguire shifted in his favorite armchair, feet propped on a tattered ottoman, watching the assassination news. All the lamps were turned off to save on the Con Ed bill. He turned his good ear to Rory as a promo for a movie called *Action in the North Atlantic* with Humphrey Bogart came on the TV, saying it would run all week next week on the *Million Dollar Movie*. Rory played with the Irish wool antimacassar that covered the frayed arm of the comfortable old couch.

"Make her laugh," Harry Maguire said.

"Yeah?"

"A girl always loves a guy who makes her laugh."

"I'll try."

"And the only thing a girl likes to hear more than that she's pretty is that she's *smart*."

"That's easy. She is real smart anyway."

"Compliment her on what's inside her, Rory. Do that and you'll be showing her what's inside of you."

"I never thought of it like that. You sure that's not too corny?"

"Girls like stuff men think is corny. That's part of what makes them different. And special. So you also talk to them differently than you talk to guys."

"Maybe I'll crack a joke about how smart she is."

Harry Maguire nodded and smiled and said, "Now you're thinking like a man instead of a kid."

"But I think she's used to guys with money," Rory said.

"Guys with money are a dime a dozen. Girls who chase them are a penny a bushel. We sailors had a saying: 'If she asks about money, find another honey.'"

Rory smiled and pushed himself up from the couch, gazing at an old framed photo on the mantel of his smiling father in his dress peacoat and watch cap, carrying his seaman's bag, his free arm slung over his mother's shoulder. It was taken before he went away to sea in World War II.

"I like that," Rory said, realizing that it was also the first time he'd ever heard his father make reference to his life as a sailor. He felt like he'd gotten a foot in the door to Harry Maguire's past, his private World War II days. "What else did you sailors say, Pop?"

"Most of what we said isn't repeatable," Harry said, with a dark chuckle.

"What did they say the day your ship got sunk?" Rory asked, trying to unlock the secrets his father held tight inside.

Harry stared deep into Rory's eyes, blinked three times, and said, "That's got nothing to do with this conversation, big guy."

Rory fell silent for a long moment as his father gazed out the window toward the cold moon over Brooklyn, a sprinkle of stars shining through the rattling windows. A high-pitched whistle of wind blew down the chimney of the now sealed flue that once served the kerosene heater before the arrival of steam heat.

"But it's *men's* talk, Pop. This is what they call a man-to-man, no? I need to know about that day. . . ."

"No you don't. I want to forget and you don't need to know."

"But, Pop . . ."

"You're going off course, Rory. No more questions, that's an order."

"Maybe if you tell me I can tell Esposito, who can tell it to a judge and . . ."

"Never question an order, mister."

Harry wasn't angry or loud. Just firm. Like the door of a bank vault slamming with an authoritative clank.

Mrs. Quigley, a downstairs neighbor, beat on a cold radiator as if it would bring forth heat. It wouldn't.

"Sorry, Pop," Rory said, and moved past his father's chair.

"One more thing," Harry Maguire said, clutching Rory's wrist in his big powerful hand and looking his son in the eyes. "This girl's father might just be trying to protect his little girl. Respect that. But if he looks down his nose at *you*, she doesn't come from much. Keep that in mind." He smiled. "And get a goddamned haircut."

13

Rory spotted her as soon as he walked into the packed church. Her long golden hair reflected the flames of hundreds of candles being held by the weeping parishioners. She was the only woman in the church without a head covering.

There was an empty seat next to Carol in the second to last pew in St. Stanislaus. Rory saw her tell a few people that it was taken. When he sat down next to her, Carol looked at him and smiled.

"You're late," she said.

"Work. Sorry."

"That's what men always say . . . working late at the office."

"Where's your hat?" he asked.

"I didn't wear one. . . ." She looked around and realized all the women were wearing them. "You're supposed to wear a hat?"

"Of course, every Catholic girl knows. . . ." Rory paused, looked at her.

She shrugged. "Sorry, Lutheran."

Rory smiled. Father O'Keefe wobbled a bit at the pulpit, and asked everyone to kneel. Rory and Carol knelt side by side. She was dressed in her third outfit of the day—a black pants suit, a long black leather coat, and black high heels. Her mix of scented soap, perfume, and skin lotions smelled like what it must smell like in heaven. Rory took a clean folded napkin from his jacket pocket and told Carol to bobby-pin it to her hair.

"You serious?" she said, almost laughing.

"No, but these people are."

Carol pinned the hankie to her head and bottled a laugh as Father O'Keefe slurred through the Confiteor in Latin. Rory had lost a lot of respect for the church two years ago, just before he quit the altar boys. Father O'Keefe had announced his "envelope deadbeat list" from the pulpit, while Rory was serving the ten o'clock Sunday mass. The priest mentioned Tara Maguire's name among those who were delinquent in kicking in weekly pledges to the building of the new Catholic high school. Just read her name out, from the altar of God, for all to hear.

After mass that day Rory turned in his cassock and surplice and said amen to this old drunk of a priest who sometimes mixed vodka with the wine that was supposed to be the blood of Christ at the daily 6:15 A.M. mass, ate bacon and eggs on meatless Fridays, and drove a car few of his parishioners could afford. Drunk. And here he was, high as a kite, leading the church in a prayer for the dead president.

"This priest looks zonked," Carol said.

"You noticed?"

"Little Stevie Wonder could see it."

Rory thought it was outrageous that Father O'Keefe couldn't stay sober even for President Kennedy's special mass.

The choir sang and Rory's eyes searched the church and he found his mother sitting on the opposite side, in the middle of the church, near the statue of St. Anthony, her favorite saint. Not even St. Anthony was going to bring back the hope she lost that afternoon in Dallas. Caitlin, Connor, and

Bridget knelt in the pew, Bridget fidgeting and growing excited when she spotted Rory on the other side of the church. Dermot was nowhere to be seen. Harry Maguire never went to church.

"Rory!" shouted Bridget through the silent church.

Rory blushed and said, "Oh, God."

Carol saw his little sister waving across the church as congregants chuckled and his mother wrestled the three-year-old straight in the pew, which was like trying to train an eel.

"That your little sister?" Carol asked.

"Don't spread it around."

"*Adorable.*"

"If we are incapable of controlling our children, perhaps we should have the courtesy to leave this solemn mass," Father O'Keefe slurred from the pulpit, and then took a sip from his glass. *Here's a common drunk, with no kids, criticizing my mother,* Rory thought. *I'd love to break his nose.*

He saw his mother leave with a wiggling Bridget and her other two kids. He felt damp now with sweat, embarrassed in front of Carol. She leaned close to his ear, her lower lip almost touching his lobe, her breath moist and hot. Thrilling him. Then he looked back at the priest.

"I'm sorry, but this priest is a jerk," she said.

"I have to go," Rory whispered.

"Wait for me."

Later, they strolled down Fourteenth Street toward Brooklyn's Fifth Avenue, which was a distant multicolored mirage of Christmas lights. Rory told Carol how Father O'Keefe, whom the altar boys nicknamed Father O'Stewed, had embarrassed his mother.

"He's a hypocrite," Rory said.

"Maybe he should see a priest," Carol said.

Rory laughed as they walked down the long street where

the blue hue of television sets glowed in every window, delivering assassination updates.

"How many kids in your family?" she asked.

"Five."

"*Wow.* I'm an only child."

He couldn't believe he was walking side by side with Carol Sturgis. He would have given a week's pay to walk up Eleventh Street with her, past all his old stickball pals— Kevin, Bobby, Willie, Timmy, Skip, Jimmy—so they could see him with her! They'd all be drooling. He didn't get to spend much time with his boyhood friends anymore, what with working every day after school and all day Saturday and homework most nights.

As they approached Fifth Avenue, she asked, "So, what does your father do?"

"Works for the state," Rory said.

"Oh. Doing what?"

"Highways."

"That's good. Keeps America rolling along."

"Yeah, but he's laid up right now. Hurt on the job."

"Sorry to hear that. He gonna be okay?"

"Sure. He's an old marine, you know."

He didn't mention that Harry Maguire was in the *merchant* marine.

"He was in World War Two?"

"Big-time."

"I bet he has a million stories."

"He doesn't tell war stories."

"Real heroes never do," she said. "I read that somewhere."

He looked at her, saw her smiling at him. *Make her laugh,* Harry Maguire said.

"All the girls as pretty and intelligent as you over in Manhattan?"

"That a trick question? I can't answer without sounding conceited."

"Which only shows how smart you are."

"You trying to make me blush?"

"Boy, that would be a switch. I'm the one who usually does. Mark Twain wrote, 'Man is the only animal that blushes. Or needs to."

She laughed. *Perfect,* he thought.

"What about Protestants, do they blush?"

She pushed her face an inch from his. "You tell me."

He wanted to kiss her. But he didn't.

As they reached the corner, Babe's red Riviera swung onto the block, window down in the cold night so that everyone could hear his radio playing "Deep Purple," by Nino Tempo and April Stevens. He squealed to a stop and revved the engine.

"Hey, sweetie, we must be destined for each other," Babe said.

"Hi, Babe," she said.

"You walkin' the champ home, make sure he gets there safe?"

Rory laughed but his guts churned.

"We're just walking," Carol said. "Gonna see the Christmas lights."

"The ones down here are lame," Babe said. "Wanna see real lights, I'll take you to Rockefeller Center see the tree get lit on Sa'day."

"Thanks, but . . ."

"Hop in, hon, I'll take you down Nathan's for a dog and a bag of fries and then spin ya home. Whadda ya say?"

"Not tonight, thanks."

"Suit yourself," Babe said with a big dopey grin. "Make sure you burp the Champ before he goes to sleep."

"Up yours, Babe," Rory said, smiling as Babe burnt rubber up Fourteenth Street.

Carol watched the Riviera race up the street. "His nickname suits him," she said.

They both laughed and Rory said, "Babe's a ballbuster, but he's an okay guy."

"He likes teasing you."

"He also likes me to help him with his term papers."

She laughed. "I bet you're good at it."

"I like to write."

"I'm not great at essays. Math and science are my forte."

"They're my weakest subjects," he said.

"Well, I want to be a doctor, so I better know science."

"I wanna be a sportswriter, so I better know nouns and verbs."

"What does Babe really want to be, you figure?" she asked.

"His father is gonna make him be a lawyer or a businessman," Rory said. "But I feel sorry for him, because he wants nothing more in the world than to be a butcher."

"Yuck."

"Yeah, but there's nothing wrong with it if that's what you want to be."

"I guess."

"Hey, we all can't be what we want to be. My father could have played major-league baseball until he got hurt in the war. . . ."

"Wow, that's sad."

"And I'd love to play center field for the Mets, but I know I'll never be good enough. But I do know I can write about the center fielder for the Mets."

"The *Mets?* Hell, *I* could play center field for the *Mets.*"

"Please, don't tell me you're a *Yankees* fan."

"I even have a pinstriped bikini."

"Get lost!"

"Seriously."

"Boy, I'd like to see that."

"Wait'll summer."

"Worth the wait. Wearing that, I might even forgive you for rooting for the Yanks."

"Forgive *me*? The Mets just had the worst season in the history of baseball."

They kept walking and he said the Dodgers beat the Yankees in the World Series and they were hijacked from Brooklyn. And she said that was pure luck. And he said, luck doesn't get you four straight. That Sandy Koufax from Coney Island set a series record with fifteen strikeouts in one game. She conceded that but asked what else Brooklyn did for the Dodgers or baseball this year. He said that Joe Pepitone, who got shot when he went to Manual Training, made the error that cost the Yankees Game Four and clinched the Series for the Dodgers.

"Okay," she said. "So you're smarter than me."

"I'm not so sure about that, Dr. Sturgis."

She stopped and looked at him, with the Christmas lights that swayed over Fifth Avenue reflecting in her eyes. "I never imagined what that would sound like," she said.

"I never met a girl who wanted to be a doctor before. Then, I never walked home from mass with a Protestant before. Can I buy you a slice of pizza, Doc?"

"Sure, Rory Maguire."

Inside Carmella's pizzeria Rory ordered two slices and asked what she wanted to drink. She declined a soda.

"I'm watching my figure," she said.

"Everyone else I know is watching your figure, too."

She laughed and punched him in the arm as they walked to a table in the rear of Carmella's pizzeria, where they talked about the great competition between Y. A. Tittle and Johnny Unitas, about what an amazing running back Jim Brown of the Cleveland Browns was, and how Jimmy Cannon had written that watching Brown run was like listening to the greatness of Caruso singing, and how he was even better than Jim Taylor. They talked about Cookie Gilchrist and this new kid coming up named Gale Sayers.

"I can't believe I met a girl who likes sports."

"I can't believe I met a guy who wants to be a sportswriter. I told you, I like *different*. If you had a column today, what would you write?"

Rory said he'd write that he thought it would be inappropriate of the NFL to play their regular games on Sunday so soon after the John Fitzgerald Kennedy assassination. Carol agreed, and they each ate a slice. He folded his and took a big bite. She baffled the pizza guy by asking for a knife and fork. Rory chewed slower, trying to mimic the grace she showed while eating her pizza.

"I admit the pizza is better in Brooklyn than in Manhattan," she said. "Certain *guys* aren't bad either."

Rory stopped chewing, because he saw that she was staring him straight in the eyes as she said it. She was so confident that she didn't even blink. He couldn't help thinking of Babe saying she made out like a French maid. He didn't believe him.

Carol reached across the table and grabbed his Coke and wrapped her lips around the straw and took a small sip. She guided the small paper cup under his mouth and he put his lips on the same straw, tasted her lipstick on his lips. It sent a thrill through his body.

"Walk me home?" she said.

"On my hands, if you want."

She laughed a second time. He couldn't wait to tell his

father he made her laugh twice and told her she was smart and that it was all working.

They walked along Fifth Avenue, looking in store windows that workers were decorating for Christmas with Santas and spray frost and garland and twinkling lights.

"Where do you hang out?" she asked.

"Eleventh Street between Fifth and Sixth," he said. "With my stickball pals, kids I grew up with. But since I started working I have less and less free time."

"Sorry, am I stealing your free time?" she asked, giving him a sly smile.

"If I was catching, I'd let you steal home in the bottom of the ninth."

"That supposed to be a sportswriter's idea of flattery?"

"Best I could do. Kinda lame, huh?"

"You know the name of the new Beatles song that's coming out next month?" she asked. "The one that's a big hit in London right now?"

"Sure. Cousin Brucie, the DJ on WABC, says it's 'I Want To Hold Your Hand' . . ."

As he said it he felt Carol take his hand in hers and she steered him with her hip up Eleventh Street.

"Why's your hand so sweaty?" she asked.

"Um, well, because . . . to be honest, you make me nervous."

"*Me?*"

He dried his hand on his pants, took a deep breath, and again clutched her hand.

"You have really big hands," she said, splicing her small, soft fingers through his much larger ones and squeezing. "You know what they say about guys with big hands?"

"No. What?"

"Oh, *God* . . . never mind."

Up ahead, Rory saw all his friends hanging out in Skip and Timmy's areaway. His heart raced. He was going to walk past them all, holding Carol Sturgis's hand. The hot new chick from Manhattan that everybody was drooling over since she crossed the Brooklyn Bridge.

"Those your friends?"

"Yeah."

"I've seen them around before."

"Sure, ogling *you.*"

She eased closer to him, striding a little sassier, swinging his hand in hers and then looping her arm around his waist as they approached the guys sitting on the stoop. Rory put his arm across Carol's shoulder and she crushed her head against him as they passed.

"What's doin', guys," Rory said. "By the way, this is Carol."

"Hi, fellas," Carol said, giving a smiling little wave with her free hand.

All the guys said hi and then fell silent.

The only thing Rory heard when they were past them was someone whisper, *"Ho-ly shit!"*

Rory and Carol walked hand in hand, turned the corner and then strolled up Tenth Street. Rory felt light-footed and excited. Now he knew what adults meant when they said they were walking on air.

As they approached the Sturgis family brownstone, Carol said, "Thanks."

"No, thank *you.*"

"Remember what Babe asked me?"

"Not really."

"He asked me to go with him to see the Rockefeller Center tree lighting next Saturday night," she said.

"Yeah, now I remember."

"I go every year, ya know."

"I haven't gone since I was nine."

"You planning, by any chance, on going next Saturday?"

He shrugged, watching her front door, terrified that her father would appear.

"I didn't make any plans or anything. . . ."

"Well, if you do decide to go, would you mind some company?"

Now he realized that she was trying to get him to ask her out on a date.

"You mean . . . like, that, maybe you would, like, go, sort of, with, ya know, *me?*"

"Jesus, I hope you write better than you ask girls out."

"I do, I swear. . . ."

"The answer is yes! I'd love to go out on a date with you, on one condition."

"Okay. What?"

"The condition is, *dummy*, that you kiss me good night right now."

Trembling, Rory gazed from the areaway gate to the front stoop door, then took Carol's hands in his and pulled her to him. He kissed her on the lips, thinking, *Nobody asked me, but . . . Carol's lips are like little silk pillows.*

"No matter whatever happens," he whispered hoarsely, "neither one of us will ever forget that we kissed for the very first time on the night President Kennedy was killed."

She reached to kiss him again, when her father appeared in the doorway and said, "Carol, in the house. *Now!*"

She winked at Rory, blew him a small kiss, and spun past her father into the brownstone. The man who earned his living by putting people in jail gave Rory the up-and-down once-over, then turned and followed his daughter into the private house and slammed the heavy door.

* * *

Rory headed home with a big, confident bebop in his step, his blood coursing in his veins like the Amazon and the Mississippi and the Nile all together.

Nobody asked me, but . . . I have an actual, honest-to-God date with Carol Sturgis, the hottest chick in the neighborhood, and life doesn't get any better than that. . . .

All Rory thought about was taking out Carol Sturgis on a date to Rockefeller Center, over in the City, holding her hand, kissing her, and seeing the lighting of the world-famous Christmas tree reflecting in those perfect blue eyes.

He quickened his pace, his skin on fire, his heart doing "Wipeout" in his chest, and then he war-whooped and threw a Sugar Ray Robinson five-punch combination into the cold night air, spun on the balls of his feet, and then just started to run so fast through the streets of Brooklyn that he thought he'd run out of his own life.

And in that moment Rory didn't think about his father living with constant pain and fighting for the disability. He didn't think about his mother aching over John Fitzgerald Kennedy. He didn't think about Lefty Hallahan threatening to use Dermot as a human shield in a rumble against the Roman Emperors unless Rory boosted Sal's gun. He didn't think about Ankles the cop trying to turn him into a rat. He didn't think about there being no money in the Maguire household for what was looking to be a miserable Christmas.

Not then, he didn't.

PART II

The Days That Followed

14

The next day the morning news broadcast pictures of John Fitzgerald Kennedy's body in repose in the East Room of the White House. Tara had pulled back all the curtains separating the railroad rooms so she could peer in from the kitchen to the living room to see the television as she served oatmeal to the kids at the kitchen table.

"Do we have an east room, Mom?" Connor asked, sitting at the table.

"Aye, in Belfast city, Connor," Tara said.

"We have a west room, too," said Dermot, digging his spoon into his oatmeal as if turning clumpy soil. "On the Bowery. And that's a step up in the world from this dump."

Tara smacked him off the back of the head with a wet dishrag. "I don't see you contributing anything but ill will to this family," Tara said. "Get you over to that fish market before someone else gets that job."

"Soon as I can sign myself out of school, I'll make my own living," Dermot said, standing from the table. "And I won't be delivering smelly fish to smelly old ladies on Fridays for nickels and dimes, tell you that right now. I'll make my own loaves and fishes miracles come true. Watch."

"Sit down and eat or you'll need a miracle to rise from the dead," Harry said.

Dermot sneered at his father and said, "Oh, yeah? Dead by who?"

Rory leaned across the table and grabbed Dermot by the shirtfront, "By me, squirt. I'll break your jaw in five places so you can't talk like that to Mom and Pop."

Caitlin and Connor trembled and Bridget started to cry. Solemn military music poured out of the TV. Images of John-John and Caroline and Jackie filled the TV screen in the living room.

Harry said, "Okay, enough, big guy."

Rory let go of Dermot, who pushed himself up from the table with a little hard-guy flourish, like one of the punk kids out of *Angels with Dirty Faces*, and grabbed his old wool overcoat from the closet behind the front door.

"He ain't such a 'big guy' out on the street," Dermot said. "Rattin' to the bulls, lettin' people call him quiff, runnin' around with girlie hair, working like a colored or a Porto for a fat, greasy wop."

Tara ran after him again, lashing him with the wet rag. "No one uses bigoted words in this house! Ever! I lived with bigotry in Belfast all my life and I'll not have it in my American home!"

Rory rose from his chair again, but Harry clamped a hand on his shoulder and snarled at Dermot. "You couldn't hold the soiled work gloves of the Negroes, Italians, and Spanish men I served with, mister."

"Hey, Pop, go tell it to the marines!" Dermot said, sneering as he buttoned his coat over his undershirt. "Make that *merchant* marines . . ."

"They don't need to be told," Harry said.

"I'll kill ya," Rory said, racing around the table, knocking over a chair, falling over it as Dermot tore out the door and down the stairs two at a time. Rory scrambled to his feet in pursuit as Bridget screamed and bawled. Tara stopped Rory at the door, slamming it and standing in front of him.

"Let him be," she said. "Please, let him be. It's only a phase. Don't ever let anyone else see the Maguires fighting amongst themselves."

Rory said, "I'll strangle that little son of a . . ."

Harry sat in helpless pain at the table, his face shrouded by the steam rising from his chipped mug of tea.

Rory pushed the bike through the Brooklyn streets all through Saturday, delivering orders, always taking Tenth Street, hoping to see Carol. He didn't see her all day. He also scoured the neighborhood searching for Dermot. He wanted to have a good private word with him. If Dermot gave him any back talk he'd give him a good ass-kicking. No matter who saw it happen. But he couldn't find his kid brother anywhere.

By two P.M. he ran into his mother in front of their apartment house, and helped her drag the garbage cans in from the curb. Inside, Caitlin mopped the hallway stairs with ammonia and pine and Connor polished the brass mailboxes with Noxon polish. The janitorial duties lopped thirty dollars a month off the seventy-dollar rent for the Maguires.

Tara asked Rory about his walk home with this girl Carol Sturgis the night before. He told her how great it went, that everything his father told him to do worked. Tara smiled in a knowing way. He told her about his date with Carol the following Saturday at Rockefeller Center. Tara declared that he'd need a suit and new shoes for the occasion.

"I know we can't afford it, but I'd love one of those collarless suits like the Beatles wear they have down Belmont's," Rory said. "And a pair of Featherweights."

"We'll do the very second best," she said. "Although I don't understand this business of collarless suit jackets at all."

"Shows off the shirt collar, Mom," he said. "With a long, skinny black tie, it's just boss as a horse."

"Who wants a horse as a boss?" she asked. "But even a horse would be better than Mr. Riley, who's a right *pig.*" She sighed. "But what's the use of being young if you can't act the *lig.*"

Rory laughed, certain that none of his other friends would know that a *lig* was an Irish expression for a fool or a clown.

At the end of the day, Rory took his two-shakes-of-a lamb's-tail bath and turned over his ten dollars' pay and twelve dollars and seventy-five cents in tips to his mother. Dermot was sleeping in his lower bunk. He smelled like puke.

"He came home at dinnertime roaring drunk with the smell of the drink on him," she said. "Vomiting all over the kip. I gave him a cup of tea and an aspirin and sent him off to bed. Leave him be. Must've been up on the factory roof all day, guzzling with that Lefty and the Shamrocks, the durty wasters."

Rory hated beer. The two times he'd tried it with the guys, the taste made him gag and puke. Like Dermot. He took clean clothes from a drawer and walked into the living room and opened the window a few inches to let the smell of vomit out.

Harry Maguire sat in front of the TV watching a replay of Jack Ruby shooting Lee Harvey Oswald that morning in a televised jail transfer in Dallas. He had a copy of *One Flew Over the Cuckoo's Nest* by Ken Kesey on his lap, which Rory had taken out of the library for him. Rory stared at the TV in disbelief. Then he heard that the NFL had decided to play their scheduled games.

"The whole country is off its rocker," Harry said.

"People are starting to talk about a conspiracy."

"I'd say it's more than talk."

"What should I do about Dermot, Pop?"

"Let him sleep."

"I mean about his whole thing with the Shamrocks, school, his attitude?"

"He's angry that I'm not who he wants me to be. That's my guess. Anger can either kill you or be a great teacher. Dermot's the kind of kid who runs away to join the circus to be the daring young man on the flying trapeze. He'll find his way home when he realizes they've made him a clown instead."

Rory nodded, dressing in clean dungarees and a pair of Keds.

"Thanks for your advice with the girl, Pop," Rory said, pulling on a sweater.

"It worked out well, then?"

"I'm taking her to see the lighting of the tree next week."

"Great stuff."

"I made her *laugh*, Pop. Three times. And I told her how *smart* she was."

Harry smiled, turning away from the TV images of the Oswald murder.

"I'm happy for you, Rory."

"Can I ask you a question, Pop?"

"Sure."

"How come you don't ever make Mom laugh anymore?"

Harry Maguire looked at Rory for a long silent moment.

"Maybe I'm not so funny anymore," he said and looked back at the TV, where Jack Ruby was now in handcuffs.

He hung out for a few hours on Timmy and Skip's stoop on Eleventh Street, jingling the three quarters his mother gave him to spend in his pocket. All the guys wanted to know about Carol. Bobby asked if she wore falsies. Willie asked if

Rory tongued with her. Kevin said he bet he just got lip action. Skip wanted to know if he copped a feel yet. Skip even suggested he paid her some of his tip money to walk hand in hand with him.

"You calling her a *who-wah?*" Rory asked.

"Well, did you even get to first base?" Skip asked.

"I didn't try anything like that," Rory said. "I like this girl. She's like, you know, *respectable*. Girlfriend material."

"She goes out with younger guys and she's *respectable?*" said Bobby. "C'mon, man, if she's a Protestant she doesn't have to go to confession, so she probably wants to deflower *you.*"

Rory pushed his chest out and stepped in front of Bobby, face-to-face, ump and manager, and told him to take it back, to never talk about Carol like that again. Bobby took it back, saying he was only goofing, that he didn't know Rory had wedding plans already.

"Who said anything about a wedding?" Rory said. "I'm just bringing her to the Rockefeller tree."

"Bull," Bobby said.

None of the other guys believed him either. Rory told them he was picking her up at eight o'clock Saturday night.

"I'll be there," Bobby said. "A slice and a Coke says you're full of bull."

"You'll see," Rory said and walked up toward Seventh Avenue.

It felt good because these were the same guys he'd always felt inadequate in front of over the years because they lived in brownstones, their fathers had full-time city jobs or worked down Wall Street, and they always had money for pizza, sodas, and when the ice cream man came around. They always had new Easter suits and the best back-to-school clothes, and they got to buy their shoes in Flagg Brothers and

Florsheim, when he bought in Mr. Gutter's and John's Bargain Store.

They also bragged about their fathers' exploits in World War II, showing off scrapbooks, Jap bayonets, Kraut helmets, medals, newspaper stories, and articles from *Stars and Stripes*. Some of them by Jimmy Cannon. They got to go to VFW Post parties and barbecues, like the one the local Stenick Post threw last Memorial Day. But merchant marine veterans of the same war were cordially *not* invited to attend. The families of his pals all had really good medical coverage. Their fathers bought their homes with veterans loans. Got good jobs after going to college on the GI Bill.

Those kids had a small piece of the middle-class American Dream that he saw on *Leave It to Beaver* and *Ozzie and Harriet*.

But now Rory had something they didn't have—a date with Carol Sturgis, who had a build like Annette Funicello and a face like a teenage Stella Stevens.

He veered over to Tenth Street and walked up Carol's block, hoping to spot her. No sign of her. He went home and climbed into bed and found Carol in the ceiling plaster.

Sunday, November 24

The next day, Mr. Gutter, who closed on Saturdays but opened early on Sunday morning, showed Rory a dozen pairs of shoes. His mother looked around, trying not to be a mother.

"I gotta have something pointier," Rory complained. "I can't wear brown round shoes. I need black and pointy, something Florsheimy or Flagg Brothery, even Thom McAny'll do. What you're showing me are all-played-out Boy Scout shoes for grown-ups."

"These are American shoes, sonny boy," Mr. Gutter said. "Not Eyetalian. The Eyetalians have little feet, like hors d'oeuvres. They can wear pointy, to kill cock-a-roaches in corners. You have big, fat Irish feet. Like your head. You need big, fat round shoes."

"They look like something Dennis the Menace's father would wear."

"What's wrong with that?" Tara asked.

"They're lame," Rory said. "Shot down. You got anything that even looks like Featherweights, Mr. Gutter?"

"Featherweights you could make out of scraps of old linoleum," Mr. Gutter said. "You walk from death row to the electric chair you get holes in them."

Mr. Gutter climbed a ladder, took a box from a high shelf, and gave it to Rory.

"Try these," he said. "I order them for gangsters too vain to wear orthopedic shoes."

Rory opened the box to find a pair of semipointy shoes with a leather heel that at least looked passable.

"He's got a big date with a girl in Rockefeller Center next week," Tara said.

"Mom, please . . ."

She laughed and Mr. Gutter waved a finger. "Shaddup, kid. It's good your mother tells me this because I have discount tickets for Radio City Music Hall for the Rockettes."

"*Really?*" Rory said.

"With a purchase of the shoes you get two discount tickets, twenty-five cents each. But you gotta go the day before to exchange the coupon for the tickets, good only the next day."

"Plus your father has a friend from Ryan's who works security at the ice-skating rink," Tara said. "He says he can sneak you and your girlfriend in."

Rory tried on the shoes and looked at them in the floor mirror. They were only half ugly. He said, "I'll take them."

Rory's mother put fifty cents down, adding to her bill for all the other kids' shoes, which she never seemed to pay off in full.

He put the wrapped shoes in a paper bag and then his mother asked Rory to go with her down to Larsen's Bakery outlet on Fifteenth Street just up from Fifth Avenue, where she needed his help carrying home three day-old cakes and five loaves of bread, including raisin bread for French toast, white bread for regular toast and grilled cheese, date nut loaf, and their delicious Viking rye that Rory loved with butter and hunks of sharp cheddar cheese from Sam Brody's corner grocery. She was able to get enough bread and desserts for the week for under a buck, all of it tied together with baker's string, because they didn't offer bags with the wholesale purchase.

Then they hurried up the block to the Catholic Charities Outlet store on Fifteenth Street and Sixth Avenue, where Rory and his mother rummaged through the bins and racks together. They were the first customers of the day and Rory hoped that no one coming from the eight-o'clock mass would spot them.

His mother found two white shirts that she made Rory try on. They fit but were wrinkled and kind of dingy. She also found a baggy black suit that she held up to him.

"Mom, I wouldn't be caught dead in that suit," he said. "In fact the last guy who wore it probably did get caught dead in it. I'd rather wear a Santa suit."

"It's a Robert Hall," she said. "I'll dazzle it up for ya."

Rory just nodded, eager to get the hell out of Catholic Charities before someone he knew spotted him. He had this roaring dread that Carol would pass in her father's brand-new Chevy on their way to Sunday mass and the whole family would spot Rory and his mother shopping in Catholic Charities like a pair of shanty Irish grubbers. Catholic

Charities was like ten steps down from John's Bargain Store, used clothes from dirty dead strangers, the place where knocked-up-unmarried-teenage-mothers and people on the home relief shopped.

As his mother haggled the old nun who ran the store down from two bucks to fifty cents for the suit and twenty-five cents for the two shirts, Rory escaped into the fresh air, carrying the day-old Larsen's bread, the ugly Mr. Gutter shoes, and the Catholic Charities clothes.

"Ho-ho-ho, lookee who's doin' his Christmas shoppin'," Lefty Hallahan shouted from across the street, walking his way with three Shamrocks who looked as if they'd been out all night. He didn't see Dermot.

"I'm with my moms, Lefty, cool it."

"Getting a few welfare vines for midnight mass? You invitin' us for dinner to eat that day-old Larsen's bread, Rory?"

"Up yours, Lefty."

"Heard you're chasin' the new chick from Tenth Street," Lefty said. "She know you're a Mr. Gutter's, Catholic Charities, Larsen's bread welfare artist?"

"Hey frig you, Lefty . . ."

Lefty said, "Woooo, you hear that guys? The welfare artist altar boy said *frig*. Better run right to confession, gory Rory."

Tara stepped out of the store and saw Lefty and the Shamrocks on the sidewalk.

"What's this?"

"Nothin', Mom."

"You're not kidding," she said.

"We were just discussing the morning sermon at St. Stans, Mrs. M.," Lefty said.

"Don't you be calling me any pet names, you big ghett," Tara said. "I'm telling you to your gub as God is my witness—

stay you away from my Dermot or you'll answer directly to me. And you won't like it when you do."

"Sorry, Mrs. Maguire. But me and your hep son here have already come to an agreement. He does something for me, I'll chase his punk kid brother home every time I see him."

"My son doesn't make pacts with the devil," Tara said. "G'wan, off with yiz, the shameful lot of yiz, disgracing us all by wearing the colors and symbols of Ireland. Shamrocks, me arse!"

"Happy Thanksgiving, Mrs. Maguire," Lefty said and then he fired an imaginary pistol at Rory again.

After Lefty and the Shamrocks left Tara asked, "What sort of deal did you make with that goon?"

"I didn't make any deal at all, Mom. Now please, let's just go home."

15

Monday, November 25

Monday was declared a National Day of Mourning as Jack Kennedy was buried.

The entire Maguire family watched the service for the murdered president, who lay in repose in the same catafalque—that was a brand-new word for Rory—as old Abe Lincoln.

Even Dermot watched. His only shoes and sneakers were now locked in his father's toolbox, which was in turn locked in the metal armoire in the back bedroom, and just Harry and Rory had keys. He wasn't allowed out.

They all watched John Fitzgerald Kennedy being moved from the White House to St. Matthew's Church for the Low Mass.

Rory's mother sobbed most of the day, almost in time to the slow beat of the muffled drums as two hundred and twenty world leaders followed the coffin through Washington, D.C., past the huge weeping crowds before burying John Fitzgerald Kennedy on a hillside in Arlington National Cemetery, overlooking the Potomac. Rory thought how sad it was that JFK was buried between the bodies of two of his and Jackie's stillborn babies. Then they lit some kind of eternal flame.

"Who's gonna pay the gas bill?" asked Connor. Rory noo-gied him.

"Nothing will ever be the same without Our Jack," Tara said, as she lit a candle on the mantel in front of a statue of the Infant of Prague.

Rory didn't say anything.

Sal didn't open Freedom Meats that day and all the schools were closed. Rory sat in the living room, reading a col-umn by Jimmy Cannon in the *Journal-American* about Jack Kennedy. The column confirmed his desire to be a newspa-per columnist. It reaffirmed Harry's statement that Jimmy Cannon wrote with lasting precision what others were only feeling. It was why Rory had used Cannon's second-person technique as the model for the essay he was writing about his father. Cannon came from the Irish West Village, the same kind of tenement neighborhood as the Maguires'. There were lines in today's Jimmy Cannon column that Rory knew he would remember forever:

"It would be impertinent for me to measure John Fitzgerald Kennedy on the sports pages. The historians will do that, and in other parts of the paper qualified reporters will describe him as a public man.

"In this department, obsessed only with the toys of the nation John Fitzgerald Kennedy represented to the world, our small laments generally sound as if they are played on kazoos. Our dirges are concerned with the insignificant regret of athletes. But I am my father's son, and John Fitzgerald Kennedy's death seems a private matter of fam-ily. Never did I meet him, but I felt close to him—he was never a stranger.

"John Fitzgerald Kennedy would have been no alien on the tenement-sad streets of my childhood where my people still live and mourn today. He was rich by inheritance, an educated man, but his ancestors suffered as we did. He was the perfection of our breed, and my affection for him was not influenced by political reasons. . . .

"John Fitzgerald Kennedy was the best of us and when he made it to the White House, we were no longer Micks. . . .

"Other reporters will describe how tall he stood against the horizon of history. I only knew that Boston voice always seemed to be talking to me and mine. . . . They weep for John Fitzgerald Kennedy today, and for him their candles burn."

Rory looked up from the newspaper to the candle flickering on the Maguire mantel. And then he looked to his silent father, who sat in his wheelchair by the window, staring out into the November skies, gripping the scuffed rawhide of a baseball. Rory knew he had to keep working on his story about his father. Jimmy Cannon would have.

No one spoke much in the Maguire home that night. Dermot lay in his bed reading old copies of *Batman* and this new comic that Rory liked called *Spider-Man*. Rory didn't speak to Dermot. Didn't want to start an argument on the day the president was buried. Hard words would only make his mother sadder.

So he sat in front of the TV, switching the channels, looking for something other than more sadness about John Fitzgerald Kennedy. He saw another *Million Dollar Movie* coming attraction for *Action in the North Atlantic* with Humphrey Bogart. It looked like merchant marines fighting Jerries at sea in World War II. It was going to air on Channel 9 every day, a few times a day and at night, for a whole week starting December 8.

"You ever see that movie, Pop?" Rory asked, excited.

"Nah."

"It's about merchant marines . . ."

"Probably just another Hollywood fairy tale, big guy, made by quick-buck artists who never served."

"I'm gonna watch it."

"Good luck."

When all the lights were out in the apartment, Rory lay on the top bunk, staring at the ceiling where the headlights of passing cars and buses splayed through the top of the curtain rod and danced in the dark. He searched for and found Carol's face and studied it until sleep pulled him under.

Tuesday, November 26

The next day, Rory saw Carol in the hallway after homeroom.

"You get in trouble the other night?"

"Not really," she said. "But my dad wasn't happy to see me kiss the boy who almost crashed into his prized Chevy."

"Did he say anything else about me?"

"He asked if you had ambitions. I told him you wanted to be a sportswriter."

"What'd he say?"

"Nothing. He just kinda snorted."

"*Snorted?*"

"A kinda scoff through his nose. As if to say 'Yeah, sure.'"

"He'll see."

"That's what I said."

Rory beamed. "Yeah?"

"Yeah. Actually I said, 'We'll see.' Same thing."

It wasn't the same thing, but at least she hadn't sided *against* him.

"Can I walk you home after school?"

"Sure," she said.

In Miss Seltzer's class Rory typed for forty straight minutes, describing the walk home from church past the Christmas lights, talking sports and music and dreams in Carmella's pizzeria, her taking his hand as they strolled past his stickball pals on Eleventh Street and the amazing kiss goodnight, making a date to see the tree and the scene with her father the D.A.

"My, my, my," Miss Seltzer said, after yanking Rory's short essay out of the typewriter and starting to read it. "We are a busy little typist today, aren't we, Mr.Maguire? But this is *not* the workbook assignment I wrote on the board. Is it?"

"No, ma'am."

"Maybe you'd like to read it to the rest of the class?"

He looked at her, and whispered. "Please don't do that to me."

She glanced up at him and continued reading his story. Rory could see her clenched little face begin to soften as she got to the part with the hand-holding and the kiss good night. There was nothing dirty in there but she took a deep breath and the paper trembled in her hands. She wore no wedding ring. She was a forty-something-year-old miss. She wasn't ugly but she wasn't what you'd call "hot" either. Rory wondered if she'd ever had a boyfriend.

Miss Seltzer finished reading, looked Rory in the eyes, removed a red pen from the bun at the back of her graying hair, circled three typos, and drew a large A– on the top of the paper. Then she scribbled a comment on the bottom of the paper.

"You're typing so fast out of your head you sometimes miss the space bar," she said. "Otherwise excellent work, Mr. Maguire. You might consider retyping and reworking it a little and handing it in as extra credit work in your English class."

"Thank you, Miss Seltzer."

"Feel free to use the machines here anytime after school."
He sat back down and read the comment at the bottom.
"Lucky girl!"

After school Rory hurried down to the street. Carol was already waiting outside on cold Seventh Avenue. In the passenger seat of Babe's red Riv! Rory's heart sank. He just stood in front of Manual wondering what to do. Should he go over and tap on the frosted window and ask her to get out of the nice, warm brand-new luxury car and walk home in the freezing cold? Or should he just act cool? And wait like nothing was bothering him until she saw him? And leave it up to her whether to get out or not?

Babe honked three times and powered down Carol's window.

"Eh, Champ, jump in the back and we'll drop you off before I drive Carol home."

Carol just smiled at Rory.

"Sorry, but I had plans to walk, Babe, thanks," Rory said.

He saw Carol turn to Babe and say something he couldn't hear. Babe made an incredulous face, hunched his shoulders, and gathered the fingers of both hands together, Italian-style, and shook them in astonishment. "You kiddin' me or what?" he said.

Rory heard Carol say, "Thanks, another time."

And then her door opened and she climbed out, dressed in a stylish Bloomingdale's cashmere coat and a plaid skirt and matching plaid beret.

Babe yelled, "My old man needs you on the double, Champ."

Then Babe squealed away as Carol walked along Seventh Avenue with Rory through the crowd of students, passing Coyle the cop, who looked at Carol and said, "Maybe you can make this mope get a haircut."

"I love it the way it is," Carol said.

That revved Rory's heart like Babe's engine.

Officer Coyle shook his head and Rory and Carol kept walking.

"I know it's corny, but lemme carry your books," Rory said, gripping his few books tighter, and grabbing hers.

"Be my guest."

"I feel terrible making you walk home in the cold," he said.

"It's okay."

"Funny how he was out there again."

"He said his father sent him looking for you."

"C'mon, Carol, he came to see you."

"Well . . . I got out early, it was cold, and he offered to let me wait for you in the warm car," she said. "He's not a bad guy."

"I told you that."

They walked in silence for another block. He wondered if she'd been making out with Babe like a French maid while she waited for him. He studied her lipstick to see if it was messed. It wasn't.

"So, all ready for the big tree?" she asked.

"Wanna see the Rockettes while we're there? Maybe go ice skating?"

Carol bumped him with her hip. "If you didn't ask I was gonna brain you."

As they neared the corner of Tenth Street, where the first Christmas tree hawkers were set up outside of Magno's Fruits and Vegetables, Carol said it might be best if they said good-bye there instead of at the gate of her house. Her father had a half day today because of John Fitzgerald Kennedy. She said she'd told her parents about the date on Saturday night but she didn't want them to think they were going steady already or anything.

Rory didn't know how to interpret that.

"Course not."

"Smell the pine?" she said. "I love the smell of Christmas. I love everything about it. I can't wait for Saturday night. I bought a brand-new outfit."

He didn't want to discuss his clothes.

"I have to warn you, I never ice skated before," he said.

"I'll teach you," she said, looping her arm around his waist. "I'll hold you up like this. If you fall, it'll be into my arms like this."

She bent and cradled him in a mock dramatic pose and kissed him. Right smackeroo in the middle of Seventh Avenue with all the students and grown-ups and buses and cars going by. One of the cars was Babe's Riviera, which seemed to be tailing them, windows open, radio up full blast. This time when Carol kissed Rory he felt her tongue pierce through his lips, just a short little dart, and his eyes popped wide and saw her blue eyes staring right into his. She broke up laughing and her eyes shifted to Babe's passing car, radio blaring Bob Dylan singing "The Times They Are A-Changin'" almost like she knew it'd be there.

"You taste good," she said.

"That was amazing," Rory said, wondering if this is what Babe meant when he said she made out like a French maid.

"That was just coming attractions," she said, and grabbed her book bag from his shoulder and strode up Tenth Street in the high black boots and black wool tights under the red-and-green plaid skirt with matching beret.

Back home he dropped off his books. Propped up on her Singer sewing machine his mother had a newspaper picture of John Lennon of the Beatles in a collarless suit. Tara was a very good seamstress, and sewed all the habits for the Dominican nuns of Holy Family elementary school in lieu of tuition for Dermot, Caitlin, and Connor. She had already taken Rory's measurements with a measuring tape, marked the black suit from Catholic Charities with tailor's chalk, and worked the steel manual foot pedal in time to Kitty Kallen's *Little Things Mean a Lot* on the old RCA Victor Victrola. The bobbin needle danced up and down the seams, and she paused only to cut hems with pinking shears, or to mark a section with straight pins she held in her uncolored lips.

"It makes me feel a wee bit better knowing this Lennon fella is Irish," Tara said, removing the pins as she tapered the pants waist. "Lots of Irish in Liverpool. They went for the work. But I'll never understand a suit without a collar any more than the music these lads sing."

"Jimmy McNab's father says you can fit half dollars up Ringo's nose," Connor said, sitting at the table eating graham crackers and milk. *Ballbuster at seven,* Rory thought. *Can't imagine what he'll be like when he's Dermot's age.*

"That's not a nice thing to say." Tara said.

"He can afford a million half dollars up there," Rory said, laughing as he saw that the two Catholic Charities white shirts were soaking in a tub of water and bleach with a small sack of stuff called "bluing" that his mother said made old shirts look like new. A box of Argo starch sat next to the tub. The ironing board was all set up.

He changed into his Freedom Meats clothes and saw his father reading the sports pages of the *Daily News* in the living room. A copy of a book called *The Sailor Who Fell from Grace with the Sea* by Yukio Mishima sat on the small table next to his chair.

"Any news?"

"Everybody wants to horse trade with the Mets for Ron Hunt . . ."

"I meant from Esposito, the lawyer?"

"Nothing. The only team doing worse than the Mets is me and him."

Harry chuckled. Then added: "But our day will come."

"Pop . . ."

"What?"

"How do you, ya know, *know* when you're in . . ."

"You know you're in love when you don't have to ask," Harry said, without looking up from the paper.

"Does that mean I'm not?"

"It means you're not sure," Harry said, turning the page. "Yet."

"Why?"

"Probably because you're not sure yet if *she* is."

Rory laughed as he tied his dirty Freedom Meat boots and said, "You know everything, man."

"I only wish that were half true," Harry said, and picked up his novel by the man with the funny Japanese name.

Rory delivered orders all over the neighborhood that afternoon, riding up Tenth Street on four different trips without seeing Carol.

Three times in the afternoon, Sal sent Rory over to see how the Bohack meat section was doing. Each time it was packed. All three times he came back and told Sal it was like a tax collector's wake.

"Must be the JFK thing," Sal said. "Business is as dead as him."

In the middle of the day Sal made delicious sirloin steak sandwiches on Robestelli's crispy seeded Italian bread, topped with fried onions and peppers. Rory wrapped his hero in butcher paper and told Sal he'd eat it on the bike as he delivered the orders.

"That's what I call a worker," Sal said, glaring at Noonz, who sat in dark silence eating his sandwich.

Rory left and stopped into Gino the shoemaker a block away and exchanged the sirloin sandwich for horseshoe taps, front and back, on his new Mr. Gutter shoes. He also asked him to remove the ugly tassels the stems wouldn't be visible.

"I make-a them look like Italiano shoes, boy," Gino promised, pouring himself a small glass of Chianti to go with the steak hero. "I spit-polish them up so you see you face."

Rory rode off hungry, but giddy that his shoes would come out looking like Italian imports.

A half hour before closing, Freedom Meats was empty. No customers. A depressed Sal told Rory to haul the stepladder and the Christmas decorations up from the cellar and had him string the garland and the Seasons Greetings signs all over the store. Rory and Noonz strung the lights in the window as Sal supervised.

"Maybe the lights'll bring people in," Sal said.

As Sal stood near the window helping Rory and Noonz center the decorations, one housewife after another pulled shopping carts past his store, laden with Bohack bags. Most of the women were Freedom Meats customers and they averted their eyes as they passed the butcher shop.

Sal lit a new Pall Mall off the butt of another. Just as Rory hung a big lighted Santa's face in the center of the window he spotted his mother and Caitlin pulling a shopping cart past the store. Dread crashed over Rory like the giant wave that almost killed him once down Coney Island.

"She doesn't buy her meat there, Sal," Rory said.

Sal said nothing, just stood staring in his private orbit of smoke.

Then Rory spotted the guy with the Plymouth that he'd seen wearing the shades, the one who Sal thought packed a rod under his sweater.

"Sal, that same guy you thought was casing the joint, he just cruised by in his Plymouth, checking the store out. Again."

"If he robs me tonight he'll be disappointed," Sal said, turning the lock on the front door, closing for the night, peering out at people heading for the subway, men carrying Christmas decorations from the hardware store, and the parade of Bohack shoppers filing past like the Jack Kennedy funeral procession. "Clean up, kid."

Rory finished scraping the blocks and washing the platters and the fat barrels and sweeping up. He was laying fresh sawdust when he heard Sal and Noonz arguing from the back room.

"I'm supposed to bail you out because you got bookies putting the hammer on you?" Sal said.

"I'm not asking for a loan no more," Noonz said. "I ast you for an early Christmas bonus. I ain't lookin for a handout. And what do I get? Fifty clams? And no card. No nice greeting wishing me and my wife and my five rabbits a merry Christmas. Just fifty friggin' clams, less than a half-week's pay, in a plain envelope after me slaving all year, six days a week here for two dollars and eight cents an hour. . . ."

"Alla sudden you know math! The valedictorian of Knock-Knock University suddenly knows how to multiply and divide?"

"I know enough 'rithmatic to know I'm getting' screwed by my own flesh and blood so bad I feel like an incense victim."

"You don't want the fifty? Good. I'll take it back."

"Good, here, shove it. Merry Christmas to you, too."

"You got anything else you wanna say?"

Rory was waiting for Noonz to tell him he quit but there was a long silence. Then he said, "Nah, I got nothin' else to say to you."

Rory liked both of them. But he wouldn't want Sal for a big brother and he never wanted to be a big brother like that to any of his own brothers and sisters. He wondered if Dermot thought he was the kind of brother Sal was to Noonz.

On the way home Rory picked up his shoes from Gino the shoemaker.

"You like?" Gino asked.

Rory grinned. "Boss as a horse on a race course," he said.

"Huh?"

"You're a maestro!"

"Bring me more steak."

When Rory got home Rico Esposito was sitting at the kitchen table with his mother and father. They were all excited. Harry had to be at the state office of workmen's compensation for something called an eligibility appeals hearing. The next day. Downtown Brooklyn, at 10 A.M. Esposito said this was what he was hoping for because once they saw how much pain Harry was in they might rule in his favor.

"These people are all appointed by the governor," he said. "They have the power over these things in their hands."

"I won't sleep a wink all night praying to St. Anthony to find a warm place in those people's hearts," Tara said.

"I'm going with you, Pop," Rory said.

"You have school . . ."

"I didn't miss one day all year and it's a half day before Thanksgiving anyway."

"Be downstairs and I'll pick you up at nine sharp," Esposito said, pushing himself up from the table where he'd had a cup of tea. "Keep your fingers crossed. Tomorrow could be the biggest day of your life."

16

Rory paced the hallway in the dilapidated state government building on Livingston Street. The walls were painted the same green as police stations. When he saw Esposito push open the door from the hearing room, and hold it for Harry, the look on his father's face said it hadn't gone great.

"So?" Rory asked.

"Had better days," Harry said.

Esposito made a "we'll see" kind of face.

Rory, Harry, and Esposito rode down in the elevator in silence amid five other people clutching canes, clamped into neck casts, or just looking plain sick.

Rory helped Harry into the front seat of Esposito's car and closed the door.

"So?"

"So the faces of the board sank when he said he originally got hurt in the merchant marines," Esposito said.

"Why?"

"People have opinions about the merchant marines."

"Based on lies," Rory said. "It isn't right. He tried to join the other services. . . ."

"He told them that," Esposito said. "So maybe that'll work in his favor. But that he has a spotty work record doesn't help."

"That's because no one'd hire merchant marines, either."

"We'll see what happens. This is the state case and he still has the final appeal on the Social Security Insurance disability. But the feds are usually tougher than the state and they've already ruled against him twice. Like the song goes, 'Que sera, sera.'"

Later, on his first order of the day for Freedom Meats, Rory pedaled to Tenth Street to see if he could spot Carol.

He saw her stepping out of Babe's Riviera in front of her house, carrying her elastic-band-bound schoolbooks from school. He felt the way he did the time he went on the parachute ride in Coney Island. *Whoosh.* He thought his heart would explode. Rory stopped a quarter of a block down and waited until the Riviera burned rubber up Tenth Street and then he pedaled hard up the block as Carol climbed her stoop.

She spotted Rory and said, "Hi."

"Hiya."

"I looked for you after school but . . ."

"I had to go somewhere with my father."

"Oh, well, anyway, Babe was nice enough to drive me home."

Rory nodded, searching her lipstick for smears. He didn't see any, but she could have made out with him like a French maid and put on fresh lipstick.

"Nice of him."

"Yeah, he was passing by and . . ."

"He always is. He gets out of school at two and rushes straight to our school. To see *you.*"

"Oh, get off it," she said, chuckling. "But he can be pretty funny, sometimes."

Girls love guys who make them laugh.

Rory said, "Yeah?"

"He told me a few funny stories about you," she said and laughed.

"Oh, yeah, like *what*?"

"I'll tell you another time," she said. "Nothing *bad*. Just funny. But anyway, you're working and I better go in and help my mom prepare for Thanksgiving."

They said good-bye in a brisk way and Rory pedaled off toward Seventh Avenue, anger fueling him like high-octane Mobil, like Pegasus, their flying-horse logo. He was mad at her. Mad at Babe. Mad at himself, for being mad at Carol. He turned onto Seventh Avenue, his heart pounding, and then he spotted Dermot. He was sneaking out of the Maguire tenement to hang out with Lefty Hallahan and the Shamrocks, who gathered in front of Sanew's candy store. Lefty, masked in dark shades, combed his greasy hair in the reflection of the store window. Rory skidded to a stop in front of his tenement, jumped off his bike, booted down the kickstand, and grabbed Dermot.

"Upstairs, asshole," Rory said. "You keep breaking the old lady's heart, I'll break your goddamned legs."

Dermot shoved back. He was strong, stronger than Rory imagined. But not strong enough. Not yet. Rory hurled him through the two unlocked tenement doors and shoved him up the stairs. Dermot kicked down at him, like a mule, catching Rory in the chest. Then Dermot scrambled up the three flights. Rory chased him. He shoved Dermot into the apartment, pushed him through the railroad rooms, and slammed him onto the lower bunk bed, yanked off his sneakers.

"You wanna hang out with that savage, do it barefoot, big shot," Rory said. "Not with shoes Mom and Pop busted their asses to put on your feet."

"Welfare shoes, anyway," Dermot said.

Rory balled his fist, cocked it, and watched his kid brother cower. He didn't throw it.

He took the sneakers and Dermot's good Mr. Gutter school shoes, and padlocked both pairs into his father's big toolbox, and locked the toolbox in the metal armoire in the little back room. Then Rory locked the door on the room so Dermot couldn't go back out. Only Harry and Rory had keys for the toolbox and the armoire.

Rory took a deep breath, his heart pumping, wondering if he'd overreacted because of his anger toward Carol and Babe. Was he taking it out on his kid brother? Was all the emotion about Jack Kennedy coming out, too? *Am I being like Sal is to Noonz right now?* he wondered. He was confused. But he knew he had to at least try to keep Dermot away from Lefty

"I'll go out barefoot," Dermot said.

"Go ahead, lamebrain. You and Tom Sawyer."

When Rory got back downstairs to his bike he noticed that all the bags had been messed with. The careful folds at the tops of the bags had been rumpled and wrinkled by greasy hands. Beef blood had been dripped on the brown paper. Lefty Hallahan stood laughing at Rory, eating a slice of baloney he'd stolen from one bag.

"Get me that rod, or I'm gonna get you fired," Lefty said, firing the imaginary pistol again. "And maybe your kid brother's gonna get himself killed."

"Too bad your mother didn't kill you in your sleep, too," Rory said.

Lefty and the Shamrocks rushed toward Rory this time but as they did Ankles screeched up in his car, jumped out, his hand on his gun. He grabbed Lefty while the other Shamrocks scattered. *Like roaches when the lights are flicked on at night,* Rory thought.

But Ankles searched Lefty, turning his pockets inside out, looking for weapons, drugs, or swag. He didn't find anything.

"This scumbag threaten you?" Ankles asked Rory.

Rory glared at Lefty for a long moment and said, "Nah."

Ankles said, "I seen them all move in on you."

"They were just messing. Playacting *West Side Story* stuff."

"If I didn't show up you'd be playacting as a corpse in Methodist Hospital."

Lefty sneered. Without warning Ankles clutched Lefty's collar with two hands and kicked him in both ankles, dropping him to the sidewalk in a wailing pile. Then he dragged him by the collar into the back of his Youth Squad detective car as citizens stopped and gaped. A few cheered.

"'Bout time someone grabbed that punk!" shouted Mrs. Sanew. "He and his punks steal money from my newspaper stand. They take comics. They scare customers."

"Throw the book at him," said an old guy with a peak cap. "Bad seed from bad family."

Lefty sneered at them, nostrils flaring.

"See ya after night court, Lefty," shouted Dermot from the top-floor window.

Lefty looked from Dermot to Rory and winked.

"Come on, tough guy, we're gonna go for a nice ride in the country," Ankles said.

Rory knew that meant Ankles was gonna take Lefty for a ride to New Jersey, where he would drop him off in the middle of a colored neighborhood in Newark with no shoes or socks or coat or money. Just by himself, freezing and alone. He'd kick him in the ankles and let him hobble home.

After he locked Lefty in the car Ankles put his face an inch from Rory's.

"This bag of human garbage ask you about a gun again?"

"Nah."

"I respect that you kicked your kid brother in the ass and took him home," Ankles said. "I don't respect you covering for this lowlife."

Rory watched Ankles climb behind his wheel and drive off as Lefty sneered and grimaced in pain in the backseat.

It took Rory about fifteen minutes to rearrange all the orders in his basket, using the item list in each bag to make sure the right people got the correct orders. Lefty had scrambled everything.

Rage bubbled through him as Rory delivered all the orders, most of them Thanksgiving turkeys, saving the Chairman's monster bird for last.

He carried the fresh-killed thirty-pound turkey up to the Ben Franklin Club and the same two flunkies answered the door.

"I really need to speak to the Chairman," Rory told them.

"Kid, don't make a pest of yourself, huh?" said the bald guy. "The Chairman got bigger fish to fry. He just buried his friend, the president. Looks like Bobby'll be out soon, too. He doesn't have time for you and your father's home-relief case. . . ."

"My father never took a dime in home relief in his life," Rory said. "He needs his rightfully due disability and workmen's comp and—"

The tall guy handed Rory his Liberty dollar plus an extra quarter for Thanksgiving.

"Kid, do this once more, come around here bustin' balls about our boss helpin' your old man, I'm calling your boss, understand? Tell your old man to go through channels or go to hell. I'm sorry. That's life, kid."

Rory said, "Yeah, my father's life. . . ."

The bald guy slammed the door.

Rory jumped on the bike and sped to Krauss the typewriter store and put the extra quarter toward his Royal. Krauss took the typewriter from the window and set it up for Rory and entered the quarter into his ledger. Rory sat down and typed.

Nobody asked me, but . . . life isn't on the level. You can't trust anybody—not girls, not the government, not the cops, not the church, not the Chairman. . . .

Krauss looked over his shoulder and shook his head.

"Careful, Maguire, some things you write with ink never go away," Krauss said, picking up the Royal typewriter to put it back in the window. Rory noticed a numbered tattoo on Krauss's arm.

"What's that tattoo, Mr. Krauss?" Rory asked.

"It's not a tattoo, boy, it's a reminder. It reminds me every day that the best part of life when it's awful is that it can only someday get better," Krauss said, shooing Rory out the door. "So go back to voik and stop feelink all the time so sorry for yourself, Maguire."

When he got back to Freedom Meats the suspicious guy with the shades who'd cased the store was wearing a badge. He and several other guys with badges were carrying records and boxes of receipts and cash registers out of the store, out of the basement office, through the store and into the street where they loaded them into the dark Plymouths.

Sal was frenzied. He was on the phone with his attorney.

"They're from the Internal Revenue," Sal said. "I need you here right now to look at this goddamned warrant. They're hauling my store out the door the day before Thanksgiving, f'Chrissakes. Like I'm some kind of crook! Registers, receipts, checkbooks, ledgers, bankbooks, bags of cash. The whole ball of wax. . . ."

Rory saw Noonz smirk as he entered the walk-in icebox. He followed him in.

"What's going on?" Rory asked, his breath frosty.

"That guy he thought was casing the joint? The guy he thought was dunning me for bad bets and overdue paper? He's a *fed*, kid. IRS as in *In Real Shit*. Someone ratted him out, all that braggin' to everybody about paying fifty grand cashola for a house over Staten Island. That's all the IRS gotta hear. A guy with a cash business buyin' a big-ticket item like a house in cash they figure he's skimming like a Vegas crap dealer." His face was flushed. "Well, now he knows how I feel. You won't see me shed no tears. And I got a Christmas bonus of my own for him, too."

"You didn't . . ."

Noonz looked at him like he was insulted.

"You askin' did I rat on my own brudda? *Never!* He's still my brudda. That don't mean I ain't enjoyin' him squirmin'. I wanna see him say 'Ho ho ho' come Christmas."

"They won't close us down, will they?"

"No, but they says they're freezing his bank accounts. Which means he won't be able to pay suppliers soon. Bang goes his credit line. Pretty soon he'll have as many people bustin' his balls for money as I do. And the troot? I love every minute of it."

Rory went into the back room, where Sal was now talking to a sobbing Babe.

"Dad, let me drop outta Poly Prep, lemme come work here for you," he said.

"No way, Babe," Sal said. "This here's just a bump in the road. I'll get it straightened out. See, this is the reason I need you to become a lawyer. So you can protect me from ghouls like this here. You stay in school. Understand? No son of Sal Russo will ever go home with blood on his shoes."

As much as he resented him that afternoon for driving Carol home, Rory admired Babe right now for wanting to do the right thing for his old man. He couldn't help feeling good about something else: That Babe might have to sell the car.

Before closing for the night, Sal gave Rory a twenty-five-pound turkey to take home.

"Here, kid, take it before these IRS bastards do," Sal said, and then Rory went home for Thanksgiving.

17

Thursday, November 28: Thanksgiving

After Tara said grace, Rory sliced the turkey. The one from Freedom Meats. The free Butterball turkey that Tara got from Bohack for buying over thirty-five dollars' worth of groceries was wrapped in towels on the cold fire escape so cats and pigeons wouldn't get at it. She'd cook that one tomorrow and for at least a week the Maguires would be eating turkey dinner, turkey sandwiches, creamed turkey on toast, turkey hash, and turkey soup.

Rory had gotten the Thanksgiving turkey-slicing job in the family because he worked for a butcher. He piled the meat on a big platter from the "good" set of dishes, the ones reserved for company and holidays. He passed it around. Caitlin, Connor, and Bridget piled their plates with meat, their eyes bigger than their bellies. A silent Dermot speared one slice of white meat and passed the platter to his father, and draped his arm over the back of the chair in a sneering way. Harry took one slice and passed the platter to Tara, who took a drumstick.

Rory sat down and took two large slices of white meat and then everyone was taking mashed potatoes, corn niblets, peas, string beans, turnips, and stuffing, the sound of clicking spoons merging with "mmmms" and "ahhhs" and the rattling of the windows and Mrs. Quigley banging on the pipes for more heat from downstairs.

Like someone trapped in a submarine sending out an S-O-S, Rory thought.

The pitcher of dark gravy circled the table and then Tara said, "Happy Thanksgiving."

And the Maguires ate in silence for the first minute, Rory thinking, *She made this feast out of nothing. How'd she do this?*

"When I sit on Santas's lap in Germaine's I'm gonna tell him I want Tiny Tears," Bridget said, her three-year-old eyes wide and green like her mother's.

"Tiny Tears dolls are too dear, love," said Tara. "Santa's on a budget this year."

"Well, I'm asking fatso for Fanner Fifties," said Connor.

"Never call anyone fatso," Tara said. "And those Fanner Fifties cap pistols are dearer than a Tiny Tears dolly. Santa can't afford them this year, either."

"Santa waiting for a settlement, too?" Connor asked.

Dermot laughed, his mouth a bitter slash. No one else did. Rory glanced at Harry who watched his kids in silence. He was chewing with his mouth closed. Dermot ate without looking at anyone, wolfing his mashed potatoes and vegetables and turkey as if consuming a last meal. Nobody spoke.

"Slow down," Tara said, as something snapped behind the stove. One tiny peep followed. Dermot dropped his fork on his plate, stopped chewing. He ejected the wad of food from his mouth and balled it into his napkin.

"Can I be excused?" Dermot asked. Harry nodded. Dermot rushed in his stockinged feet into the bathroom and closed and locked the door.

Harry kept chewing, glancing around the wordless table at his wife and children, his eyes meeting Rory's. Then Rory saw his father look down at his plate and scoop up some mashed potatoes with dark gravy.

Happy Thanksgiving, Dad, Rory thought.

18

The next morning Rory awakened a little past six A.M. and pulled on his red flannel robe. Freedom Meats was closed the day after Thanksgiving. When he walked into the kitchen his father sat alone at the kitchen table, sipping a cup of steaming tea. A library copy of *Catch-22* by Joseph Heller sat on the tabletop. His mother was already gone, working an extra shift at Mayflower Laundry. Dermot and the rest of the kids were sleeping.

Rory relieved himself, washed his hands with cold water, and went out and poured himself a cup of tea from the pot that sat on the kitchen table with the Irish knit pot holder on top to keep it warm. He added milk and sugar.

"I heard on the news last night that Notre Dame won," Rory said.

"Good."

"Navy, too."

Harry nodded. "Great."

"Merchant marines ever have a football team, Pop?"

"Yeah, in Kings Point and state maritime schools. I never played."

"How come?"

"There was a war on."

"Can you tell me about that? What you did in the war?"

Harry sipped his tea in silence for a long moment. Morning sun gleaming on the frosted window burst a little rainbow onto the Formica tabletop.

"Rory . . ."

"Yeah, Pop."

"I just want you to know how much I appreciate all you do for this family."

"It's our family, Pop."

"All ready for your big date, then?"

Harry drank more tea and nodded to a baby roach walking through the Formica rainbow. Rory knocked it off the table onto the floor. He pretended to step on it, and watched it wander under the table.

Rory said, "I guess."

Harry pushed himself up from the table, leaned on his crutches, put his finger to his lips, and nodded with his head for Rory to follow him. They moved through the rooms, thick with windowless darkness and the phlegmy sounds of sleeping children, and into the tiny back bedroom. Below them, Seventh Avenue was coming awake.

Harry took a ring of keys from his robe pocket, unlocked the padlock on the chain on the tin armoire, and opened it. He removed a hanger holding a piece of clothing wrapped in S&S French Dry Cleaner's paper. He handed it to Rory. This wasn't a suit. It was bigger and bulkier and Rory knew what it was.

Rory backed away and said, "Aw, Pop . . ."

"C'mon, open it."

Rory ripped the paper off the dress peacoat like a kid opening a Christmas toy. It hung on the hanger, a little faded by the salty sea and the sun, but as clean and spotless as any coat he'd ever seen. The gleaming navy-blue bone buttons were new and imprinted with anchors and the collar was high and proud.

Harry said, "A man needs a man's coat."

When his father called him a man, Rory blinked, planted his feet into the floor. "Pop, really, I can't. This is *your* prized coat. . . ."

"I wore it alongside the best men I've ever known." His father leaned the crutches against the armoire, braced his back on the door frame and held the coat up for Rory, who glided his arms into the satin-lined sleeves.

"Oh man, oh man, oh man . . ."

Rory buttoned it with precise care, shrugged his shoulders to heft the weight of the fine fit, shooting the cuffs and pulling the collar up. He looked at himself in the wavy mirror on the wall. Harry grabbed his crutches.

"I know you've been after that leather job down in Belmont's window," Harry said. "That's not gonna happen. Not this year, anyway."

"This is *perfect*, Pop."

"I was gonna give it to you Christmas morning but I know you have the big date on Saturday night. It kept me warm many a cold night at sea. It probably saved my life. And I'd be honored if you wore it, big guy."

"The honor's all mine, Pop."

Harry smiled and said, "Now you can do something for me."

"Name it, Pop."

Harry leaned his crutches against the armoire again and grabbed Rory by the shoulders.

"I need you to help me use my legs again," Harry said. "So I can get back to work."

Rory nodded and held his father under his arms, helping him find his center of gravity, the smell of his sweat like the magical scent of manhood. Harry floundered and then fixed his balance on his unstable feet. He spread his arms like a tightrope walker and Rory very slowly let go. He stepped backward five steps from his father, holding out his work-strong arms as Harry had done for him when Rory was a toddler. And then Harry took a step. He paused, grimaced in pain, hesitated, wobbled, and steadied himself again. Then he took another step. And another. Until Harry Maguire had walked five steps into the arms of his son.

"Christ, but the pain is awful," Harry said as Rory helped him into his wheelchair. "Tomorrow we'll try for ten."

Saturday, November 30

All morning business stunk in Freedom Meats. Even Rory's orders were way down, from over thirty to under twenty. Rory knew that all the regular customers couldn't be living just on turkey leftovers, like the Maguires. Rory knew business was hurting because more and more people were going to Bohack.

But as the wall clock neared noon the only thing Rory could really think about was his date with Carol in four hours. He wondered what she'd wear. She always looked so hot. Her mother took her shopping in some place called Bloomingdale's in the City where no one else in Brooklyn shopped, so no matter what she wore it would be different. He projected, imagining walking through the Christmas Manhattan crowds with Carol, holding hands, making other guys gape and turn their heads to stare in envy.

Noonz walked around all day with a big smile on his face, even when Sal barked orders at him, giving him "busy work" to do while business was slow.

"Anything you say, big brudda," Noonz said, when Sal told him to go into the walk-in box and grind 100 pounds of chuck chop, which meant he'd be in the freezing icebox for over an hour. Rory brought him in the can of Rheingold from Karl the deli guy. Noonz didn't even call Karl a kraut SOB. He kept smiling, drinking his beer as if in private celebration.

Around one P.M. Rory picked up the new window sales signs from the one-armed sign painter who shook his hand and saluted. Rory and Noonz taped the signs in the front window. To compete with Bohack, Sal had cut his prices by a third, even a half on some items, and promised that anyone who bought thirty-five dollars' worth of his meat would get a free canned ham for Christmas. He was declaring a price war with Bohack.

By 3 P.M. word had spread on the neighborhood tom-toms and Freedom Meats was packed, a line going out the front doors. Sal and Tony worked the customers as fast as they could. Some of the regular customers requested Noonz. Sal sent Rory into the walk-in box to get Noonz.

Noonz walked out with a big smile on his face, gulping from a can of Rheingold. Sal looked at him in astonishment.

"Get rid of that beer and get to work," Sal said.

Rory watched Noonz drain the beer, bang the empty on top of the showcase, and belch in Sal's face. He then removed his apron, balled it, and threw it at Sal's feet.

"See ya around, big brudda," Noonz said, pulling on his coat.

"Where the hell you think you're going?" Sal said, in front of the embarrassed customers watching the family melodrama.

"Me, I'm going to woik for the *Bohack*, baby, fifty bucks more a week than you pay me," Noonz said with a smile. "And you? You can go to hell."

Noonz yanked open the front door, the bells dinging, and made a left and walked toward Bohack. Rory watched Sal gape in astonishment.

* * *

After closing, Rory washed the platters by hand in the back room as the linen and sawdust guys made their weekly deliveries. The scale adjusters and knife sharpener were also there. As they worked, Rory scrubbed platters and knives when he overheard Sal and Babe talking in Sal's cellar office directly below the flimsy floorboards.

"I'm between the rock and the hard place, Babe," Sal said. "I'm being squeezed by the Bohack and the IRS."

"Let me help, Dad, please, let me help. I'll replace Uncle Noonz. I'm good. . . ."

"I can hire another butcher," he said. "But right now I need a ten grand operating loan. But every bank I ask says no because now I have an IRS lien."

"So what are you sayin', Dad?"

"Well, we might have to forget about the new house on Staten Island."

"So what? We stay where we are in Bensonhurst."

"I might have to trade in the Caddy for something smaller."

"You sayin' I have to give up my Riv?"

"If business don't pick up, yeah, I might even have to put a lock on the door."

"Jesus Christ, Dad," Babe said. "You can save money today by lettin' me drop outta Poly. I'll work six days a week here *free* to keep my Riv. To save the store. You're my father. Someday I wanna run this store, you gotta let me help you now."

"You gotta stay in school so you never get in a bind like I'm in here," Sal said.

Rory felt sorry for them both, washing blood from the platters down the drain.

"Look, Dad," Babe said. "I got a few hundred in allowance saved . . ."

"You use that for Christmas," Sal said. "Buy this girl you like something nice. Take her dancing. I'll do what I gotta do to figure all this out."

Rory knew Sal must be talking about Carol.

"I'm gonna go upstairs and work and—"

"Enough! Sal Russo's son will never go home with blood on his shoes!"

"Well, one way or the other I'm gonna help," Babe said. "I'll sell the Riv. I'll get a job somewhere else. I'll think of something!"

When Babe came upstairs he passed the sawdust guys, the scale adjusters, the linen deliverers, and Rory and headed toward the bathroom. He looked like he'd been crying. Rory was scraping the blocks and Babe came out of the bathroom, said nothing, and left with everyone else.

Rory finished cleaning up the store. Sal and Tony looked glum and exhausted by the six-o'clock closing time. Levitsky the tailor appeared at the door as usual around 6:15 with his leather schoolbag filled with catalogues and samples. Rory let him in.

Sal sat on a customer's chair, smoking a Pall Mall, lost in smoky silence.

"So what do you need to wear for Christmas mass, Sal?"

"Nothing this year, Sol."

"Nothink? Whadda ya mean nothink? Sal Russo always needs somethink."

Sal looked a little embarrassed, cleared his throat and waved his hand.

"Please, good night, Sol, huh?"

"Maybe it's a bad time," Sol said.

"Yeah," Sal said.

Rory let Sol out the front door, walking off in a disappointed shuffle.

Rory laid the fresh sawdust and Sal gave him his ten dollars pay.

"Good night, kid."

"Good night, Sal," Rory said and left. For the first time ever he felt sorry for Sal Russo, who'd always seemed to him like the man who had everything.

19

Rory finished his bath and stepped out of the bathroom, shivering in the red flannel robe. His mother had the pants of the altered Catholic Charities suit up on the ironing board, a flattened brown paper bag over one leg to protect it from searing as she pushed an iron over it like a little steam locomotive.

When she was done Tara lifted the pants with a flourish, the creases as sharp and true as Sal Russo's favorite knife. Harry sat at the table smiling as Caitlin stood by the RCA Victor radio singing along with Ruby and the Romantics' "Our Day Will Come." Rory took the pants, turned his back to his parents, and put them on. The fit was perfect, just the right four-inch, high-water hem with no cuff above the shoe. Harry tossed Rory a pair of brand-new black Banlon socks with the store sticker still on them, a Father's Day gift he'd never had reason to wear. Rory flashed his father a thumbs-up and pulled them on and then removed the robe, standing bare-chested and rippling with muscle. He donned a fresh undershirt and then his mother held out one of the Catholic Charity white shirts that was now as snowy white as one right off the shelf of Abraham & Strauss. The collar and cuffs and button line were as stiff as cardboard. His mother had moved the shirt collar button closer to the edge to allow him to button the shirt around his thickening neck. He tied on a long thin black tie and then examined the jacket. The stitching was flawless.

"You should've been a plastic surgeon, Mom," Rory said, going to the bathroom mirror, beaming as he saw himself with the stiff starched shirt collar protruding from the black suit.

Gino the shoemaker had dazzled up the plain round Mr. Gutter shoes to give them an Italiano look. Rory slid his feet with the new Banlons into the shoes and clickety-clacked the horseshoe taps on the worn linoleum and then stepped up onto the ceramic tiles of the bathroom to give a real loud little tap dance.

"Boss-o," screamed Caitlin, who couldn't wait to be a teenager.

"I hate ties," said Conner, who wore a clip-on job to his third grade class in Catholic school every day.

Tara held up the *Daily News* photo of John Lennon.

"Ladies and gentlemen," Caitlin said, using a milk bottle as a microphone. "Introducing the fifth Beatle from Brooklyn, New York: Rory Maguire!"

With his mop-top hair and identical Beatles suit he played an imaginary guitar and sang, *"I wanna hold your haaaaaand! I wanna hold your hand!"*

Everyone laughed. Even Dermot couldn't stifle a small smile as he walked barefoot to the fridge and grabbed himself an apple.

Then a loud knock came upon the front door. The family looked at one another. No one was expecting company. Tara folded the ironing board and had the kids clear off the table in case it was the landlord or important company. A second, louder knock came. Tara smoothed her hair and apron. Rory opened the door.

Ankles said, "Just the punk I was looking for."

"Watch who you're calling 'punk,' Tufano," Harry said, from his seat at the table, grabbing his crutches.

Behind Ankles stood two silent uniformed cops and Sal Russo, looking a little surprised as he gazed around the kitchen.

"What do you want with my Rory?" Tara said.

"What's this all about?" Harry demanded.

"Sal Russo's thirty-eight-caliber pistol is missing," Ankles said.

"Rory knew where I kept it," Sal said, twirling his hat in embarrassment.

"What are you talking about, Sal?" Rory said. "You think *I* took your *gun?*"

"We're talking about a felony here," Ankles said. "Stealing a licensed firearm. And if you gave it to someone else, kid, and it's used in the course of crime, you can add another felony. Maybe a few more."

"C'mon, kid," Sal said, trying to sound reasonable. "You knew where it was. . . ."

"And I know that Lefty Hallahan has been pressuring you to swipe it for him," Ankles said. "For this rumble they got planned with the Roman Emperors. You know—as soon as their leader, Pee Wee Carbo, gets out of Rikers next week."

Dermot looked at Rory, his eyes cloudy with a sense of dread and guilt.

Sal kept glancing around the apartment, as if amazed that people still lived in this kind of poverty just blocks from his store.

"My son would never do anything like this," Tara said. "Sal, you know this is a great kid. . . ."

"I didn't take your gun, Sal," Rory said, stepping in front of his distraught mother. "No way, not in ten million years."

"You're gonna have to come down the Seven-Two to talk, kid," Ankles said. "And if I could, I'd take you, too, Dermot. You're in with Lefty and the other creeps he runs with."

"No way," Rory said. "I have a date. At eight sharp."

"Where'd you get the dough for all the new vines, kid?" Ankles said, grabbing Rory by the elbow.

"His whole outfit cost two dollars," Tara said.

"And I just married Elizabeth Taylor," Ankles said, yanking Rory toward the door, the uniformed cops flanking him on either side. "Let's go, kid. . . ."

Tara whispered, "Jesus Mary and Joseph . . ."

Harry stood from the table, swung across the kitchen on his crutches. "You take my son over my dead body," Harry said, brandishing a crutch at Ankles. A uniformed cop grabbed the crutch and he and Harry struggled. Harry, his upper body stronger from hauling himself on the crutches for six months, flung the cop against the wall, knocking off the pictures of John Fitzgerald Kennedy, Pope John XXIII, and the Sacred Heart. Harry stood on his own, wobbling, brandishing his fists. The second cop waded in with a pair of handcuffs, knocking Harry off balance, and wrestled him to the floor.

Caitlin, Connor, and Bridget sobbed for their pained and manhandled father.

Then from the far side of the kitchen came a resounding metallic snap. Like a pistol being cocked. Spooked, the second uniformed cop pulled his gun, aiming toward the stove. Ankles reached for his gun. Sal raced into the hallway for cover.

Then they heard the doomed mouse squealing in the mousetrap. One cop exhaled.

The tense quiet moment was broken when Rory said, "Okay! Enough! Leave my father alone and I'll go with you."

"No!" Harry said.

Ankles nodded. The uniformed cops let go of Harry. Dermot and Tara helped him to his wheelchair.

"Say nothing to this shower of bastards until Esposito gets there, Rory," Harry shouted.

Downstairs a small crowd gathered on the sidewalk of Seventh Avenue in front of the Maguire tenement as Rory was led by Ankles and the two patrolmen toward the radio car with flashing lights. Just before his head was lowered into the backseat Rory made eye contact with one face on the edge of the crowd—Jim Sturgis. His heart fell into his belly.

Carol's father had just left the fish market on the corner and craned his neck to get a look at this new skell he might be arraigning in the morning.

After the door slammed Rory saw Sal Russo chatting with Mr. Sturgis, both stealing glances at Rory in the backseat of the squad car that was pulling away from the curb.

In the precinct, Ankles interrogated Rory for almost an hour before Esposito showed up and told him to either charge his client or let him go. Rory kept looking at the clock as it inched toward eight o'clock. It was 7:54 when Esposito said, "A slew of other potential suspects were in that back room and had access to that gun. Sal's brother Nunzio, who happened to quit that afternoon in a public huff. The sawdust guys. The knife-sharpener. The scale adjuster. Sal's own son, Sal Jr.—or Babe—and the linen guy who could have found it because the gun was kept under the linen. . . ."

One by one Sal dismissed these suspects as the clock on the wall ticked. Rory held out hope that he could explain to Mr. Sturgis that this was all a big mistake and still get to take Carol to see the lighting of the tree.

"But you can't prove for a minute that Rowdy Maguire took this gun," said Esposito. "So either book him or say good night."

Ankles looked at Sal as if to say Esposito was right. Sal shook his head in sad disbelief.

"I'm sorry kid," Sal said. "I always liked you. But don't bother coming back to my store no more."

"You're firing me for something I didn't even do?" Rory said. "Right before Christmas? This isn't right."

"Scram," Ankles said, leaning his face an inch from Rory's. "But remember: I'm gonna be on you like wrinkles on old ladies."

Esposito gave Rory a ride from the 72nd Precinct to Eleventh Street and Seventh Avenue. By the time Rory hopped out of the car it was 8:14. He ran the rest of the way to Tenth Street and up to Carol's house.

As he approached the Sturgis brownstone, out of breath and frantic, Rory ducked behind a big Norwegian elm when he saw Carol dressed in a gorgeous new green velour dress and long green leather coat with matching boots. She was climbing into the front seat of Babe's red Riviera. To his horror Rory also saw his stickball pals—Kevin, Willie, Timmy, Skip, Bobby—gathered like a cheering section beside a parked truck on the other side of the street waiting to see for themselves if Rory had a big date with Carol Sturgis. They snickered and slapped five as Babe closed the car door for Carol. When Babe circled to the driver's side of his Riviera, Jim Sturgis called to him, "Remember, Babe, hands to *yourself*. And have her home not one minute past midnight. Hear me, pal?"

"Loud and clear, Mr. S," Babe said, and climbed into the Riviera.

Before he entered his house, Mr. Sturgis heard Rory's pals goofing on Rory from across the street. Mr. Sturgis looked at them and then spotted Rory standing by the tree, watching

Carol leave in Babe's car. He came down the stoop in a firm authoritative swagger, pointing a finger at Rory.

"*You*," Mr. Sturgis said. "I just saw you in handcuffs! I know the whole story."

"It was a mistake . . ."

"Mistake, my ass," Mr. Sturgis said. "Your boss's gun is missing. I know all about it. I don't want to hear any bullcrap stories. Just stay away from Carol, you shanty little turd."

"I didn't steal any gun . . . I never stole anything from any-one. . . ."

"Stay away from Carol or I'll find a way of personally pros-ecuting you," Mr. Sturgis said.

"What is it you got against me?" Rory asked, flapping his arms. "What did I ever do to you? What, I'm not good enough for your daughter? That it? Because I live in a tenement? Because I'm an order boy? Tell me. You don't even know me. So what makes you better than me?"

"Just stay away from Carol," Mr. Sturgis said in a firm, lower voice.

Mr. Sturgis climbed the stoop. Rory stood in his Catholic Charity suit, his Mr. Gutter shoes, and his father's hand-me-down peacoat.

"Hey, Mr. Sturgis . . ."

"You have something else to say to me?"

"Yeah, I am not *shanty*," Rory said, his father's wisdom guiding him. "I don't know how you were dragged up, but I was raised better. You're a D.A. but you judge people on zero evidence. What's that? That's not justice. So no offense to Carol, or her mother, but she doesn't come from much of a father."

Mr. Sturgis moved his gnashing teeth but no more words came out. Rory looked him square in the eyes, the way his father looked in the Chairman's that night in 1960.

Then Rory turned and walked down the street, his dream date with Carol ruined. And like his father, he no longer had a job.

His so-called buddies, the ones he fought with many times over the years for goofing on his merchant marine father, now goofed on him from across the street about making up the date with Carol Sturgis. Rory flipped them the bird and started walking toward Seventh Avenue.

And then Rory started to run, thinking, *This'll be the worst Christmas of my life.*

20

Monday, December 2

Rory searched for Carol in school all day but didn't see her. After his final class, he waited for her outside school in the rain. But she never showed. Rory passed Freedom Meats on the way home and felt strange seeing the place without being a part of it anymore. He trotted past it on the other side of the street as rain peppered Seventh Avenue.

When he got home he felt strange not having to change into his Freedom Meat clothes. *Gotta get a job*, he thought. *Gotta get a job.* He felt something heavy in the damp chilly air of the apartment. The smell of burning wax was like a requiem mass. The candle had been lit since Jack Kennedy died. His mother was bent on one knee in the corner of her bedroom, praying to her small statue of St. Anthony and the Infant of Prague. The light of the candle danced on his mother's face. He could tell she'd been crying when she walked into the kitchen.

"Mom, what's wrong?"

She nodded toward two pieces of mail on the kitchen table. Rory opened the first envelope that was from the state workmen's compensation board. He scanned the letter and his eyes focused on only one word: DENIED.

The second envelope contained his father's $44 unemployment check. There was also a note saying this was the last check for which Harry Maguire was eligible.

Anger rose in Rory. Anger about the bad hand dealt to Harry Maguire. Anger at Carol. And her asshole father. And Babe. And Sal. Anger at his own foolish self. No girl. No job. No joy.

"Don't cry, Mom."

"It's all so unfair."

"I'll find another job."

She nodded and laughed. "What else can go wrong, right?"

Rory smiled and said, "We could be the Kennedys with all their millions and be a lot worse off, right?"

"Aye." She gathered herself, dried her eyes with the sleeves of her dress.

"I'm gonna go out today and look for a job," Rory said.

"I'm going in early today myself," she said. "Ebenezer Riley is giving me some overtime."

"See, there's hope, Mom."

He kissed her forehead and walked through the rooms. His father sat in his wheelchair by the front window in the living room, clutching a baseball in his right hand, staring out at the drizzly Brooklyn sky. The television set was off.

"Sorry, Dad."

Harry didn't hear him yet as his deaf ear was turned to him. Rory stared at his father, sitting in the wheelchair, half-deaf, his body broken, his youthful dreams smashed, hope shattered, pride ebbing. He ran his fingers over the smooth stitches of the baseball of his youth as if trying to summon hidden powers from a sorcerer's magic orb.

Rory didn't repeat what he'd said. He just stared at his father as he gazed into the tireless rain. Then Rory whisked through the curtain and went out to look for work for Christmas.

Tuesday, December 3

When he asked about the job in the fish store he learned that Minogue, the loudmouth from the football team, had already gotten it.

Rory put his name in for jobs at several of the other groceries and small markets along Seventh Avenue. But word had already spread that he'd been fired from Freedom Meats for stealing Sal Russo's gun.

When he left for school in the morning Ankles was parked outside of his building. The big cop cruised alongside him as Rory walked to Manual, a cat and mouse game that attracted a lot of attention from nosy, gossipy neighbors. It was like being branded as a felon without being charged with anything.

Ankles parked outside of Manual while Rory joined the line to enter. He saw the big cop get out of his car and speak to Mr. Sears, throwing glances at Rory.

In school Rory spotted Carol twice, among the more than two thousand students moving through the corridors. Once she ducked into the girls' room to avoid him. The second time she surrounded herself with girl classmates to shield herself from him.

Rory received extra credit in English class for the paper he had written in typing and then rewrote and retyped and handed in to Mrs. Florence Mondry, his English teacher. She gave him an A-plus. Rory thought how odd it was to get back a paper about his first kiss with a girl who now avoided him in the hallways. At last, after the fifth period, he ran into Carol on the stairs. Her eyes were evasive and glittery with doubt and embarrassment and annoyance. Rory showed her the A-plus paper. She seemed flattered that he had written about her, but her eyes seemed to be scanning his words, without absorbing them.

"This is really nice, Rory," she said. "But maybe it was a mistake, me and you."

Other students hurried past, loud, giggling, goofing on each other. A few couples held hands. One couple made out as they walked, oblivious to the sixth-period bell.

"No, don't say that. At least let me explain why I stood you up. I didn't really stand you up, anyway. I got there late. . . ."

"I know why. My father told me. He also told me you said that he was dragged up and that I didn't come from much of a father."

"I was wrong, but I was mad. He called me a shanty turd. But the reason I was late . . ."

"I know the reason. The whole *neighborhood,* the whole school, knows. Like a real jerk you stole your boss's *gun.*"

"I did *not* steal any gun. I swear."

"Babe says everyone says you stole his father's gun. . . ."

"Babe couldn't *spell* gun with a gun to his head!"

Carol broke up laughing. Rory was relieved. *Girls always like guys who make them laugh.*

"You swear you didn't take it?"

"Swear."

"On who?"

"Anyone you want. My mom, my dad, my baby sister."

"Swear on the person who means the most to you right now."

"Okay, I swear on *you.*"

"*Yeah?*"

He nodded. She looked flattered. Mixed up. Gorgeous. Maybe a conniving, two-timing game-player, too.

"My father despises you."

"I know."

"Which makes it difficult."

"Yeah."

"But kinda *exciting.*"

"I just want to see you, Carol. I still want to take you out. I don't care if it's Romeo and Juliet style. . . ."

She smiled in a sly way. "Protestant and Catholic," she said. "Bad boy and prosecutor's daughter. Montagues and Capulets. I'll let you know." She put the A-plus essay in her book bag. "I need time to think it over. If my dad caught me with you anytime soon he'd keep me in right over the holidays."

"Are you . . . and Babe . . ."

"We went on that *one* date when you stood me up," she said. "He asked me out again. I told *him* I'd think it over."

"So, what? You're gonna decide between him and me?"

I should let Babe have her, he thought. *Let's see how long she lasts when he shows up on a Schwinn instead of in a Riviera.*

But he wanted her. Part of him wanted to prove to himself and her father that he was good enough to have her. The other part of him really liked her. Liked her so much he wondered if it was that other thing called love.

"I'd like to see *you,* but I *can't,*" she said. "I *can* see Babe but I don't really want to. I'm mixed up. You don't make it easy, Rory. I need *time.* Time to think about all this. Meanwhile, I better get to class. And please don't wait for me after school today because my father's picking me up."

Rory stepped aside and let her go by.

Friday, December 6

At home, no one ever spoke about Christmas. The Maguires treated the coming Christmas like a day to get past, hoping the next one would be better. The kids fantasized about what they would get for Christmas '64.

Dermot was still being kept in after school, his shoes and sneakers locked up in the toolbox. The only thing that brought Dermot home after school each day was the Catholic school uniform, in which he wouldn't be caught dead hanging out after school. But he'd caused plenty of mayhem from home. On Wednesday, a bright and sunny day, Dermot took the big mirror off the living room wall and propped it in the front window in such a way that it reflected the bright sun straight into the window of Joe the barber across the street. That in turn exploded the blinding rays off every mirror in the store, turning it into a box of blinding sun. Joe was shaving a guy with a straight razor and gave him a bad nick on one ear. His partner, Mario, fresh off the boat from Palermo, was so blinded that he cut off most of a balding customer's combover by mistake. Both customers went ape shit, and Joe and Mario and the two customers in their aprons ran out onto the sidewalk, screaming up at the Maguire window where the mirror was causing all the trouble.

Coyle the beat cop came bounding up to the Maguire apartment, huffing and screaming at Harry and Tara but by then the mirror was back on the wall and Dermot was feigning sleep in the top bunk bed.

The next day Dermot made a life-size dummy out of some of Harry's old seaman clothes, stuffing the arms, legs, and torso with rags and newspapers, and using a mop and a stuffed ski mask for a head. He then jammed the front of Rory's old Mr. Gutter shoes with toilet paper and tiptoed up the stairs to the roof, leaned over the edge of the building wearing a second ski mask.

"I can't take this life anymore," Dermot shouted. "I'm gonna jump!"

A big crowd gathered. Someone pulled the handle on a fire alarm box. Another neighbor called the cops. Fire engines, an ambulance, and patrol cars raced to the scene, lights and sirens at full tilt. The avenue was a ghoulish mob scene.

"I can't handle it anymore," he shouted.

After ten minutes of threats to jump, Dermot stepped back from the edge, counted to five-Mississippi and heaved the dummy off the roof right into the path of an oncoming B-67 Seventh Avenue bus that screeched to a halt, throwing everyone out of their seats.

Screams echoed along the avenue. Two women, including Mrs. Sanew from the candy store, fainted. In the pandemonium Dermot leaped over an air shaft separating two buildings, and snuck down the stairs of another tenement on Eleventh Street to hang out with Lefty and the Shamrocks, who robed him a new pair of sneakers.

Coyle the cop banged on the Maguire door.

"That Dermot of yours is gonna wind up in Youth House for criminal mischief and disturbing the peace," Coyle said. "I'm warning you. Control him, or get ready for monthly visits."

Meanwhile, Rory was desperate for a job. He filled out applications in Germaine's Department Store and Platt's Toy Store and J. Michael's Furniture store and Whelan Drugs and a few other stores along Fifth Avenue. And although the Christmas lights were strung across the avenue and Christmas decorations bubbled in the store windows, none of them were hiring new holiday help. All those jobs were lined up in August.

Rory had avoided his stickball pals ever since they goofed on him about making up the date with Carol Sturgis.

He spotted Carol a few times from his top-floor window, walking with her father or mother, dressed in suggestive fashions, her elegant strut turning heads of even dirty grown men. He saw her glance up at his window a couple of times. But they never made eye contact. When Rory saw her in school, they smiled and nodded, but he stayed out of her way. After school he saw Babe offer her lifts in his Riviera. Once, when it was raining, she got in. Once she didn't.

Rory kept his distance, giving Carol the time she said she needed to think things over. But he was calmer now, more indifferent. He began to notice other girls in the hallways of Manual Training. Like LuLu McNab, who was a little nutty but who had developed a great body, and made the cheer-leaders. And Susie Lawrence, who was on the debate team, who everyone said was a brownnose but had a pretty face under the harlequin glasses. He had lunch with her and dis-cussed Jimmy Breslin's column about John Fitzgerald Kennedy's gravedigger that a lot of people were talking about.

While he waited for Carol's answer, Rory was thinking things over, too.

On the way home from school on Friday he ran into Esposito. The lawyer asked if there were any other repercus-sions over the gun.

"Detective Tufano follows me all the time," Rory said.

"He's allowed to do that. It's his job."

"It makes everyone think I'm a criminal."

"It'll pass in time."

"Is there anything else we can do about my father's case?"

"He doesn't have a case anymore, Rowdy. It's over."

"No where else to turn for my pop?"

"Like I told you before, the only one who can help Harry Maguire now is a politician," Esposito said.

21

With no job and no money and still embarrassed to be seen by his friends, Rory spent Saturday night at home. Before leaving for work at the Mayflower Laundry, Tara made a large pot of beef stew and after dinner Bridget was put to sleep with a big bottle of milk while Caitlin and Connor went out to the hallway to play on the stairs leading to the roof, reading comics, singing along with the pop songs on the transistor radio and playing with dolls and toy soldiers.

Dermot lay in his top bunk, pretending to be reading his catechism, covered in a Catholic school book cover fashioned from a brown paper bag. Rory knew it was actually a copy of *Naked Lunch* by William Burroughs, a nutso story written by a heroin junkie in a dirty hotel room in Tangier, which his father had read after the book triggered a big obscenity trial in Boston. Dermot was probably skimming it, looking for the sex scenes. Rory was all for Dermot reading anything, rather than hanging with Lefty. Rory had tried reading the scandalous novel a few times. He loved the way the guy wrote but he couldn't follow it. Too weird. And creepy, and not sexy at all.

Rory and his father sat in the living room, drinking steaming tea and eating day-old Larsen's chocolate layer cake, watching Joey Giardello win a fifteen-round decision over Dick Tiger of Nigeria.

During the prefight introductions, Rory had helped his father take baby steps again. This time Harry took sixteen very slow ones, across the length of the living room and back again. If he couldn't get proper medical therapy Harry Maguire was determined to walk again on his own so he could get some kind of factory job.

During the bout, as he always did when watching a fight, Rory held a pad and pen on his lap, keeping a round-by-round score, and writing a brief synopsis of each round the way Dick Young did in the *Daily News*. He tried to describe the combinations, the left hooks, the overhand rights, the bobbing and weaving.

"Writing about boxing is as close to real human drama as you'll ever get in sport," Harry said, a bookmarker-in-the-middle of *The Naked and the Dead* by Norman Mailer on the snack table next to his chair. "It's primal. It's one-on-one. That's why Cannon loves pugs. You don't have to be afraid of hyperbole when you use words like *courage, destiny, character,* or *heart,* describing a fighter. No golfer was ever brave swinging at a little ball."

Rory walked to the overflowing bookcase in the corner of the living room, asked his father how to spell *hyperbole,* and then looked the word up in the big *Webster's* dictionary. "What about baseball, Pop?"

"Baseball is about dreams," Harry said. "Boxing is about life. A man getting off the canvas and reaching down deep inside of him to find the reservoir of courage it takes to get up and fight on, and sometimes to win, is what you call a microcosm of life itself. So boxing can teach you about many things. Including how to write, because writing is also a lonely, disciplined, individual trade. Baseball, on the other hand, is a team sport, and it teaches you how to *belong.* To a team. Or a crew. Or family or a company or a society. No one is good at every baseball position, but the game tells you where and how you fit into the scheme of things."

Rory figured that when Harry Maguire lost baseball, he didn't know anymore where he fit into the scheme of things.

Rory wrote down the word *hyperbole* and the synonym *exaggeration.* He also looked up *microcosm* and wrote down the definition as "world in miniature."

After the final bell both agreed Giardello had won the decision. But as the officials collected the cards and the TV went to a Gillette commercial, Rory mentioned that he had never heard of an athlete from Nigeria before.

"Quite a place," his father said.

"You were there?" Rory asked, excited.

"Sure."

"When?"

"It was September 16, 1942," Harry said, looking at Rory and then his eyes seemed to go waxy and distant. "We were aboard a Liberty ship named the *Stephen O'Hara,* steaming out of Lagos, through the Gulf of Guinea to Gibraltar, carrying a cargo of cocoa and bauxite to make aluminum for fighter planes. The *O'Hara,* God rest her brave and sorry soul, was a specially armed freighter with forty-five merchant mariners and a fifteen-man U.S. Navy Armed Guard gunner crew. And we were steaming full steam ahead in the foggy dawn when out of the soup comes a German raider named the *Stine,* and . . ."

Rory sat on the edge of his chair, leaning closer to his father so he would not miss a word. His father was talking about his World War II experiences. At last. Maybe he was even talking about the day his ship was sunk. The day he almost died. The day that changed his life forever.

"Anyway, there we were, like sitting ducks, when—"

On the TV a series of bells rang. Johnny Addie the ring announcer was about to announce the decision. The time-keeper hammered the bell over and over. And as he continued to bang that bell, Rory saw his father jump at each gong as if he'd been electrified. He covered his ears with his hands, his body convulsed by spasms.

"Ahhhhh," Harry screamed as Johnny Addie announced the unanimous decision for Giardello. Then in a frightened, whispery voice Harry said, "Quiet! Turn it off! Turn off the bells! Turn off the sirens! Turn them off!"

Rory turned off the sound of the TV but Harry writhed in his chair and stood without crutches, short-circuited by the bells and sirens in his head. After he rose, he held his ears and took three aimless steps, then swayed, and his ruined back and ankles seemed to go in opposite directions. He fell in sections, slamming into a snack tray, his cup of tea and cake smashing to the floor.

He bounced off the coffee table with a loud yowl. Rory dove to catch his father before he landed on his back, throwing his arms under him to cushion his fall. Then silence. Rory cradled his father in his arms. Harry cupped his ears, moaning in agonizing pain.

"The hell's going on?" Dermot shouted through the curtain from the bedroom.

"C'mere, quick!" Rory shouted.

After several seconds Rory was able to kneel up straight, lifting his father onto his lap. And then Dermot rushed in, and together he and Rory lifted their father onto his wheelchair, his living hearse.

Harry sat in hot white pain for several seconds as Rory sent Dermot to fetch some aspirins from the kitchen. Harry had prescriptions for stronger painkillers but they were too expensive and he refused to have them filled.

"Pop, you okay?" Rory asked.

Harry nodded in a humiliated way.

"You want me to go downstairs and use Quigley's phone to call an ambulance?"

"No!"

Dermot came back with the aspirins and a glass of water. Harry placed them on his tongue and sipped the water.

"Pop, the bells from the fight did it to you," Rory whispered into his good ear. "Did bells and sirens go off that day on the *Stephen O'Hara?* Before she went down?"

Harry faced his sons in an angry way, then spun his wheelchair and rolled himself through the curtains, through the kids' bedroom, and into his own darkened bedroom. Rory and Dermot sat facing each other in the living room, hearing their father grunt his way out of the chair and into bed.

"This is life played fair and square?" Dermot asked and walked through the curtain and flopped into the lower of the bunk beds.

Rory sat alone in silence because he didn't have an answer for his brother. Just as his father had none for him.

Sunday, December 8

In the morning Mrs. Quigley from downstairs knocked on the door and said that Rory's mother had called at six A.M. to say someone from the morning shift at the Mayflower Laundry had been fired. Tara volunteered to work her shift. Rory and Caitlin should get the kids their breakfast and reheat last night's stew for lunch.

"What are we gonna do about the goddamned heat?" Mrs. Quigley asked a yawning Rory. "I even got the dogs in goddamned sweaters. They sleep under the blankets with me. The only ones the cold don't seem to bother is the friggin' mice and roaches. They probably have their own radiators in their friggin' nests. I'd rather have the old kerosene heaters any day."

"Mr. Kernis has the thermostat on a fixed temperature Mrs. Quigley, and it only comes on certain hours of the day," Rory said.

"Yeah, February Twenny-ninth, every leap year. C'mon, youse is the supers."

"There's a lock on the thermostat. We don't have access."

"Eskimos get more steam heat," said Mrs. Quigley, and she went back downstairs.

When they awakened, Rory made grilled cheese for all the kids which they ate while watching Sunday morning cartoons on the TV. He brought his father a sandwich, aspirins and tea to bed, where he lay in the dark, still in pain.

Rory fried another grilled cheese sandwich, sealed it in wax paper, bound it in a clean dishtowel to keep it warm, cut and wrapped a hunk of Larsen's pound cake, filled a Miracle Whip mayonnaise jar with tea mixed with milk and sugar, and jammed it all into a brown paper bag. As the kids ate breakfast, Rory left Dermot in charge and hurried downstairs and trotted all the way to Prospect Avenue, and the laundry.

Ankles climbed out of his car as Rory turned the corner. Rory paused as Ankles grabbed the paper bag and searched the contents. Rory stared at him as Ankles handed back the bag.

"Don't you have any other cases?" Rory asked.

"When there's a loose gun on my stomping ground, it's my main case, before it becomes a murder case," Ankles said, folding himself back into his car. "I told you I'd be on you like ringworm. I will get you."

The austere dirty brick Mayflower Laundry building stood like some medieval castle from *The Count of Monte Cristo*, its smokestacks wheezing soot and steam into the overcast winter sky. Men sipping coffee and smoking cigarettes watched their helpers load the trucks with bags and parcels of laundry for the morning run. When Rory turned sixteen his mother said maybe she'd ask Mr. Riley to give him a helper's job. That's if Rory didn't land a copyboy's job at the *Daily News*, like Jimmy Cannon did when he was fifteen.

Rory had walked his mother to the gates many times, but he'd never entered the big plant, where women toiled day and night to help feed the tenement families.

On the loading dock the same fat truck driver he'd seen before puffed an unfiltered cigarette and sipped a cardboard container of coffee imprinted with an illustration of the Acropolis. He spoke to the same short wiry guy with the crew-cut red hair and pressed khaki uniform who checked each truck off on a clipboard. The name Riley was stenciled on his pocket.

" . . . any progress on them ones you're oilin' yet?" the truck driver asked.

"Soon," Riley said, counting laundry bags being loaded by the helper and making marks on his clipboard. "Getting' near hump or dump time, Chubby."

"Put out or get out, baby. Lemme know when you homer. *Again*."

"Figure I give them all these extra hours they can throw me one measly one, here and there, no? So, I made my holiday list, I'm checking it twice, Chubby. I'll let ya know who's been naughty . . . or *too* nice."

Chubby laughed as Riley moved to the next truck, counting bags and marking his clipboard. Rory had a half an idea what they'd been talking about. Men's talk. Like most men, of any age, they were talking about women. *Nobody asked me, but . . . Men who had a hard time getting women spent more time talking to other men about being with women than the guys who got women.*

Rory waited until Riley moved on before he approached the fat guy named Chubby.

He asked where the night-shift women worked and Chubby pointed to a metal staircase in the rear of a small quadrangle. Rory clanged up the steps where the steel door was jambed open six inches for ventilation even in the biting winter cold.

He stepped inside to the blast of heat, the air dense with steam and dust, the roar of over three hundred machines spinning and sloshing and tumbling at once, louder than ten subway trains. Hundreds of pipes and big thick duct vents crisscrossed the twenty-foot-high ceilings. Washers and dryers ringed the two-hundred-by-three-hundred-foot room, a room bigger than a football field, with a hundred long sorting tables clogging the center where the women sorted and folded and ironed and pressed and packaged clothes and linens.

Rory searched the faces of the women, their hair tied up in nets or babushkas, all wearing Mayflower aprons, none wearing jewelry, makeup, or smiles. He didn't smell any perfume. These were the washerwomen who cleaned the soiled clothes of well-to-do strangers through the Brooklyn night in order to put dinner on the table for their tenement children.

Rory'd brought lunch to his father on several job sites over the years. But this was the first time he'd ever brought anything to his mother at work. He had no choice. She was on her way to working sixteen straight hours and she would never spend the money to eat out, never ate out once in all the time he could remember. But she needed something to eat. And the magic elixir of her life—a cup of hot tea.

Rory searched the crumpled faces of the women, hard and bony, some ravaged by booze and cigarettes and poverty and illness and beatings and time. There were a few pretty young Spanish women and two Negresses. He spotted four young neighborhood women who he knew got knocked up in high school by guys who never married them. Or by guys who were doing time upstate. Or by guys who were dead. Most of the women had Irish faces, holy-statue-white or oinky-pink and worry-bitten, many with false or rotting teeth. He'd held the gold plate under many of these faces as these women knelt at the St. Stanislaus altar rail. Their eyes shut tight. Their ugly tongues stuck out, while booze-faced Father O'Keefe served them communion at the 6:15 A.M. mass, on their way home from the night shift here at Mayflower. If they were delinquent in their pledge envelopes, O'Keefe would whisper a terse reminder at the railing as he gave them the body and blood of Christ. *He would do anything for God except get sober,* Rory thought. *Or a job.*

None of these Mayflower Laundry women were the mothers of Rory's stickball friends from Eleventh Street. Most of those women were housewives who stayed home all day and took care of their houses and kids. They were all nice ladies but they had no idea what working the night shift at Mayflower was like. Never would. In fact, a few of them had laundry picked up and delivered by Mayflower trucks and so his mother probably washed and dried and folded their clothes, the dungarees and polo shirts his pals wore when they ranked on his father for being a merchant marine.

Finally, among this gallery of women's faces, he spotted his mother's. After the hot Puerto Rican chick in the second aisle and the Italian honey with the big knockers under the big clock in the rear, he thought his mother was the prettiest face in the big, loud room. All green in the eyes and strong in the jaw, squinting as she folded clothes in a neat stack and wrapped the stack with brown paper and string like a

Christmas present. He saw her singing as she worked, which made him smile, because it meant there was still music in her head and she had told him many times that life without music wasn't life at all, but purgatory.

She looked stray-dog tired, as she would always say, little dark circles under her eyes and a resigned stoop in her shoulders like the one Yogi Berra had when he watched Bill Mazeroski's seventh-game home run sail over the left-field wall to win the 1960 World Series for Pittsburgh. He'd never seen that stoop on his mother before. She spent half her life telling her kids to straighten up, shoulders back, head high. In this place, Tara Donovan Maguire, without her kids around, looked a little older in a funny kind of way.

Rory approached her through the crowd and when she looked up and saw him she looked startled, and put her hand over her heart like she was pledging allegiance, and drew a deep breath and held it.

"Mother of Jesus suffering on the Holy Cross, please don't be bringing me any more bad news, son. . . ."

"I just brought you some breakfast, Mom."

Tara exhaled like a drowning man he'd once seen coming up for air from the sixteen-foot-deep pool in Sunset Park. Tears juiced up her eyes and she gripped the countertop of her workstation. Riley, the foreman came by, banging his clipboard against his right leg, looking from Rory to Tara.

He asked, "Everything okay, Tara?"

She nodded and turned her back to blot her eyes dry with a clean corner of her apron. She composed herself, turned around, and introduced Rory.

"Nice to meet ya," Riley said. "But you gotta take your shoes for a walk, kid. Insurance thing."

Rory stared into the little man's eyes until Riley walked to another table, checking on the progress of another wash-woman. Riley was no taller than Rory but he walked and talked like a big shot. *Nobody asked me, but . . . Being the boss is like having a second set of muscles.*

Rory kissed his mother on the forehead as the other mothers watched, smiling as they worked.

"Thank you, Rory. You're a love."

"See ya, Mom."

"Tell your daddy I'll be home by two-fifteen. I'll make the five-o'clock mass."

"Mom, what were you singing?"

She waved her hand and smiled and said, "Och, you'd never believe it if I said."

"What?"

"'I wanna hold your ha-a-a-a-and,'" she sang, ruffling his mop top. " 'I wanna hold your hand.'"

Rory stood in the cold for a minute, peering through the ajar door, watching his mother work. She started to sing again. Rory smiled. Then he saw Riley walk up behind her, real close, and whisper something in her ear. She stopped singing. Spun. Spoke to Riley in a controlled but angry way. Riley just smiled. And said something back in her ear. Rory's mother turned and went back to work. Rory watched Riley bop through the washroom, passing one of the neighborhood Spanish girls who Rory knew was raising a baby alone. Riley tapped his clipboard off her behind. She turned and Riley winked.

Rage bubbled in Rory's brain, like a ham in a pot. He looked back at his mother at her workstation. She wasn't singing anymore.

He ran all the way home. Ankles was parked across the street from his tenement, wordless, just staring.

* * *

At midnight *Action in the North Atlantic* with Humphrey Bogart came on the *Million Dollar Movie* for the third time that day. Rory couldn't watch it earlier with the kids awake. Besides, on Sunday nights in the Maguire house the TV stayed on CBS to watch *Lassie*, *My Favorite Martian*, *The Ed Sullivan Show*, *The Judy Garland Show*, and *Candid Camera*.

Then everyone went to bed. His mother had passed out in the middle of *Ed Sullivan* and had to be back at work at six A.M. to work another extra shift.

His father watched ten minutes of *Candid Camera*, said that like everything else it was rigged, a hoax and a setup. "That *My Favorite Martian* is more realistic," Harry said, and went into bed next to Rory's mother. Dermot and the kids were already asleep.

Then Rory changed to Channel 7 to watch Kevin Kennedy deliver the news about the kidnapping of nineteen-year-old Frank Sinatra Jr. in some casino hotel in some place called Lake Tahoe. Gloria Ochron gave the weather forecast. Then a sportscaster gave highlights of Cookie Gilchrist rushing for two hundred and forty-three yards and scoring five touchdowns against the Jets. It was too depressing to watch again. Rory slipped out the back door so he wouldn't awaken anybody and walked through the tenement hallway and entered the front door to the kitchen to make himself a cup of tea, and to grab what his mother called "Sam's compliments"—the free day-old crullers and Danish from Sam Brody's corner grocery. Sam was taking a worse shellacking from Bohack's than Freedom Meats.

But Rory's mother still used Brody's because for all these years Sam gave her credit and let her buy things on "the bill," when times were tough. As they always were. And because of Sam's compliments. Rory's mother would take the hardened

Danish or other pastries, put them in a plain brown bag, wet the bag under the faucet, and then place the bag into a hot oven for five minutes until the pastries came back to soft, luscious life.

By the time *Action in the North Atlantic* came on, Rory sat alone in the darkened living room, eating his Sam's compliments pineapple Danish, and sipping his mug of hot sweet tea.

As the movie started Rory kept the sound low, sitting close to the TV on the ottoman in his red flannel robe, an army-surplus blanket over his shoulders, cupping the mug in both hands for additional warmth. Hail nibbled at the shuddering windows, sounding like a kid grating a stick along a picket fence.

Then the opening credits and images began to roll: IN THE TRADITION OF *SGT. YORK* AND *AIR FORCE* WARNER BROS. PRESENTS THE IMPERISHABLE STORY OF THE MERCHANT MARINE.

His father was forever correcting him and telling him the organization was called the merchant marine and that the sailors were *merchant mariners,* not marines. But everyone else in Brooklyn called it the merchant marines, so Rory did, too.

Whatever you called it, Rory's flesh pebbled as the merchant marine was compared to the other true heroes of World War I and World War II.

Then foghorns. Fog. Night. Humphrey Bogart as First Mate Joe Rossi stood on the deck of a tanker called the *Northern Star,* "steaming North, with 100,000 slopping barrels of fuel oil to make tanks roll and planes fly . . ." for the war effort. Rory watched Bogart complain to Raymond Massey, the captain, that he had a toothache. Rory knew how bad that could be. Bogart said, "Like a mouthful of little dwarfs with red-hot pickaxes." *Wow,* he thought. *That's as good as Jimmy Cannon.*

Rory grabbed his notebook and pen and started taking notes. Massey told Bogart to see a dentist as soon as they reached port. "When I get to port I'm gonna see someone better looking than a dentist," Bogart said.

And Rory thought of Riley. Men's talk. And to chase it away he thought of Carol, and imagined what it would be like coming home from a long sea voyage, from *war*, to find Carol waiting on the dock, wearing the green leather coat and matching boots. He wondered what it was like when his father came home from sea, from *war*, and found his Tara waiting for him. Did she wait on the dock? Or did she wait at home? He never asked. *Carol Sturgis didn't wait for me for fifteen minutes*, he thought.

On the TV a young deck cadet, fresh out of Kings Point Merchant Marine Academy, came up on the bridge to discuss some business with Massey. Massey gave him an order. The second mate asked for an explanation. Massey said, "There's an old law of the seas, mister, 'Don't ask questions when given an order.'"

He'd heard his father say that a thousand times. Now he knew where it came from. Not the movie. The sea. Then the scene shifted to the crew's messroom in the belly of the boat, where all the merchant mariners sat around playing cards, goofing on the cook, talking about dames in different ports. He wondered if his father had one in every port. Men always talked about women.

Then one guy, with a Brooklyn accent thicker than Noonz's, said he was a sailor to protect his business and home back in Brooklyn and said that he signed up for duty because 'I got faith in God, President Roosevelt, and the Brooklyn Dodgers, in that order of importance.'"

Rory laughed out loud, imagining his father arguing with guys from all over the country about how good the Dodgers were, and how he'd turned down a chance to play in their farm system in order to do his bit for the service of his country in World War II. The line made Rory stand up, clutching his tea. This was gonna be a great picture. And then another guy played "Home on the Range" on an old-fashioned wind-up Victrola and then the scene shifted to a German sub. The Jerries spoke in German and the captain of the U–boat, part of what was called a wolf pack, got the *Northern Star* in its periscope. And then all hell broke loose.

"Watch out!" Rory screamed as the Nazi torpedo was fired and sped through the water straight for the American ship. His heart raced and panic sizzled in his blood. He imagined his father, Harry Maguire, in the belly of that ship, as the silent torpedo whispered through the first foggy light of dawn.

Then KABOOM!

The ship was in flames, under attack and Rory was screaming. "Get out! Get out!"

The men on the screen scrambled through the guts of the ship where fires raged and pipes burst and steam shot out in a zillion different directions as the ship took on endless gallons of water.

Harry whooshed through the curtains, crutches squeaking and thumping, saying, "For Christ sake, Rory, I'm half deaf and that TV woke me up so turn it d—"

Rory turned and saw his father propped on his crutches, unshaved, his hair sleep-tousled. Harry stopped in midsentence as he stared at the screen in the dark living room.

He watched the German U-boat fire another "tin fish" as the merchant marines scrambled to the fiery deck and slid big flat floating rafts into the roiled sea. Then Bogart and Massey boarded a lifeboat with a dozen men and lowered it into the flaming Atlantic. Rory looked from the TV to his father, where the flickering images reflected in his gaping eyes like little peepholes into hell. The oil spilled out of the tanker and the fire spread on the ocean and now two merchant mariners left behind on the *Northern Star* dove into the ignited waves and swam underwater to the thrashing lifeboat.

Rory looked from the frenzied TV to a silent Harry and back and forth as the men in the water were rescued by the men on the lifeboat.

"Pop . . ."

Harry didn't respond. Kept gaping at the images on the screen, not blinking, not moving, suspended on his crutches like a scarecrow in some overgrown field.

"Pop," Rory said, his voice falling to a whisper. "Is this what it was really like?"

Harry didn't answer as he stared at the cold, wet, scared men huddled in the lifeboat as the U-boat surfaced, and blew the remains of the blazing *Northern Star* out of the water with 88mm D.P. quick-firing rifle fire, and then rammed the little rowboat. The frantic merchant marines dove overboard and swam to avoid the ferocious propellers of the U-boat.

And then the men made it to one of the flat floating rafts, where they spun adrift on the endless sea.

"Was it, Pop? Was it really anything like that, Pop?"

Harry stared for one more long rueful moment and said, "Turn it down. It'll wake up your mother."

And then Rory watched Harry turn on his crutches and hobble into his bedroom.

22

Monday, December 9

Everyone on the TV and radio talked about the FBI report that said Lee Harvey Oswald acted alone and that he had no ties to Jack Ruby.

But Rory half listened. In school Carol smiled at him twice in the hallways, which Rory figured meant that maybe she wanted to see him again. After school Babe showed up to offer her a ride home. She turned it down. That made Rory's heart soar. He walked her home anyway, without asking if he could. She handed him her books, which made it official, and as they passed Bohack, Rory spotted Babe parked outside. *Probably checking on the meat section for his father,* Rory thought.

"What are you doing for your birthday?" she asked.

"Getting another year older. Thank God."

"Plans?"

"No."

"Good."

"Why?"

She smiled and shrugged and he walked her as far as Ninth Street. Then she gave him a quick kiss and hurried off with a giggle. Thrilled, he ran all the way to the big library at Grand Army Plaza and checked the card drawers for a book on the merchant marine. He couldn't find any. He asked the librarian, Mrs. Fitzpatrick, if she could help.

"How do I find out about a particular ship named the *Stephen O'Hara* that got sunk on September 16, 1942?"

She took him to the microfiche machine, which he already knew how to work, and told him to look up September 16, 1942. There was a tiny little news brief a week later that said that the *Stephen O'Hara* had been sunk but there were no details.

"You might check the A.B.S. Register, Lloyd's Register and Merchants Vessels of the United States for 1942," Mrs. Fitzpatrick said. "You might also check the declassified report of the War Shipping Administration of June 1946. You might also check the Customs House library across from Battery Park. But if I were you, Rory, to save some time and possible clearances because of your age, I think you should first try the library at the Seafarers' Union on Fourth Avenue and Twentieth Street right here in Brooklyn. I know that they publish their own weekly newspaper named *The Log* and I'm sure they have back issues with accounts of that ship in their library."

"You mean the merchant marine has its own library?"

"Oh, sure. I'm sure your parents could get you access with a simple note."

Rory sat in the library of the Seafarers' Union, notebook and pen in hand, going through a brief history of the merchant marine in World War II. Rory's mother had sent Rory with a note, giving his father's merchant marine identifying Z-number, explaining to the gray-haired Seafarers' librarian that Rory was working on a school report.

The librarian was a bit surprised by the request.

This was the first time a high school student had ever asked to use the facilities to research a paper on World War

II. "Are you sure you don't want the United States Marines?" she asked.

Rory assured her he wanted to know all about the United States Merchant Marine.

She explained that he had no appointment and that she was in the middle of filing and that she was very busy because the whole facility would shut down for two weeks for the coming holidays. Rory told her that he wanted to check a general history of the merchant marine in World War II and then he wanted to check on one particular ship.

"I can give you the history first," she said. "I can't get individual case files until I finish my own filing. Those are kept in a vault in the basement. Is that okay for now?"

Rory said fine.

He sat for three hours in the Seafarers' library learning things he never knew about the merchant marine, stuff he couldn't wait to throw in the faces of his Eleventh-Street pals, who had goofed on his father for being a merchant mariner in World War II.

Rory took notes. He learned that 243,000 men served in the merchant marine in World War II and that 9, 497 died, a ratio of one in twenty-six. That was higher than any branch of the military. One in thirty-four of the 669,108 regular United States Marines died. One in forty-eight of the 11,268,000 soldiers in the U.S. Army died. One of every 114 of the 4,183,466 U.S. Navy sailors died.

Percentage-wise, the U.S. Merchant Marine suffered the highest losses of World War II. Another 12,000 merchant marines, like his father, were wounded and 661 were incarcerated in POW camps, and another 1,100 died in public health hospitals.

But these were general facts and figures. He needed to know details about a particular ship. He asked the librarian about the *Stephen O'Hara*. The librarian looked at him and said, "You don't actually know somebody who survived the *O'Hara*, do you?"

"Maybe?"

"I'd like to shake his hand," she said.

"Why?"

"That was one of the worst battles of the war involving a cargo ship," she said. "Every one who survived is a bona fide hero. Not that many of them ever received a medal, mind you. Most of the real medals went to members of the U.S. Navy Armed Guard who were on board. But a few of the merchant mariners deserved the highest medal in the land. Wait here."

The librarian disappeared down a flight of stairs and about ten minutes later she climbed the steps with a couple of bound volumes of *The Log,* the Seafarers' newspaper, from November of 1942 and a big official file filled with papers.

"None of these are classified anymore," she said. "But if you want an actual account of that battle I suggest you read the one in *The Log* from October of forty-two. I'll be closing in about a half hour, so try to be quick."

Rory leafed through the heavy official file, a lot of it written in the seamen's jargon and legalese. If he had time and a dictionary he could decipher it. But he didn't, so he decided to search for the account of the *Stephen O'Hara* in *The Log.* In a back issue he found the story he was looking for, copying it word for word into his spiral notebook.

THE SAGA OF THE *STEPHEN O'HARA*

By Maurice Devlin

The sea was tranquil at 0900 on Sept. 16, 1942 as the *Stephen O'Hara* steamed from Lagos, past Gibraltar into the open

Atlantic carrying a cargo of Nigerian bauxite and cocoa beans bound for New York's Red Hook when from the north a strange ship bore down upon her about three points off starboard bow just as a sudden rainsquall began to build.

The *O'Hara* had a crew of 45 Merchant Mariners and 15 US Navy Armed Guard assigned to man the four-inch gun in case they ran into hostile German ships or one of the dreaded U-boats from Hitler's notorious Wolf Pack.

Capt. John Hood looked through his binoculars from the top of the pilot house of the *O'Hara* and told his third mate to sound the general alarm. In moments the deafening clanging of bells roused the crew from their bunks and sent US Navy and Merchant Mariners dashing to their posts, donning life jackets and helmets.

Even in the rainy morning the captain could make out the Nazi flag billowing above the *Stine*.

The *O'Hara* was armed with a four-inch gun aft and a pair of 37-mm guns and four 50-caliber and two 30-caliber machine guns. These were like David's slingshots against the Nazi Goliath called the *Stine* with her mighty 5.9-inch guns. But the merchant seamen helped load the shells into the breech of the *O'Hara's* four-inch gun as the *Stine* fired. The first shot managed to hit the *Stine* but the return fire from her bigger guns rocked the *O'Hara* that erupted in flames. Machine gun fire tore deadly holes through two thirds of the US Navy gun crew.

Bells clanged and whistles wailed under the roar of the big guns.

Down below, the *O'Hara* mess room was turned into a floating hospital as seamen ripped open by shrapnel lay bleeding and dying on the table tops. The *O'Hara* was fast taking on water as the *Stine* closed in for the kill. Casualties were mounting as round after round pierced the hull of the *O'Hara*. Capt. Hood ordered lifeboats and rafts to be lowered and all hands to abandon ship.

In the engine room a just turned 19-year-old wiper named Harry Maguire raced up to the deck, passing through the shooting steam pipes, and over the mangled bodies of dead comrades. As the *Stine* moved in to within 1000 yards of the *O'Hara*, Maguire—with just two weeks training on the gun under his belt—cleared the brave dead Navy men from its base. He moved the one wounded US Navy ensign to a seated position and asked him for instructions while he manned the gun.

By this time the *Stine* was firing on the men in the lifeboats with machinegun fire, also killing those unarmed sailors clinging to dear life on the raft, all part of the new standing order from Hitler to leave no merchant seaman alive.

A horrified Maguire watched as dozens of his fellow seamen were cut down like fish in a barrel, calling out the names of their children, their mothers and wives and other loved ones.

Sharks circled in the sea.

Then as the wounded US Navy Ensign gave faint instructions, barely audible under the roar of the assault, Maguire wheeled the four-inch gun into direct aim at the *Stine*. He fired. The blast trembled what was left of the doomed *O'Hara* and flung Maguire onto the slanting deck. He then proceeded to load another shell into the breech and as the wounded ensign gasped weak instructions, Maguire fired again, into amidships and the magazine, causing the *Stine* to light up like the Fourth of July over New York, from which the young wiper named Maguire hails.

Before the *O'Hara* sank, Maguire managed to haul the wounded ensign overboard into the roiled and cold

Atlantic, swimming one-armed to a nearby raft, where
nine survivors embraced him.

The raft drifted for 27 days before it was picked up by
a British naval ship. Of eleven people initially on the raft,
nine were saved, including the ensign whose name
remains classified but who was likely to be awarded the
Navy Silver Star.

Further details of the entire rescue were presented to
the US War Department by the unnamed ensign but are
also considered classified at the time of this writing.

Rory sat marbled in pride. He had to reread the story twice to
believe it, and made sure he had copied every single word.

The librarian walked over and told him it was almost time
to close. Rory asked if there was any way to get actual copies
of some of these documents. She said that he could put in a
request for a back issue of *The Log* but the fee was two dollars
and because of the holidays it would take about a month to
get it from the warehouse. He had thirty-five cents in his
pocket and didn't place an order.

He did ask for ten more minutes and the librarian said that
would be fine.

When she walked away Rory once again opened up the
official file on the *Stephen O'Hara*. Then he found a document marked DECLASSIFIED in 1946. It had been signed
by President Roosevelt in 1942, awarding the Navy Silver
Star to the wounded U.S. Navy ensign whose life Rory's
father had saved.

The name of the ensign stopped Rory's heart.

He copied down all the numbers and dates and other
information on the document. Adrenaline raced in his blood,
but not nearly as fast as it must have in his father's veins on
that day on the *Stephen O'Hara*. For the first time in his

young life Rory Maguire felt like a real *reporter*. He had put in the legwork. He'd asked the right questions. He'd read the right clips. He'd dug and found the buried document that gave him the truth and the whole story.

Then he read again the name of the young Navy officer whose life was saved by Harry Maguire.

Ensign Charles Pergola Jr.

The Chairman's son, Rory thought.

23

Rory didn't mention what he'd learned to his father. Not yet. He was waiting for the right moment. He needed to let it stew in his own brain first. He also wanted to discuss it with his mother, but she was working all these crazy extra shifts and was either at the laundry or buried in deep, exhausted sleep as soon as she got home.

At school, he saw Carol during lunch, where she had milk and an apple, and nothing else. Pretty girls were weird like that. Rory had an egg-salad sandwich, a Devil Dog, and a container of milk.

"You ever play hooky?" Carol asked.

Rory never had, but said, "Oh, sure."

"Maybe someday we can play hooky together."

"Maybe," he said.

"I'm kidding. Just wanted to see what you'd say."

He leaned in close like he was about to divulge atomic secrets.

"I found out my father was a hero," he whispered, showing her his handwritten papers in the spiral notebook.

She whispered back, "So why are you whispering?"

"I don't know," he whispered and they both laughed.

That afternoon he walked her most of the way home again. And as they passed Bohack he saw Babe sitting behind the wheel of his Riviera parked in the bus stop behind a Wells Fargo armored truck into which armed guards loaded bags of cash from the supermarket. Babe stared at Rory walking with Carol. For the first time Rory could remember Babe didn't smile that goofy grin. He just stared.

Rory also saw Noonz walking into Bohack and as he did he gave Rory a little wave and shook a finger of caution.

"Careful!" he shouted. "Amemba what I warned ya, kid."

"What's he talking about?" Carol asked.

"He knocked up his wife when she was like fifteen."

"He thinks we go all the way?"

"I never told him anything like that."

"You better not."

They walked another block. "Did you ever go all the way, Rory?"

Panic seized him. He didn't want her to think he was a virgin. He also didn't want her to think that all he was after was to get in her pants.

"My father says a real man never kisses and tells."

"I like that," she said, bumping him with her hip.

At Ninth Street he saw all his stickball buddies pile out of a candy store, leafing through Marvel comics and eating potato chips and unwrapping candy bars. They saw Rory walking with Carol, and they all stopped and stared. He heard a few comments about the flunky carrying her books. About the lost puppy following his mistress.

Carol stopped Rory by the mailbox, and in front of his pals, she grabbed his face in her small hands and kissed him. A big, wet kiss. A French kiss. Making out with Rory for all of them to see. The snide comments stopped as Rory's pals gaped.

"Don't tell anybody, baby," Carol said, winking and taking her books from him and strutting off toward Tenth Street.

"I don't believe what I just saw," Bobby said with awe in his voice.

"She as hot as she looks?" asked Kevin.

Rory tried to hide the excitement in his loins and took a deep breath. *Change the subject,* he told himself. *Throw a change-up. Talk about something else. As if kissing Carol was a daily routine. Talk about something big. Something important.*

"Hey, did you guys know that the United States Merchant Marine lost more men per capita than any of the armed services in World War II?" Rory asked.

"What's a capita?" asked Skip.

"It's when a guy gets his head cut off, dumbbell," said Timmy.

"One in twenty-six merchant marines died in World War II," Rory said.

"When did she start French-kissing you, man?" asked Willie. Relentless.

"A real man, the son of a *merchant marine,* never kisses and tells," Rory said. "Did you know that over nine thousand merchant marines died in World War II? And that fifteen thousand were injured? That seven hundred and thirteen merchant marine ships were sunk? That two hundred and fifty men froze to death on the Russian-Finnish border? And that nine hundred were held in POW camps. . . ."

Thinking: *That's what's important, guys. That's the world.*

"Did you get to second base, yet, man?" Tommy asked. "Did you touch skin?"

Rory ignored him and all the other questions about Carol Sturgis and continued his lecture on the heroics of "the imperishable merchant marine," and then marched home.

* * *

That night Rory went to bed during *The Red Skelton Show*, right after the Freddie the Freeloader skit. He awakened around midnight, needing to relieve himself. He knew his mother was working the midnight shift at Mayflower Laundry, putting up with nasty Riley. After returning from the cold bathroom his eyes adjusted to the dark, and as he brushed past the plastic glow-in-the-dark pull-chain handle dangling from the overhead light, he noticed that his father was not in his bed.

He squeaked through his own room, where Dermot and the other three kids slept, emitting mucusy winter wheezes and pulled aside the heavy purple drape to the living room. His father sat on his ottoman in the darkened room, blanket draped over his shoulders, silhouetted against the silver glow of the silent TV. Harry's crutches were propped on the ottoman next to him.

Rory stood for a long moment looking at the back of his father's head, wondering what went on inside of it. How did he live with all the loud and screaming secrets locked inside for all these years? What kind of hero does not come out and take a bow?

Rory walked across the linoleum floor of the living room and sat down on the couch facing Harry's good ear.

Rory looked at the TV and was stunned. Harry Maguire was watching *Action in the North Atlantic* on the oft-repeated *Million Dollar Movie*. No sound. *He doesn't need any*, Rory thought. *He has all the sound he needs inside that noble head. Bells and sirens and explosions and machine-gun fire and the sounds of men calling the names of their children and their wives and their mothers and fathers and brothers and loved ones as the machine-gun bullets from the Stine tore into them. . . .*

Harry never turned to his son, instead just watched Bogart

and his crew fight a pitched battle with the Luftwaffe and a U-boat. In black and white.

"Pop . . ."

Harry didn't answer and now Rory saw that his father twirled the baseball in his right hand, turning it over and over, gripping it with two fingers, and three, and then all five, and on the stitches and across the stitches, going through his repertoire of fastballs, curves, splitters, fork balls, change-ups. All gone. All vanished. Like the men on the *Stine*. All that remained were the bells and the sirens and the drowning sounds of the dying.

"Pop, I know about the *O'Hara* and the *Stine*," Rory said, and paused. "I know you might get mad. But I did some research, Pop. I know that you saved those other ten men. I know that one of them was the Chairman's son. I know that you're a *hero*, Pop."

Without turning from the screen, Harry said, "*Hero* is a four-letter word we use to make hell sound like heaven, big guy."

"Yeah, maybe, Pop, but . . ."

"We might be going through a tough time, but I came *home*, Rory. I got to come home. I have a great wife. I have wonderful kids, none perfect, but I love every one. I have *you*. All of which makes me filthy rich with life."

"Pop, you saved the Chairman's son. You saved Charlie Pergola Jr. His father *owes* you. They gave his son the Silver Star but you were the real hero. . . ."

"If you want to find real heroes from September 16, 1942, you'll find thirty-seven of them at the bottom of the sea. Not one of them, or the nine thousand other heroes of the merchant marine, has his name engraved in government granite. That's why it's better to forget, so that you don't have to remember that everyone else did."

"Nine thousand, four hundred and ninety-seven, Pop."

Harry looked from the screen for the first time to Rory. He reached across and patted him on the cheek and then made a fist and fake punched him.

"Like I said," Harry said. "As long as I have you and the brood I'm blessed."

Harry grabbed his crutches and pushed himself to his feet.

"What about Charles Pergola Jr., Pop? Maybe he can talk to the Chairman, and . . ."

"The Chairman and his son haven't spoken in a dozen years," Harry said. "Which means they're a lot poorer than us. Good night, big guy."

Rory watched his father thump his way to the curtain separating the rooms. He stopped, held both crutches in one hand, balancing on his own legs, and took a last glance over his shoulder.

"That movie's not half bad," he said, tossed the crutches ahead of him, and tottered six independent steps into the black hole of his bedroom.

24

Rory stayed after school and Miss Seltzer let him type up the story he'd hand copied from *The Log*, along with all the information on the Silver Star authorization. He also had a stack of correspondence between Esposito the lawyer and the disability and workmen's compensation boards. Miss Seltzer let Rory make five mimeographed copies of everything on the school machine. Rory stapled each set together.

Rory took the new papers to Esposito. The lawyer looked them over, and sighed.

"I wish I knew all this stuff from the beginning," Esposito said. "Still, these aren't official documents, Rowdy."

Rory said that the lawyer could get the official documents from the Seafarers' Union.

"Don't you understand? Even if I did, it's *too late*. The case is closed." Esposito glanced out the window at the gray day. "Your father needs to put his pride in his pocket, go to welfare, get himself into a city hospital, have the operation he needs, and when he goes home, find himself a job. The disability case is closed. The workmen's comp case is shut. Only a politician can reopen them."

"But look at the last *page*," Rory said, heat rising in his voice. "My father saved the Chairman's son."

Esposito shook his head. "Under ordinary circumstances, I'd say this meant something," Esposito said. "But everyone knows the Chairman and his only son haven't spoken since the 1952 election, over eleven years. For God's sake, the Chairman's son publicly embarrassed the old man in an election, cost him a congressional seat, and that was it. They severed all ties. Sorry, kid, this is just another dead end."

Friday, December 13

Rory Maguire turned fifteen. Jimmy Cannon was fifteen when he dropped out of school and took a copyboy's job at the *Daily News*, where he worked his way up to a column. *Nobody asked me, but . . . being fifteen is not the same as being sixteen, but it's better than being fourteen. Especially with Carol Sturgis in your life.*

On Friday afternoon Rory told Carol he couldn't walk her home because he had an important errand to run.

"Can you meet me later?" she asked. "I have something for your birthday."

"Absolutely."

They agreed to meet on Seventh Avenue and Ninth Street at seven.

Rory knew that the Chairman waited for the Freedom Meats delivery every Friday afternoon so he could make the big pot of sausages and meatballs for his cronies at the Ben Franklin Club. Rory was now betting that the Chairman's flunkies didn't know that he'd been fired. He folded two sets of his letter addressed to President John Fitzgerald Kennedy and his "You're Harry Maguire" essay into a white envelope and slid it into the inside pocket of his father's peacoat. Then he opened a plain brown paper bag he'd taken with him from home that morning and stuffed it with balled up newspapers and wrote on the outside in dark pencil: THE CHAIRMAN.

He hurried to Union Street and rang the bell of the big ornate brownstone with the gargoyles carved into the eaves. The cronies he came to think of as Bald and Tall answered the door.

"How much?" Bald asked.

"I have to use your bathroom . . . *bad*," Rory said. "Please, man . . ."

"Sorry, kid," said Tall.

"It's gonna run down my leg!"

"All right," said the bald guy. "Make it snappy. Put the meat in the kitchen and then use the upstairs bathroom, first door to the right of the Chairman's office."

Rory put the bogus bag in the kitchen and bounded up the stairs and without any hesitation he pushed open the big oak door to the Chairman's office, and entered the oak-walled room where this powerful man made all the smoky deals that affected the lives of millions of Brooklynites, and in some cases the whole city, state, and country because he manipulated councilmen, mayors, state legislators, governors, congressmen, senators. Even presidents like John Fitzgerald Kennedy. And now Lyndon Baines Johnson.

"You lost, kid?" the Chairman said, leaning back in his leather swivel chair, the six-inch cigar clasped between his big, thick fingers, a diamond the size of a glass eye gleaming from a pinkie ring. A fire crackled in a five-foot-wide fireplace behind him. In the flicker of the flames, Rory saw Mr. Krauss repairing a beautiful Olympus desktop typewriter.

"Not anymore," Rory said.

"*Maguire?*" said Mr. Krauss. "What are you doink here, boy?"

"You know this kid?" the Chairman said. "*Maguire?* Why do I know that name?"

"He wants to write the sports pages."

"I'm here about my father," Rory said, a million words trying to escape from his mouth at the same time. "His name is Harry Maguire and he was wounded in World War II and he saved lives and he's a war hero and then when he came home he couldn't play baseball anymore and he couldn't get a job and then he finally got one, filling potholes, but he fell, fell off an overpass from the dizzy spells from the war, and broke his back and ankles, but his boss, one of your guys, Vermillier, Chuck Vermillier, said he was drinking, but I know my father wasn't drinking that day because I saw him myself when I brought him a grilled cheese sandwich that my mother, who voted for JFK, made him at home because it's too dear to eat out and I wasn't the only one who saw him, because Ankles the cop, real name Detective Anthony Tufano, from the Seven-Two, who doesn't even like me, he saw it too and you could ask him the truth, sir, but the disability and workmen's comp turned my father down on Chuck Vermillier's dirty word and because they said my father wasn't in the real service and now the unemployment ran out and he lost his disability and workmen's comp appeals and Christmas is coming and . . ."

The Chairman stood, held up a hand with the unlit cigar, and shot his cuffs. He stared at Rory. He straightened his silk tie, realigned his diamond-studded alligator tie clasp, buttoned his double-breasted pinstriped suit, walked from behind his desk, passing a wall of leather-bound books, lit the big cigar with a gold butane lighter. His eyes remained on Rory. A little placard on the desk read YEA I WALKED

THROUGH THE VALLEY OF DEATH BUT I WAS THE TOUGHEST S.O.B. IN THE VALLEY.

"Hold the phone, kid," the Chairman said, his voice like a bulldog's growl. "First you tell me your old man was a war hero. Then you said he couldn't get a job. All vets in Charlie Pergola's Brooklyn work. Period."

"He was a merchant marine and . . ."

"Oh, okay, so that explains it." The Chairman blew a stream of smoke toward the wood-beamed ceiling, like a human smokestack.

"No, it doesn't, because the merchant marine had the highest per-capita losses of any service in World War II, one in twenty-six of the two hundred and forty-three thousand merchant mariners who served were killed in the line of duty—"

"*Mariners*, huh?"

" . . . yeah, and another six hundred and sixty-three were taken prisoner in POW camps where sixty-six died, and another estimated eleven hundred died in public service hospitals because they weren't allowed into the much better veterans' hospitals . . ."

Rory walked across the thick rug and handed the Chairman the envelope containing the letter addressed to President John Fitzgerald Kennedy and the "You're Harry Maguire" essay that explained his father's life and his failed battle with the bureaucracy, and a whole section about him being a war hero and the one about Charles Pergola Jr.'s Silver Star at the back of the sheaf. The Chairman sat on the edge of his desk, leafing through the pages, listening to Rory, puffing on his cigar in a blue cloud of power, like Zeus on Olympus when Thor came to visit in the Marvel comics.

"I was gonna send this letter to Our Jack," Rory said. "Which is what my mother called President Kennedy. After November Twenty-second, I never got to send it to him. But

I think if he'd read it, being a navy war hero himself, he would have done something for Harry Maguire."

"*Harry Maguire?*" The Chairman said, staring at the beamed ceiling. "*Harry Maguire* . . . hey, didn't I meet a *Harry Maguire* once?"

Rory remained silent.

"Sure I did. Outside the JFK storefront on election night, 1960," The Chairman said, snapping his fingers. "You're just a little kid then. Sure. I remember your old man now. Swaggering up Seventh Avenue in the watch cap and peacoat . . . peacoat like the one you're wearing right now, matter fact. With a merchant marine pin on his hat. I go to pin a JFK button on him. He refuses it. Tells me he isn't a registered Democrat. Or Republican. Says he doesn't vote at all because it only encouraged the *bums.* I'm a Democratic donkey, kid, but I got a memory like an *elephant.*"

"Yeah, but my Pop never voted against Jack Kennedy, either, and he said if he hadn't been killed he might've voted for Kennedy's reelection and . . ."

"And now you bust in here?" the Chairman said, ruffling through the mimeographed papers. "Asking me to help a guy who *snubbed* me? A guy who fell off a job and got hurt where one of my own guys says he was stewed? A guy who probably ducked the draft in World War II by going in the merchant marine . . ."

"That's a lie! My father's a hero! If you remember that night you met him he told you he was on the same ship as your son! The *Stephen O'Hara.*"

The Chairman looked at Rory with a flicker of recognition. He shivered, as if some old ghost had just rustled through the room. "Tall tales!"

"My father saved your son's life! There's proof, Chairman. Read what I *gave* you . . ."

"You think you can sneak in here and talk to me like that, you little punk?" the Chairman said. "With a bunch of hand-typed crapola?"

"I'm not a punk," Rory said. "And my father *is* a hero."

"Maybe you should calm down, Maguire," Mr. Krauss said. "Go home . . ."

Bald and Tall rushed into the room, and the tall guy grabbed Rory by the arm.

"The real kid from Freedom Meats just showed up," Bald said. "Sorry, Boss."

"I called your *ex*-boss," said Tall. "You were fired for steal-ing his *gun*."

"That's a lie, too." Rory shouted.

"Get this little pain in the ass outta my office," the Chairman said, balling the mimeographed papers and tossing them into the roaring fire. Rory watched them curl and burst to flame and thought of the flaming seas in *Action in the North Atlantic*. "Outta my sight. I have no time for tall tales and thieves. Why'd you mopes ever let him in here? What if he came in here with this gun?"

The cronies grabbed Rory under each arm and trundled him down the stairs in a bum's rush.

"You wouldn't even have a son if it wasn't for my father," Rory screamed over his shoulder. "They gave your son the medal but my father was the real hero! You sit up there like the Wizard of Oz, behind your curtain, playing God with people's lives. But you wouldn't even have a son to *hate* if it wasn't for my father!"

The Chairman's flunkies ushered Rory down the stairs and out onto the stoop, where a thin shawl of twilight fell on the city. Christmas lights twinkled in the windows of the brownstones along Union Street.

Ankles stood at the bottom of the stoop, a much cheaper cigar than the Chairman's clamped in his mouth.

He grabbed Rory and banged him against the wrought-iron fence and pointed the lit cigar at his face. "Listen to me, dipstick. The Shamrocks and the Emperors rumbled about a half hour ago . . ."

Oh, my God, Rory thought. *Dermot* . . .

"A kid was *shot!*"

"Oh, Jesus Christ . . . please, don't tell me . . ."

"Unidentified so far," Ankles said. "Just got the call. They're rushing him to the emergency room right now. If it turns out the bullet was a thirty-eight, you're on top of my hit parade, punk. I think you gave Sal Russo's gun to Lefty Hallahan and I think he used it to shoot a kid . . ."

"I swear to God I never took any gun . . ."

"And the A.D.A. Jim Sturgis, who's prosecuting this case, wants to nail you so bad to the cross he's out buying a new hammer as we speak. Your little honey's old man. Deck the halls with that, Maguire."

Ankles gave Rory a half kick in one ankle before driving off.

Rory raced through the streets, his heart pounding, the twinkling Christmas lights in the store windows along Seventh Avenue like a passing streak, like his life flashing before the eyes of a dead man, running the entire mile home to his tenement. He bounded up the stairs, gulping for air. He burst open the door of his apartment. Silence. Rory didn't have the air to shout Dermot's name. His mother was at work. He swiped the curtain aside and bolted through his parents' room, where the candle for Jack Kennedy still flickered by St. Anthony and the Infant of Prague.

He pulled aside the second curtain. And saw Dermot lying on Rory's top bunk, reading a Batman comic book. Rory walked to him, grabbed him by his shirt front, and yanked him off the bed.

"What the hell," Dermot said. "I was only lying on your bed because the light's better. Been here all afternoon . . ."

Rory slapped him off the back of the head and wrapped his arms around his kid brother. And hugged him. Squeezed him with every muscle in his body. He kissed the top of Dermot's head the way his father often kissed his. He saw his father turn to the commotion from the living room, reading, rolling the baseball in his right hand.

"What the freak you doing?" Dermot said. "Goin' quiff on your birthday?"

"Everything okay?" his father asked.

"Great," Rory said, but wouldn't let go of his little brother Dermot. "Couldn't be any better."

At seven on the dot, after a bath and changing his clothes, Rory met Carol on Seventh Avenue as planned. She kissed him. Her soft lips and the aroma of her perfume made his blood boil.

"I told you I got you something for your birthday."

"Carol, I don't expect . . ."

"It's in my house," she said, taking his hand. "C'mon."

"You *crazy?*"

"My dad had to go do some preliminary work on a shooting and then he and my mom went to meet some friends in Manhattan for dinner. Won't be back until nine."

"If your father ever caught me in your house he'd . . ."

"Come on," she said, grabbing him by the hand. "Live dangerously."

Rory followed her up Tenth Street, looking over his shoulder for nosy neighbors as she unlocked the front door. The street was empty in the cold. She led him inside. Carol hung up her cashmere coat on a vestibule peg. She was wearing a plain, short black dress held up by two simple shoulder straps.

The house smelled like flowers and home cooking. As he stepped into the foyer his feet wobbled on the deep pile rug. One of those Arabic rugs, a magic carpet kind of rug. The only other places where he'd stepped on rugs like this were in movie theaters, doctors' offices and the Chairman's house. A small chandelier hung over the foyer.

"Wow," he said, looking at the expensive wallpaper in the dining room and sponge-painted walls in the living room.

The living room had polished wood floors, those little squares they called parquet, and thick Arabic area rugs over them. He looked at a big leather recliner chair facing a mahogany color Magnavox TV/Hi Fi stereo cabinet. He traced a finger across one of two tan suede couches and a smaller suede chair, which he figured was for Mrs. Sturgis. Heavy brown velour drapes covered the windows and a wacky-eyed Van Gogh self-portrait glared down at him from the wall. Rory preferred the other framed posters from the Museum of Modern Art, big bold abstract paintings that he didn't quite understand. *Nobody asked me, but . . . Jackson Pollock is like rock and roll in a frame . . .*

The Christmas tree in one corner of the room was at least nine feet tall, dripping with expensive balls and flickering lights and colored tinsel. Gold and silver, green and red, and blue and yellow. A gold illuminated angel glowed at the top of the tree. Lionel train tracks circled the tree stand and inside the tracks lay dozens of gift-wrapped presents. A big elaborate manger, a huge Waldorf Astoria of mangers, sat on the oak mantel over the fireplace, where logs waited to be lit. Rory thought: *It's like a store window.*

He followed Carol through the dining room, catching his reflection in the gleaming ten-foot polished teak dining table, hearing the crystals of the overhanging chandelier tinkle from the vibrations as he walked. The fine china and crystal glasses in the matching teak hutch also rattled and caused him to tiptoe the rest of the way into the country kitchen. Figures from the American Revolution battled across the wallpaper. He didn't see a single roach. Or a bookcase.

Carol smiled in a conspiratorial way and took two seven-ounce bottles of Bud from the fridge. She popped the caps. They clinked. He hated beer but took a sip, grimaced as he swallowed, and said, "Ahhhhh," because that's what they did in movies.

He looked around, felt the cozy heat of the house. He gazed out the thermal back windows and saw two squirrels chasing each other on the limbs of a leafless peach tree, scampering over a picnic table, and a covered barbecue, then around the edges of a covered aboveground swimming pool. Then the chase was over. They foraged for winter food on the yellow lawn.

"Place is beautiful," Rory said. "Assistant D.A.s must get paid plenty . . ."

"Nah. My grandmother, my mother's mother, bought them the house. She's filthy rich. She owns like a gazillion in AT&T stocks that she inherited from my grandfather, who was a big shot on Wall Street. Someday, when his D.A. days are over and he makes all the connections he needs, my dad will make lots of money as a private lawyer. I hear them talking about it. Plus, my mom just took the test to become a real-estate broker. She thinks Brooklyn, especially neighborhoods like this and Brooklyn Heights, could be the next real-estate bonanza."

She gulped her beer and kissed him, then put her hand on his lower back and pulled him to her. He glanced at the front door, an uneasiness rumbling in his gut.

"Don't worry," she said.

She took his damp hand and led him up the carpeted

stairs into her bedroom, where her lace-covered canopy bed was piled with teddy bears and cutsie little throw pillows. Matching lace curtains covered the shaded windows. Her own portable color TV sat on top of her dresser. Posters of the Beatles and Bob Dylan and the Beach Boys were tacked to the walls. She opened the top drawer of her dresser and took out a small wrapped gift, tied with a little bow. The size and weight of it made him think it was a watch. *Oh, man, how can I give her back something as good for Christmas?*

"Go ahead, open it," she said, standing behind him, her breath warm on his neck.

He tore open the package and saw the black velour box with the word BULOVA etched into it in gold.

"Carol, I can't . . ."

"Look inside," she whispered into his ear, still behind him.

He opened it and his heart began to pound. He lifted the foil wrapped Trojan condom out of the box with a slack-jawed smile. A little card read: "Happy Birthday, Rory. It's about time! Carol."

He turned to her. Her short black dress was heaped around her ankles. Rory's eyes popped. His heart thumped. She pushed him onto the bed. "You never went all the way before, did you?" she asked.

Rory didn't have enough saliva in his mouth to answer.

She took the condom out of his hand and said, "Let me show you how it works."

It was over so fast that it reminded him of a two-shakes-of-a-lamb's-tail bath.

"Oh, my God," she said, laughing. "That might've been world-record time."

Rory swirled in a jumble of shame, conquest, embarrassment, exhilaration, and disappointment. It had always been so much better when he imagined doing it with Carol in the cracked plaster of the night ceiling.

"I'm sorry . . . I couldn't . . . it just . . ."

"You did fine. You're a *man*, now, Rory Maguire."

"I don't know about that," he said. "But at least we're the same age now."

"I have a confession to make," she said, snuggling him. "I'm not fifteen. I'm sixteen. Got left back once for truancy. Got kicked out of private school."

"*Sixteen?* Holy, God . . ."

"We're going to my grandma Muller's house in the country for the weekend, " Carol said. "Now, you better go before my parents get home." She laughed as Rory dressed at almost the same supersonic speed with which he'd lost his boyhood.

When he got home Rory opened the door to the darkened kitchen. Then Caitlin walked out of his parents' bedroom carrying a full Larsen's cake ablaze with fifteen candles as the Maguires—except Dermot, who was missing—sang "Happy Birthday."

"We've been waiting for you," his mother said. "Where've you been?"

"Running around, Mom."

"Sorry. Have to run," she said. "I'm late and Riley'll be having kittens . . ."

He kissed his mother good-bye and sat down and ate the Larsen's cake with his family, but could not get the images of Carol out of his mind.

He was fifteen. He was no longer a virgin. And both his father and Carol Sturgis had called him a man.

That night, in his top bunk, staring at the ceiling, Rory kept thinking about Carol. But not in a sexy way. He didn't recall or relive what they'd done together. Something else nagged him. It was odd. They had done *it*. He'd gone all the way. But he didn't feel like he loved Carol any more than before. If anything, he felt oddly disconnected from her. Suspicious. Maybe it was the old altar boy in him that he couldn't shake loose. *Nobody asked me, but . . . If Carol was that easy with me, why wouldn't she be even easier with other guys? More experienced guys? Older guys? Guys like Babe. . . .*

25

Monday, December 16

The knock on the door in the morning was too soft to be
Ankles', so Rory opened it. Carol stood in the tenement hallway, dressed in a red wool coat and a green beret and matching
scarf, as Christmassy as a Rockette. Morning light pushed
down through the smoked dirty glass of the skylight. The hallway was the usual commotion of people shouting, doors slamming, dogs barking. In that setting, Rory thought Carol fit to a
tee the new word he'd learned reading Red Smith in his
father's favorite newspaper, the *Herald Tribune: incongruous*.

"Hi."

"*Carol?* Holy . . ." Rory hadn't seen her over the weekend,
not since they did it.

"Can I come in?"

He hesitated, embarrassed to invite the brownstone girl
into the tenement flat.

The younger kids dressed in the bedroom. Harry watched
the *Today* show in the living room. Rory's mother wasn't yet
home from working the midnight to 8 A.M. overtime shift,
after working all day as well.

On the stove, H-O oatmeal bubbled in a pot with a burnt
plastic handle.

"Sure, come in."

Carol entered and sat on one of the metal-framed and vinyl-covered chairs and plopped her books on the Formica table.

"Cup of tea?"

"No, thanks."

"How ya doing?"

"Good," she whispered. "Wanna play hooky?"

"For real?"

"A little hooky after a little nooky," she whispered. "Rockefeller Center, window shop in the Fifth Avenue stores . . ."

Rory put his doubts aside and became excited. She was treating him like her steady. No way was he going to say no.

"I'm in," he said.

The bathroom door banged open and Dermot stepped out, dressed in school pants and a strapped undershirt and barefoot. He was starting to develop a rippling set of muscles in his natural athlete's build. He stared at Carol.

"Hi," she said.

"Hi," Dermot said and looked at Rory.

"This is Carol. Carol, Dermot."

"*Hot,*" Dermot said.

"Shut up, lamebrain!" Rory said, laughing and banging gluey oatmeal into bowls.

Carol laughed and said, "Thanks. I guess."

"All Rory ever talks about is how hot you are."

"I'll break your arm in two places," Rory said, laughing.

"He's right, too," Dermot said, bare feet slapping across the linoleum that was worn to the dark petroleum base and brushing through the floral curtain to the middle rooms. "See ya later, toots, I gotta get dressed to go play hooky."

"You better not!" Rory shouted.

"I just heard you two say you were," Dermot shouted.

Now the other kids came out of the bedrooms dressed in their Catholic-school uniforms. Rory introduced them to Carol and they grunted bashful hellos.

"I like your clothes," Caitlin said.

"Thanks," Carol said.

"I bet you don't shop in Catholic Charities," Connor said.

Caitlin smacked the back of his hand with her oatmeal spoon.

"Swine," Connor shouted. "Did you know my sister got her freckles when God threw poop through heaven's screen door?"

Rory grabbed his coat as his father crutched his way through the rooms into the kitchen, unshaven, wearing a cardigan over his tea-stained undershirt.

"Good morning," he said. "Excuse my appearance. Wasn't expecting company."

Rory introduced them.

"My son speaks very highly of you," Harry said.

"Does he?" Carol asked, smiling.

"I can see why," Harry said.

The door opened and Tara stepped in, looking exhausted and upset. When she saw Carol she forced a smile. Rory introduced her. Tara said hello, said she'd heard all good things about her. Rory grabbed his books. Eager to leave while the going was good.

"Everything okay, Mom?"

"Grand," Tara said, the word lost in a sigh.

"We have to go."

Then: SNAP!

"We bagged another one, Mom!" Connor shouted. "That's six this week!"

Carol's eyes popped and her mouth opened when she heard the squealing of the trapped mouse, dragging the wooden trap around under the sink in fitful desperate circles. Dermot, dressed now, hurried into the kitchen and spooned out some oatmeal without acknowledging the mouse.

Rory looked at the tableau of the Maguire family, imagining how it looked through Carol's big blue brownstone eyes. Then he nudged her out the door.

On the D train into the City, Rory fingered the forty cents change from the silver dollar he'd spent on four fifteen-cent tokens. He'd been saving the final Liberty buck for his father but he couldn't blow a second chance to see the tree with Carol. Besides, they'd *done it*. She owned a piece of him no one else would ever have. He wondered who *her* first guy was. *Was it Babe?* he wondered.

She didn't mention the mouse or his family or their encounter on his birthday. Neither did Rory.

A passenger who got off at Jay Street and Boro Hall left behind his *Daily News*. Rory grabbed it and searched through the paper for a story about the shooting in Brooklyn. There wasn't one. In a funny kind of way he was disappointed. He wanted to see his neighborhood in the news. It hadn't been since December 16, 1960, when a United Airlines DC-8 screamed low over Holy Family School before crashing into the Pillar of Fire church on Seventh Avenue and Sterling Place, killing seventy-seven people.

After they pulled out of Jay Street and Borough Hall, Carol said, "After he came home last night, I heard my father talking on the phone with a detective. They both think you stole your boss's gun and gave it to some gang guy who shot another kid."

"It's totally untrue."

"I want to believe you or else I wouldn't be here."

"Thanks."

"But if my father ever found out I played hooky with you he'd kill me."

"Hey, this wasn't my idea. Same with the thing we did the other night."

She smiled and said, "I didn't hear you saying no either time."

She took his hand and as they sat on the rattan subway seats into the City, Rory enjoyed watching all the different guys getting on and off stealing glances at his beautiful girlfriend. He was amazed that so many grown men also seemed to ogle her. One red-haired, middle-aged guy reminded him of Riley. He felt like punching him in the face.

Rockefeller Center was packed with tourists, Santas ringing bells, Salvation Army volunteers, and pretzel and chestnut hawkers. Cops watched for pickpockets and young couples and whole families lined up for Radio City Music Hall, and for the ice-skating rink. As Rory and Carol passed the tree, huge and brilliant as any skyscraper, he stopped and kissed her. He touched her cheeks, rouged with winter cold, and stared into her sparkling blue eyes. Carol said she loved chestnuts and so Rory bought a bag for quarter, which he thought was highway robbery.

They shared the chestnuts and then they jaywalked across Fifth Avenue, hand in hand, dodging buses and Checker cabs and climbed the wide stone steps of St. Patrick's Cathedral. Inside, Carol said she'd already prayed in the Protestant church in Brooklyn but wanted to light a Catholic candle for her mother, who was praying that she would pass the test for her real estate broker's license.

"There's a donation box," she whispered in the massive church. "Catholics charge for prayers?"

"They charge for everything," Rory said. "Baptisms, weddings, funerals. My father says they get you coming and going."

She laughed and asked if Rory would put something in the donation box for her.

"Sure," he said, fishing the nickel from his pocket but not letting her see what it was as he pushed it into the slot.

"President Johnson authorized new Jack Kennedy half dollars, ya know," he said as a cover for the nickel.

Carol lit the candle in front of a statue of St. Joseph and knelt and prayed while Rory gazed around the massive church, dripping with gold and stained glass and sanctified opulence. *They don't need my nickel*, he thought.

As Carol prayed, Rory drifted through the church, the horseshoe taps on his Mr. Gutter shoes echoing off the vaulted ceilings. He stopped in front of St. Anthony. He blessed himself, and said a silent prayer for his mother, who believed in him, to find a way for his father to have his operation so that he could get better so he could go back to work so that the next Christmas wouldn't be as bad as this one.

"Amen and over and out," he said aloud.

"What?" Carol said, standing behind him.

"I was just talking to St. Tony."

She grabbed his arm, checked her gold watch, and led him out of the church and over to Saks Fifth Avenue. *Nobody asked me, but . . . Looking into department store windows is like a peep show for girls.* Carol saw coats and bags and dresses and boots that she liked. She fawned over the little elves and Santas and reindeer that adorned each window panel.

Then, when they approached one window display in the center of the store, Carol's frozen breath was taken away.

"Oh . . . my . . . God . . ." she said, putting her leather-gloved hand to her mouth. "I've been searching high and low for something to wear to midnight mass. Bloomies, Macy's, B. Altman's. And here it is. It's me. It's . . . just . . . *me.*"

A whippet-thin mannequin wore a brown velour pants suit with padded shoulders, trimmed with black velour and pearl buttons. It had a matching tight vest and ruffled white tapered blouse, and a matching black velour beret and black ankle boots.

The price tag said it was on sale at $189.99.

Rory did the rough math in his head and realized it cost almost five months of what the Maguires paid in rent.

"How much would you love that on me?" she asked.

"It's nice," he said. "But I love anything on you."

"Do you think I'm worth it?"

He thought for a minute that she was hinting for him to buy it for her for Christmas. But then he dismissed the idea, thinking she couldn't be serious.

She checked her watch again.

"They should be here any minute," Carol said.

"They? Who's they?"

"I told my friends from uptown to meet us by the skating rink at eleven."

"*Oh.*"

"Didn't I tell you?"

"No."

"Oh, sorry. I guess it skipped my mind."

Two couples leaned over the brass railings watching the ice skaters spin on the world famous rink that was sunken into the middle of Rockefeller Center like a giant glittering silver eye. People passed the tree, surrounded by the flapping flags of hundreds of nations, as tourists waited on long lines to have their photographs taken as they spun on the rink. Carol rushed to meet her girlfriends, who she said were sixteen, and their boyfriends, who were even older.

"Janey! Kaye!" Carol shouted. The two girls embraced Carol, doing a little arms-linked dance in the crowd. Janey was blond and wore a sheepskin-lined suede coat and Kaye, the redhead, sported a ritzy-looking full-length Irish tweed coat with a white Irish wool hat. Both of the boyfriends wore long real leather coats, one black, the other brown, same style, and khaki chinos and oxblood penny loafers.

Moolah, Rory thought.

Carol also knew the guys, both of whom she said were seventeen. Brad, who went out with Janey, the blonde, wore a high school graduation ring and was a freshman at Columbia University.

"This is Rory," Carol said. "We go to the same school in Brooklyn."

Rory nodded and Jack, the guy with Kaye, said. "Like Rory *Calhoun,* the third-rate actor?"

Rory shrugged. "No, like in Maguire. Me."

"So, Rory," Brad said, fingering the under collar of Rory's peacoat. "The 'Popeye look' in style over in Brooklyn this season?"

Everybody laughed.

"It was in style when my father wore it in World War II," Rory said.

"Just kidding, old sport," Brad said.

Rory thought about *The Great Gatsby* by F. Scott Fitzgerald, which his father had given him to read. Gatsby used to say "old sport," too. He nodded and stamped his feet to keep warm, the horseshoe taps clacking.

"Those tap shoes?" asked Jack.

Everyone laughed again. Rory faked a chuckle himself.

The girls drifted to a gossipy knot by the railing, leaving the three guys together.

"So I hear from Janey that Carol says you want to be a sportswriter," said Brad. "You write for the school paper, then, huh?"

"We don't have one."

Brad and Jack smiled at each other.

"But I had an essay published in the *World Telegram*," Rory said.

"The *Telegram*?" Jack asked. "They still publish that?"

"They read it in the boroughs," said Brad.

From behind him Rory heard one girl ask Carol, "So is he like your date or are you baby-sitting?" Then he heard Carol use the word *cherry*.

And then the girls all laughed.

"So," Brad said, leaning close to Rory. "She did it?"

"Did what?" Rory asked.

"Janey and Kaye dared her to take a cherry before the New Year," Jack said. "They call it the Cherry Picking Club. She picked you as her dare. So, she do it yet?"

Rory fingered the dime and two tokens in his pants pocket. He felt short of breath. Sweat broke on his skin even in the freezing cold morning.

"I don't kiss and tell," Rory said.

"Oh, Christ," Brad said. "Come on, man. She didn't tell you why her parents moved her out of Manhattan to Brooklyn?"

"Knock it off," Rory said. "You guys are just jealous."

"Bet we can guess what she gave you for your birthday, Rory," said Jack.

"Did it come in a Bulova box?" asked Jack.

"As in a good time?" said Brad, and he and Jack broke up laughing.

Carol walked over in a gushy flourish and took Rory's arm.

"We're going ice skating first," she said. "Then maybe we'll catch the Rockettes and lunch afterwards at Lindy's."

"Sounds good," said Brad.

Jack concurred. Rory took a deep breath and nodded for Carol to walk off to the side with him. "Something wrong?" Carol asked.

"I kinda can't go," he said.

"There's no age requirement for the Rockettes, *Calhoun*," Brad shouted after them.

"I can't afford to do all that stuff," Rory said. Thinking: *I'd like to knock Brad's Dentyne teeth out.*

Carol said, "What?"

"I only had a dollar when we went out this morning," he said. "Tokens, chestnuts. Poor box. I don't have enough for skating, lunch, Radio City. I did the night of our big date. But the discount tickets for Radio City expired and the rest of the dough is, ya know, just *gone*."

"What about the money you made working? Didn't you save any?"

"Goes into the house."

"For *what*?"

"Food, gas, electric, rent, whatever, like that."

Carol looked at him, flabbergasted. "*You* pay house bills? But why didn't you tell me all this before you said yes to coming here today, Rory?"

"I dunno. I thought, it was just you and me, hooky kinda thing. Sorry."

"*Christ* . . . Wait here."

Carol walked back to her friends, checked her watch in front of them. *Probably making up some other lame story,* Rory thought.

Rory and Carol didn't talk much at all on the subway ride home to Brooklyn. They got off at the Seventh Avenue stop. Rory walked her to Tenth Street and kissed her good-bye. Her lips were taut and cold.

She said, "Bye."

He nodded and watched her walk up Tenth Street and wondered if she'd ever speak to him again. He thought about everything Brad and Jack had said about Carol. He thought about how disappointed she'd been when he told her he didn't have enough money to do all the things she wanted to do. He turned up his collar to the icy wind, jammed his cold hands in his father's peacoat pockets. A line kept going through his head: *If she asks about money, pick another honey.*

26

Tuesday, December 17

Rory always knew his mother was upset it she didn't hum or sing when she ironed. At home the next morning his mother was quiet. Withdrawn. She ironed Connor a shirt for school before leaving for work at the Mayflower Laundry but the only thing Rory heard was the steam sighing from the iron, before zapping into infinity in the cold kitchen air.

"You okay, Mom?" Rory asked.

"Fine."

He watched her, as she flattened the collar. The other kids ate and bickered at the breakfast table. Harry looked at her, as silent as the steam from his tea. He hadn't shaved for two days. Dermot read a Classic comic illustrating the story of Ivanhoe.

Rory and his father exchanged a wordless glance.

Rory said, "Work going okay, Mom?"

"Eat your oatmeal, love. Get to school."

She kept ironing. She didn't sing.

At school, Rory didn't seek out Carol. He didn't want to look like some pining, sad-eyed puppy. But when he passed her in the halls she nodded and either ducked into a classroom or the girls' room.

After school he thought of waiting for her but saw her mother sitting in the family Chevy outside the school, the motor running.

Rory went straight to the Grand Army Plaza library, where Mrs. Fitzpatrick helped him do a microfiche search on Charles Pergola Sr. and Charles Pergola Jr. He found a story from the *Daily News* in a 1952 column called City Hall Stuff. It told all about how in the mid-1930s Charles Pergola Sr. had become the boss of the Brooklyn Democratic Party, the most powerful Democratic county in the state and the second largest in the nation, through a series of maneuvers and favors as a district leader and calling in his markers when the reigning boss died.

Then in 1938, his son, Charles Pergola Jr., went to Annapolis, came out as an ensign, and was assigned to a U.S. Navy Armed Guard unit aboard a Liberty ship. They didn't name the ship. The story said that Ensign Pergola Jr. had won a Silver Star in a sea battle in 1942 in which he helped rescue several other shipmates.

There was no mention of Harry Maguire.

After his discharge, Charles Pergola Jr.'s father steered him toward a life in politics, hoping one day to make him the first Italian U.S. senator and maybe even president. The young Pergola started out running for the city council in Brooklyn, where he served one term, then ran and won a state assembly seat, where he served two terms.

In 1952, father and son had a bitter public falling-out when Charles Jr. turned down his father's machine-brokered opportunity to run for the United States congress. "The seat was being given to him gift-wrapped," the column said. But Junior had decided that a life in politics was not for him, choosing instead to go into a private life in the insurance industry, to spend more time with his young wife and start a family.

When the disappointed Chairman chose an incompetent machine hack puppet to replace his son in the congressional seat, his sacrilegious son crossed party lines and backed a Republican candidate, another World War II hero.

"You mean he actually came out in public and supported a Republican candidate?" Rory asked Mrs. Fitzgerald, as he took notes from the microfiche screen.

"Yes, Rory," she said. "It looks like he endorsed a candidate he knew from veterans' circles. A Republican! But with Charles Pergola Jr.'s public support in the community, the Republican won! Which made Junior's father furious."

"I guess it embarrassed the Chairman," Rory said.

"Sure, plus it cost him some power for the two terms the Republican served," the librarian said. "And the father took it as a public ridicule."

"It says here the father and son just stopped talking," Rory said.

"The son moved away, and the family has been split since."

"Why would a family ever split over something stupid like politics?" Rory asked.

"You know what's funny," Mrs. Fitzgerald said. "Charles Pergola runs the Benjamin Franklin Club. And it's ironic that Ben Franklin and his son had a lifelong feud over politics. The son supported the British during the American Revolution. And Ben Franklin was a rebel and a founding father of the republic."

Rory asked Mrs. Fitzgerald how he could get in touch with Charles Pergola Jr. She said the story in the *Daily News* said he moved away to Elizabeth, New Jersey, where he worked for Allstate.

"To get started, I'd call Allstate in Elizabeth," Mrs. Fitzgerald said. "We have out-of-state phone books where you could look the number up."

Rory thanked Mrs. Fitzgerald and took more notes from the microfiche screen and then spent another fifteen minutes looking through the Yellow Pages until he found one for Elizabeth, New Jersey. He found a main number for Allstate and wrote down the name and address in his notebook.

Rory then went to Mr. B's candy store, and with a quarter his mother had given him for lunch, he called the number of Allstate in New Jersey.

"Can I speak to Charles Pergola Jr., please?" Rory asked the Allstate receptionist, trying to deepen his voice.

"Whom shall I tell Vice President Pergola is calling, please?"

"Well, my name is Rory Maguire, from Brooklyn, and well, see, my father saved Mr. Pergola's life once and then last May my father fell from an overpass on the Prospect Expressway . . ."

"I see . . ."

"And well, his boss, Mr. Vermillier, he says that my father was drinking, and so now they won't give my dad the disability or the workmen's comp . . .'

"Does your father have a personal injury policy with Allstate?"

"No . . ."

"So what exactly do you need to speak to Mr. Pergola about?"

"Well, Mr. Esposito, that's my father's lawyer, he's a Republican, like the candidate Mr. Pergola backed in 1952 when he dropped out of the race . . ."

"Excuse me, son, maybe I should speak with your father," the woman said. "Or have his attorney contact our legal division. I can give you that number if you like. But I'm afraid Mr. Pergola is busy and can't come to the phone and . . ."

"No, you don't understand, the only one who can help my father is a politician, and I figure the most powerful one over here in Brooklyn is the Chairman, Mr. Pergola Jr.'s father, Charles Pergola Sr.—"

"I have another call coming in, can you hold a moment, please? . . ."

Rory held on, standing in the phone booth, the little fan whirring over his head. He checked the coin return to see if anyone had overlooked a nickel or a dime. It was empty. He opened the folding door for more air. His heart thumped as he waited and then he heard his quarter drop in the phone, like a guillotine.

A recorded voice came on, saying, "You must deposit another five cents for the next three minutes or your call will be interrupted."

"Mr. B, Mr. B, please, can you lend me a nickel?"

"Are you brain damaged? I'd bet on the Mets foist."

The Allstate secretary came back on and said, "I'm sorry . . . now, where were we? Oh, yes, you wanted to speak with Mr. Pergola. I'm afraid this isn't possible at this time. Perhaps you can drop him a note or have your father's lawyer . . ."

Her voice was cut off as the phone went dead.

"If you're done, good-bye," Mr. B said. "Don't stand around freeloadin' my steam heat."

Rory left. He looked both ways on the frigid avenue. He couldn't see Carol. He didn't want to see his pals on Eleventh Street. He had no job. He went home.

He was surprised to see his mother sitting at the kitchen table, facing his father. His mother seemed despondent. Above her, on top of the fridge, was a manger with little statues of the Baby Jesus, Mary, Joseph, a few lambs, a cow, a mule, and the three wise men, one of them colored, bearing gifts. A single red bulb glowed from the back of the scene that was at least eight years old. He saw a roach, shiny and plump, its feelers probing before it dart into the coiled straw of the manger. There was no money for a Christmas tree, which were expensive this year. Maybe they'd get one in the last-minute sales.

"Home early, Mom?

"Aye."

"Sick?"

She looked at him, gave him a soft half-smile that almost cracked her face. He could see the pain in her eyes, sunken and bloodshot, like she'd been crying earlier. Her face overwhelmed Rory with a wave of sadness, a suffocating, inescapable fog.

Rory looked then at his father, who sat with a cardigan hanging over his T-shirt, unshaved. Rage blazed in his eyes. Rory knew: *More bad news.*

"The bastard," Harry said, rising on the crutches. He slammed the crutches to the floor, balanced himself on his wobbly legs, and punched the refrigerator with shocking violence. The delivery shifted the refrigerator and knocked Harry off balance. Rory rushed to him, grabbing him before he fell. Rory felt heat radiating off him like steam off an engine. Then Harry bent, grabbed his crutches and thumped into the living room. "Filthy fucking bastard," Harry said, hurling a crutch like a javelin into the curtain separating the rooms.

His mother called after him, "Harry, don't . . ."

Rory had never seen his father lose his temper or swear like that before. He sat alone with his mother for a long chilly moment.

"Something happen at the laundry, Mom?"

She nodded, gulping from her tea mug as if it were an antidote to a poison.

"Riley?" he asked.

Her head bowed, she glanced up at him, as if shamed, then gazed out through the rattling window at the pigeons flying over the clotheslines and the rooftops of the two-story houses on the side streets and into the skeletal trees of dusk. Lady Liberty was a dirty green toy in the distant harbor.

"He said business was slow," she said. "So he was letting me go."

Rory remembered Riley saying how they couldn't handle all the business. He remembered the rest of his dirty little conversation with the fat guy named Chubby. He remembered Riley whispering into his mother's ear at her workstation and his mother stopping her singing and waving a finger in Riley's face. And Riley smirking and walking off and patting the Spanish girl on the behind with his clipboard.

He remembered that for the first time in his life he had looked at his mother as a *girl*, as a *woman*, in a sexy way, the way other men might see her. Rory had always only looked at her as his *mother*. That night, in his top bunk, he imagined himself as Riley, gaping at Tara Maguire, undressing her with his eyes. The way he had seen Carol. It nauseated him that another man beside his father thought of his mother like that and wanted to do something about it. It gave him the jim-jams. It made him feel helpless. It made him feel like a *kid* again.

Which made rage bubble in Rory because more than ever, right now, with Christmas coming and his family in defeated tatters, he needed to be a *man*.

Wednesday, December 18

Rory hadn't slept much the night before. He searched for Carol in the ceiling plaster but all he could find was Riley's smirking little red-haired mick face.

He tossed and turned and thought of ways to get in touch with Charles Pergola Jr. If he wrote him a letter his secretary would screen it, and throw it in the garbage. Or send him a form letter in return. He had no way of getting to Elizabeth, New Jersey. He'd checked. Counting tokens and the Trailways bus, it would cost about three bucks. If he had three dollars he'd buy Christmas presents for Caitlin, Connor, and Bridget. Or a tree. Or Evening in Paris perfume for his mother or a bottle of Old Spice for his father.

He drifted off to sleep about three A.M. and was up at seven and in school by eight.

He yawned through most of his classes. He saw Carol three times in the hallways. She ignored him. After the final bell, he waited for her in the lobby, by the front doors.

"Just tell me, what's wrong?" he asked.

"First, remember you said you never kissed and told? You mean that, right?"

"Of course."

"Promise, no matter what?"

"Promise, absolutely, on my word. Why?"

"Well, my father found out we played hooky," Carol said.

"We?"

"Yeah. Someone spotted us together. Bad enough I got caught playing the hook. But doing it with you, my father said made it a double felony."

He laughed. Rory suspected Babe must have seen them together.

"It's funny but it's not funny, too," she said.

"Sorry."

"I'm punished," she said. "I'm not allowed out until after New Year's."

"The whole Christmas vacation?"

"With one exception."

"What?"

Carol checked her gold watch, pushed open the front door, and they stepped out onto Seventh Avenue. "The only boy my father will let me see is Babe."

Rory's heart ripped like a muscle-bound guy tearing a phone book in half.

"Aww, Carol . . ."

"Because he goes to Poly Prep and because he picks me up and takes me home in a car, on time, and because he's polite and has a future, as a lawyer, and all of that. . . ."

"You don't even like Babe."

"I never said that. Besides, at least he didn't steal a frigging gun!"

"I didn't, either."

"Rory, not for nothing or nothing, but I saw how you people . . . how your family *lives*. I know your dad is hurt, can't work, that your mom works in a laundry. But if you're thinking of robbing somebody or something, I have to warn you, my father is personally keeping his eyes peeled for your name reaching his desk. He's convinced you're connected to that kid's shooting."

"Hey, Carol, you seriously think I'd rob a gun to do a stickup? That I'd get involved in gang wars? I swore on my parents, my brothers and sisters, swore on *you* that I didn't take that gun. . . ."

"Those were just words."

"*Just words?* Words *mean* something! At least my *word* does. I just gave you my word about the other thing we did."

She checked her watch again, annoyed. "Look, I don't want to argue with you, Rory. I didn't mean to insult you. But no way am I gonna be kept in and punished through my entire Christmas vacation. I just don't want Babe to know that we *did* it."

"So that means you're gonna go out with Babe, then?"

The red Riviera pulled up, shiny and sleek. Like it did almost every day after school. And Babe got out dressed in his full-length Belmont's leather and his Featherweights with horseshoe taps and clacked around the car holding a large parcel behind his back, grinning like the Joker in *Batman*.

He ignored Rory and opened the passenger door for Carol. The radio played Perry Como singing "It's Beginning to Look a Lot Like Christmas."

He whipped the parcel from behind his back and handed it to Carol, tied with a ribbon and wrapped in Saks Fifth Avenue paper.

"You didn't?" she said.

"You'll be the best-dressed dame in midnight mass," said Babe.

Carol looked at Rory, gave him a small shrug, and said, "Bye, Rory."

PART III

Christmas Week

27

Friday, December 20

There wasn't enough money in the Maguire household to buy a Christmas tree, never mind presents to put under it. For Christmas, Rory's mother had hung stockings from the mantelpiece in the living room over the old sealed-up kerosene stove fireplace flue. They were empty.

When Rory got home from school, his mother asked him to go down into the cellar to get some of the other Christmas decorations out of the wood bin—plastic Santas, Frosty, wooden soldiers, illuminated angels. And boxes of lights and balls in case they wound up getting a tree in the Christmas Eve sales.

In the dank tenement cellar he heard grunting and the clanging of steel plates. Rory ducked under soffits and exposed pipe and BX cable, passing the fuse boxes and an ancient hot water heater and an oil burner with a thermostat that was locked in a steel box. The room smelled of molting roaches and wet plaster and mold. Two twenty-five-watt lightbulbs lit the open space like a pair of guttering candles in a giant cave. Along one wall was a bank of storage spaces, called wood bins, from the old days when firewood was stored in them. Each tenant was assigned a five-by-five-foot storage space for old baby carriages, books, clothes, cribs, sleds, tricycles. The Maguires had bin number four, padlocked, full.

In the center of the cellar, Dermot lay on a crude homemade free weight bench made of milk boxes and old planks, bench-pressing one hundred pounds on a long weight bar. Rory was impressed. His kid brother's pectorals, biceps, and triceps bulged under his strapless T-shirt.

"Looking good, Derm."

"Kick your ass soon."

"You and what army?"

"You'll see."

Rory smiled, they slap boxed in a brief playful exchange, and then Rory punched him in the shoulder.

"Think maybe you can give them a break for Christmas?" Rory asked. "It's a tough time, man. Mom and Pop don't need to worry about you and Lefty and the Shamrocks. They heard about the kid from the Roman Emperors getting shot."

"I wasn't there," Dermot said, laying back down and hefting the weight bar again and grunting it up. "Unfortunately . . ."

When Dermot depressed the bar, Rory grabbed it and pressed it into Dermot's chest. Rory noticed an infected purple friction burn with a yolk of yellow puss screaming from the back of Dermot's left hand.

"*Unfortunately?*" Rory said. "Some sixteen-year-old kid's lying in a coma in Methodist, dying, with his parents totally destroyed for Christmas, and you think it's *unfortunate* you weren't there to watch him get shot? What the hell's wrong with you?"

"I . . . can't . . . breathe . . ."

"Neither can Mommy and Pop, worrying themselves sick over you're bullcrap tough-guy routine. I know what that is on the back of your hand, Derm. It's a punk test. Part of the

Shamrock's initiation. Next comes running the gauntlet where they whip you with rubber hoses, bats, car antennas, garrison belts, pounding your head with the Yellow Pages, and punching and kicking you. Then you gotta go hit an Italian, any Italian, with a goddamned baseball bat. You think I don't know the deal? You think I'm some lame?"

"Please . . . Ror . . . lift . . . the . . . bar . . ."

Rory curled the bar one handed, twice, dangling it over Dermot's face, before dropping it into the metal hasps with a loud rattle. Dermot looked stunned.

"This Christmas is gonna suck enough," Rory said. "You aren't gonna screw it up anymore for Mom and Pop and those kids upstairs. You understand me?"

"You think you're gonna kick my ass into grinning and bearing the way we live? Lefty has a color TV, Ror. He has leather coats, a gold watch. He eats in the Cube Steak or Sun Joy or Bickford's whenever he feels like it. He has chicks. He buys them jewelry. They put out for him. He's gonna buy a four-door GTO with a V-8 engine. You got squat for your birthday and we can't even afford a Christmas tree and you expect me to just say, okay, follow the old man's footsteps? Guess what? If I follow his footsteps I'll be on crutches too! If I get in the Shamrocks, I get to share in the profits."

"Profits from what? Robberies? Burglaries? What's next? Selling reefer? You're gonna go to the can!"

"I can help get the family out of this dump. Projects coloreds on welfare have apartments with hot showers, for Christ sakes, Rory. They have rooms with windows and doors on them! Exterminators. Steam heat all day. We're living like freakin' animals, here. And you think an order boy's job is the ticket out? Daydreaming about covering the World Series for the *Daily News* or the *Telegram*? Come on, Rory, get real."

"The only *real* life Lefty and his wolf pack will ever see is a *life* sentence."

"Let me ask you something, Rory. That girl you like, Carol. Hot. Sweet. Fine. A real spider, right? And who's she running around with now instead of you? Babe! Whose father fired your ass. Because he drives a Riv and you push a bike. Well, me, I'm not gonna let anyone humiliate me like that. I'm not gonna dream about the future like you. I'm gonna do something now!"

Rory grabbed Dermot under the arm and yanked him to his feet.

"The only thing you're gonna do right now, tough guy," Rory said, "is help me carry the Christmas decorations upstairs."

He shoved Dermot to the wood bin marked MAGUIRE, telling him some of what he'd learned about their father and the battle on the *Stephen O'Hara*. Dermot stopped in front of the wood bin door, blinking, moved.

"*Really?* The old man did all that? In the *merchant* marines?"

"Yep," Rory said, opening the padlock with a key on his ring.

Dermot seemed lost in thought, pulled open the wood bin door and yanked on the light chain. They found the boxes marked XMAS on the floor near the wall. Dermot lifted one and then heard a squeal and a mad scramble and he tossed the box in the air. It landed at Rory's feet and a twelve-inch rat bolted out, its long tail slurping around the base of the doorframe as it disappeared into the shadows of the cellar.

Dermot and Rory looked at each other. Both were breathing hard.

"This is how heroes live," Dermot said, kicking the Christmas box for more rats.

*   *   *

Friday evening was also payday at Mayflower. After bringing up the Christmas decorations with Dermot, Rory wouldn't let his mother go and pick up her pay. He insisted on going.

He found Riley on the busy loading dock. He was dressed in his starched khakis, standing behind his clipboard as if it were a portable pulpit. Rory stared Riley in the little blue eyes with the red lashes and told him who he was.

"I came for my mother's pay," Rory said. He had decided on the way up there that he would look Riley right in the eyes and never look away. Right into the cocky eyes, the way Sonny Liston glared at Floyd Patterson before he flattened him twice.

Riley gave Rory a manila envelope. Rory counted out the sixty-two dollars and fifty cents, which included overtime. He knew the numbers. Forty dollars for rent, three dollars for Brooklyn Union Gas, five bucks toward Con Ed. His mother had also given him a list and some coupons for Bohack's and asked Rory to bring home some groceries and she had worked out to the penny the cost: nine dollars and eighty seven cents.

"Tell your mother I says merry Christmas, no hard feelings, kid, hah," Riley said.

Rory stared into Riley's eyes, and when he did, without breaking the man's stare for even a nanosecond, he detected a scribble of fear. Rory knew it from dealing with the stray dogs that always followed him around when he was on the Freedom Meats bike, barking after the blood-dripping meat. Like certain prizefighters, some dogs you could send away whimpering with a glare. They were spirit-broken mutts, sapped of courage except in a pack. Others, even small ones, would be provoked with a direct look in the eyes, and come right at you, like Sonny Liston, teeth gnashing, all alone, ferocious. Rory was convinced those dogs were direct descendants of the proud regal wolf. *If Riley were a dog he'd slink off with his tail between his legs,* Rory thought. *Like a mutt.*

"Why'd you lay my mother off?" Rory said.

Riley couldn't look Rory in the eyes.

"Let's just say she's not a team player," Riley said.

"Meaning what?"

"Incompatible, kid," he said, scribbling on his clipboard which he used as a prop.

"I still don't understand," Rory said, although he thought he did.

"Someday when you grow up you'll understand, kid."

"I don't think so," Rory said. "When I grow up I intend to be a man. . . ." Riley blinked. "Not a dog like you."

He turned and left. *Like a man,* he thought.

In Bohack Rory grabbed a prepackaged pound of chuck chop from the meat-display counter, getting jostled by swarming housewives who picked through the meat as if they were panning for gold, when he heard his name called.

"Rory, *kid*," said Noonz, stepping through the door from the butchering section.

"Hey, Noonz, merry Christmas."

"Yeah, I might actually have one now," Noonz said. "The extra few bucks keep the wolves from the door. How you?"

Rory shrugged.

"I hoid about the thing with the fat man's rod," he said. "He blamed me."

"I know," Noonz said, leaning closer. "So, someday if I need it maybe you could lend it to me."

"*Me*, lend it to *you? Noonz* . . . I didn't take Sal's gun, Noonz. I thought maybe you . . ."

"You crazy? I'd be afraid I'd use it! On him. Or a siggie collector."

"Maybe it was the sawdust guy. Or the scale guy. Who knows, maybe Babe."

"Babe couldn't load a water pistol in Niagara Falls."

"Anyway, Noonz, I gotta get some stuff for my mother."

"You find another job?"

"Nah."

"Want one?"

Rory's eyes popped. "You kidding me?"

"We need an extra order boy and kid for the butcher department. You know the ropes. Pay's fifteen clams."

"When can I start?"

"Go home and put on your woik clothes," Noonz said.

Saturday, December 21

Rory's parents were thrilled with him getting a new job, some little oasis of hope in a desert of bad luck. He would work every day but Monday from three P.M. to nine and all day Saturday.

He spent most of Saturday morning learning to package meat, grinding chuck chop, slicing cold cuts, scouring fat bins, and delivering orders on the Bohack bike. He didn't bring his transistor radio because he needed to construct a special holder for it in the big basket. Otherwise it was the same streets patrolled for Freedom Meats, even a lot of Sal's old customers who'd followed Noonz to Bohack. With one difference. He couldn't get over how busy Bohack was. Unlike Freedom Meats, where the customers came in waves, this was a steady rollicking stream of customers who flowed in all day long. Which was fine with him. It sure beat not working.

"Business is so good they gotta collect the money twice a week in an armored car," Noonz said, cutting shoulder pork chops on a band saw. Rory scraped the chops with a special three-ringed marrow scraper and arranged them six-to-a-cardboard-platter and sent them through the cellophane-wrapping machine that also weighed, dated and priced them. "They even deliver the Green Stamps the housewives paste in the books for toasters and bathroom scales in the armored car."

"Amazing," Rory said.

"I never knew there was enough money in this neighborhood for an armored car," Noonz said. "Now twice a week they come and cart away tens of thousands of dollars. Makes me daydream of one day hijacking one of them and driving straight to Mexico."

Rory laughed, finished wrapping the pork chops and told Noonz he had to go deliver some orders.

He put on his ski mask and heavy work gloves and rode through the freezing streets, dropping off cardboard boxes of groceries, most to old widows on Social Security who couldn't pull shopping carts. The tips weren't as good as Freedom Meats, but there were more orders so he made up for it. Plus the pay was five bucks higher a week.

As he spun through the streets he spotted Lefty Hallahan and the Shamrocks on the corner of Ninth Street and Eighth Avenue, outside Bennie's candy store. A few of them were wearing ski masks in the cold. Dermot was with Lefty, smoking a cigarette. When he saw Rory, Dermot ducked down the subway entrance on the corner.

Rory had no time to chase him on the busy Saturday before Christmas.

"You let me down, Rory," Lefty shouted. "You let me down."

Rory kept pedaling. When he got back to Bohack's he noticed Babe's red Riviera double-parked a little in front of the Wells Fargo armored car that was taking out a load of cash. When Rory chained his bike to a No Parking pole, Babe climbed out of the Riviera and approached him.

"Hey, Champ."

"Babe," Rory said, snapping the padlock on the security chain.

"Glad to see you got a job."

"Noonz hired me."

Babe nodded, watched the guard cart the money out of the store, and said, "Them armed guards might just as well walk into my old man's store and stick him up."

"Yeah, they do well here."

"You ain't kidding. By sundown every day they make more than my old man makes in a week—just on meat."

"Times change."

"People, too."

"I guess. Listen, I gotta go back in. . . ."

"I just wanted to say I hope there's no hard feelings between you and me."

"You didn't fire me, your father did."

"No, I meant about Carol. I know you kinda had the hots for her."

Rory shrugged. "It was more than that, Babe."

"Well, you know what I mean."

"Yeah, I guess."

"She's probably too old for you anyway, man."

"Maybe she's too smart for you."

Babe held out his palm to slap five. Rory slapped. "You always did have the smooth-o words, Champ. . . ."

"I don't have a boss-a new Riv and a Belmont's leather, so we're even."

They laughed. But Rory did resent him for coming between him and Carol.

"For whatever it's worth," Babe said. "I feel bad you got fired."

"For whatever it's worth, I never took your old man's gun."

Babe nodded and said, "Well, my father's just goin' through a hard time."

He frowned at the armed guards loading the last bags and slamming the steel plated back doors of the truck.

"Yeah, well, I got a good job now," Rory said. "Good luck."

The armored-car driver beeped for Babe to move his Riviera, which blocked his path. Babe jingled his keys in one hand and held out the other to Rory and said, "Merry Christmas, Champ?"

Rory shook it and said, "Merry Christmas, Babe."

Then Babe hurried to his Riviera, horseshoe taps on his Featherweights clacking.

Sunday, December 22

On Sunday Rory went to St. Stanislaus with his mother, listening to Father O'Stewed slur his way through the ten o'clock mass.

After mass Tara took the younger kids to Mr. Gutter's for shoes for Christmas. Rory walked home along Seventh Avenue. When he got to Thirteenth Street he heard screams and moans and general commotion coming from the interior quadrangle of the Ansonia Clock factory.

Rory crossed the street and shoved his way through the crowd and slinked through two bent steel bars of the gate. He entered the quadrangle that was surrounded by four eight-storey-high walls of dirty red brick with exterior battleship-gray metal staircases leading to adjoining roofs A small ghoulish crowd gathered at the big locked gate that sealed off the driveway.

On the far side of the quadrangle he saw Dermot running the Shamrocks' gauntlet, gang guys beating him over the head with Yellow Pages, thwacking stickball bats across his arms, and lashing rubber hoses across his legs.

"Okay, my turn, get away from him," Lefty said, and then he stepped in, whipping Dermot with a car antenna like a man trained in the bullwhip. He lashed it across Dermot's legs, ripping slashes in his pants. He sliced straight tears in his long-sleeved shirt, blood staining the fabric. Dermot covered his face and Lefty whipped the backs of his hands until the flesh tore and blood leaked, bursting the scab on the infected punk test.

"Say it!" Lefty commanded. "Say Shamrocks rule!"

"Shamrocks rule!" Dermot said, trying not to let his voice crack.

"Now say 'My brother Rory is a faggot!'" Lefty said.

Dermot remained mute. Looked up, shaking his head. Lefty whipped his cheek. Then Dermot covered his face and Lefty lashed him until Dermot's hands bled.

"Say it! 'Rory is faggot and Lefty is my ruler!' Say it!"

"Up yours!" Dermot said. And Lefty switched him again.

And now Rory charged across the quadrangle, shouting, "Try me, Lefty!"

Two Shamrocks rushed Rory, flailing bats and hoses. One bat broke across Rory's back. Rory punched that Shamrock square in his face. He went down like a tackle dummy. Rory buried a short, wicked left hook into the second guy's ribs, and he plopped into a seated position and started to gasp and whimper and wheeze, clutching broken ribs.

From behind, a third Shamrock took Rory's legs out from under him with a bat. Then Lefty waded in slicing the air before him with the antenna, the wicked lashing sound like wind screaming under a door.

Dermot stood from his gauntlet crouch, his bloodied clothes in ribbons, his arms legs and hands bleeding. As Lefty lifted his arm to lash Rory, Dermot grabbed it. Spun Lefty around. He punched the taller but skinnier Lefty flush in the nose. Bones crunched and blood burst. Lefty Hallahan staggered backward and Dermot bull-rushed him.

Two more Shamrocks went after Dermot as Rory pushed himself to his feet. He saw Lefty reaching for something in his jacket pocket.

He withdrew his hand when he saw the factory watchman swing open the big gate. Ankles's detective car raced into the entranceway, blocking egress. He jumped out of the car, gun drawn.

"Drop the antenna, tough guy," Ankles said to Lefty.

Lefty dropped it. The other Shamrocks froze.

"Go ahead, kid," Ankles said to Dermot. "Finish what you started. Fair one."

Dermot looked at Rory as if for permission. Rory nodded and then Dermot lifted his hands and charged at Lefty Hallahan. Lefty backed up in astonishment as Dermot winged wild punches. He caught a bloody Lefty in the temple and he went down to one knee like a clubbed calf. And then he scrambled to get away, but his Featherweights slipped on the smooth cobblestones and he fell on his face. Dermot kicked him in the ass.

"Get up, punk," Dermot said.

"No feet," Ankles said.

Dermot pulled Lefty by the hair to his feet. Lefty covered his head and face with his hands as Dermot punched him in the ribs. And as Lefty scrambled across the cobblestone a crude, handmade .22-caliber zip gun dropped out of his coat pocket. Lefty dove for it. But Ankles snatched it up as Dermot jumped on a cowering Lefty and battered his eyes and bloodied his nose and mouth.

"I deuce!" Lefty shouted. "I give up! No more! Please, Ankles, make him stop."

Ankles took out a pair of handcuffs and cuffed Lefty.

"That kid in Methodist was shot with a twenty-two, Lefty," Ankles said, holding the edge of the zip gun with a hankie. "My guess, this one. If he dies, which looks like he will, you're going away for m-u-r-d-e-r, baby. Some of these clowns are going as accomplices. But tell you what. If you get your ass kicked by a thirteen-year-old out here, you'll be wearing high heels inside for twenty-five to life, sweetie pie."

Ankles made the other Shamrocks lie down spreadeagle on the cobblestone courtyard as he walked to his detective car and radioed for a squad car and a paddy wagon.

Ankles then patted Rory down, still searching for the .38. He didn't find it.

"Take your dopey brother and scram," he said to Rory.

Rory shoved Dermot ahead of him, out the gates of the factory, then draped an arm over his shoulder as he walked him home.

"How many days was the old man out on that raft?" Dermot asked.

"Twenty-seven . . ."

"And he sank that kraut ship by himself?"

"Yep," Rory said, dabbing Dermot's bloody lip with a tissue, giving him another tissue to dab his bloodied hand.

"Our old man? Harry Maguire? *Pop*? You're sure?"

"Uh huh."

"Not bad, huh?" Dermot said, holding out his palm for five.

"Not bad at all," Rory said, slapping his bloody kid brother five on their way home and punching him in the arm.

28

Rory placed his first Bohack pay of seven dollars and fifty cents for a half week and about twelve bucks in tips on the kitchen table in front of his mother.

"You are one of the wise men," his mother said.

"I got Dermot a job packing bags at Bohack," Rory said. "Off the books, a buck an hour, but what the hell. Sometimes you even get tips."

"That's two wise men," said Tara. "Having him away from Lefty Hallahan is a better gift than I could have ever expected for Christmas."

Rory didn't tell her about the three bucks he kept for himself.

"I'll be gone most of the day," Rory said.

"Where you off to on your day off?" Harry asked, using just one crutch now as he entered the kitchen, growing a fraction steadier on his legs each day.

"I won't jinx it by saying, Pop."

Tara folded the money, put it into her apron pocket, tears welling in her eyes.

"Och, I'm being the lig," she said, thanked and kissed Rory and rushed into the bathroom and locked the door. He heard the faucet turn on.

"What's wrong with her?" Rory asked his father.

"Christmas blues, big guy," Harry said. "It's why I hate this holiday. Like Jimmy Cannon wrote once, 'This, not T.S. Eliot's April, is the cruelest month.' It makes bad times only worse. You give her twenty and she realizes she needs fifty just to pay all the bills. That's not counting a tree and presents for the little ones."

"Next year, Pop. Next year will be a good one."

Rory bought the *Daily News* and the *Journal-American* to read on the subway ride to the Port Authority in Manhattan, where he caught the Trailways bus to Elizabeth, New Jersey. The round-trip bus was two dollars and fifty cents and the tokens were fifteen cents each, which left him twenty cents for newspapers.

Rory read the stories about the San Diego Chargers clinching the AFL Western Division championship by beating the Denver Broncos 58–20 the day before. Rory figured the Chargers would probably beat the Boston Patriots in the AFL championship game in January.

The ride on the Trailways bus through the Lincoln Tunnel was smooth and fast with big cushioned seats and a bathroom. He didn't even have to go but Rory just wanted to see what a bathroom on a bus was like so he went in and washed his hands with the little towelettes they had in a rack. He looked in the mirror as he crossed state lines. Maybe it was the mop top, maybe it was turning fifteen, maybe it was losing his boyhood to an older woman, whatever it was, he thought he looked somehow older, like his mother did at work.

When he got to the Elizabeth bus station he was told he would have to walk about a mile to get to the address he'd written down. But he gave himself plenty of time, stopped and asked directions twice, once from a cop and once from a mailman, and found the Allstate Tower where the clock at the top said it was 11:10 A.M. A big fenced-in pine tree in the center of the Allstate Plaza was decorated with Christmas lights. Christmas carols echoed from outdoor speakers.

The old story in the *Daily News* said that Charles Pergola Jr. was a carbon copy of his father, just younger and thinner. The picture they ran of the Chairman and his son in happier days showed what he looked like. Rory had the face imprinted in his brain. But he would be about a dozen years older now.

He went into the lobby, looked around, a security guard asked him what he wanted. Rory said he wanted to talk to Mr. Pergola for a school report. The guard said he came down at 12:05 P.M. every day and ate the blue plate special at the Seven Seas diner across the street. Rory thanked the guard and leaned against a fence surrounding the big Christmas tree and read the rest of the New York newspapers as he waited. The forecast in the *Daily News* weather page said there could be a white Christmas. The snow predicted for Christmas Eve night might have a downside: it could put a damper on traveling and shopping.

The next time Rory checked the clock on the tower of the Allstate building it read 12:04. Rory became nervous. He paced. He thought of what to say. He thought he'd try to soft soap him at first, before letting him know who he was.

A minute later Charles Pergola Jr. walked out of the building, alone. The stocky man was dressed in a conservative gray suit, no hat, which was part of the Jack Kennedy legacy, his rugged face the same as it was in the old *Daily News* photo but his hair a steel gray.

Rory approached him, trying to get all the things he needed to say straight in his head.

"Mr. Pergola, you don't know me, but I'm a high school student doing a school report on the *Stephen O'Hara*," Rory said. "When I was doing research I found out you won the Navy Cross for bravery in the fight against the German *Stine*."

Charles Pergola Jr. seemed astonished that this kid knew about his World War II past.

"What did you say your name was?"

"I read that you spent almost a month at sea on a raft. . . ."

They stood in the icy-cold plaza, an American flag snapping from a pole above them, Christmas lights glowing in the big blue spruce.

"Actually, son, I won a medal but there were braver men than me on the *Stephen O'Hara* that day."

"Oh, yeah, like who?"

"Well, in particular there was a merchant marine named Harry Maguire. He was a true American hero."

"*Really?*"

"Yeah," said Pergola. "He's the guy you should talk to. I've tried to find him. I know he lives in Brooklyn somewhere. But he's not listed in the phonebook. He was what you call a wiper, a young guy low on the totem pole, working in the engine room. But that day on the *O'Hara*, this wiper, Harry Maguire, he rose to the occasion, above and beyond the call, I'll tell ya. He was strong as an ox and braver than a bull. He loaded shells single-handedly into the breech of a four-inch gun and fired at the *Stine*. And, by God, he sank her. I was badly wounded, and so was he."

"How did he get wounded?"

"Shrapnel tore into his skull," Pergola said. "Then we set adrift at sea . . . listen, son, I was just going to grab a bite to eat, want to join me?"

Rory had no money to chip in so he shook his head and said, "No thanks."

"Well, Harry Maguire helped me overboard, onto a raft. Luckily there was a medic aboard. He kept most of us alive. We rationed food and water to six ounces per man per day. Harry Maguire bathed his and my wounds in salt water every day. But a week after we went adrift, a man named Gene Davies, a second cook and baker, died of his wounds. We buried him at sea. Two days later a man named Romero Napoli, a steward's utility man, died. We buried him in a glorious sunset, into heaven itself. His only possession was a wedding ring from a wife who'd died six years earlier. Two weeks after we set adrift Harry Maguire took a turn for the worse. The medic operated without anesthesia, removing large hunks of shell from his skull and shoulder. Two days after that, we saw green flares from an unseen ship. I fired what you call a Very pistol. But they never found us. On our twenty-seventh day on the raft, we got picked up by a British ship. Good thing, too, because Harry Maguire almost didn't make it."

Rory didn't know this part of the story. His heart thumped. He licked his dry lips and said, "What happened to him?"

"Well, they put a plate in his head," he said. "He was hospitalized for almost three months."

"How come Harry Maguire didn't get any medals? Didn't get any parades?"

"Because he wasn't in the U.S. Navy, son," Charles Pergola Jr. said. "Merchant marines just weren't treated the same. Totally unfair . . . Listen kid, I'm freezing my bunions off out here. How about I buy you lunch?"

"Actually what I want to say won't take long."

"Oh, I thought you wanted to ask me a list of questions."

"Just one more. Then I have to catch a bus back to the City."

"Sure. Go ahead."

"Will you help my father?"

"Who's your father? He an Allstate client?"

"No. My father is Harry Maguire."

Charles Pergola Jr. stared at Rory for a long flabbergasted moment, his ears like little red stop signs in the late-December cold. Rory showed him his Brooklyn Public Library Card as ID and his father's name on the front page of the sheaf of papers he had brought along with him.

"Ohmigod," Charles Pergola Jr. said. "Why the ruse, son?"

"I wanted to see where you stood on my father first," Rory said. "I tried calling your office. But your secretary wouldn't put me through and—"

"That was *you?* She told me about some kid from Brooklyn. What's it all about?"

Rory handed him his stack of mimeographed papers, detailing Harry Maguire's fight with the bureaucracy, and the judgments against him. He had all the medical paperwork saying that Harry Maguire needed several operations, including a spinal fusion, to correct the damage done in the fall but that he had no coverage because he was accused of being drunk when he fell. He also gave him a copy of his essay, "You're Harry Maguire."

"His fall can probably be traced to the war injury," Charles Pergola Jr. said. "I'd bet my house on it."

Rory told him right now his father wasn't even getting unemployment anymore. That they'd reached the end of the road.

"That's why I need your help."

"What can I do? I'm not a rich man, but I'd be glad to write him a personal check to help him through a tough time."

Rory stared at him, shaking his head. "My father doesn't accept charity," Rory said. "He never took the home relief or the welfare. He just wants what's rightfully coming to him. His disability, his workmen's comp, and medical coverage so he can get the operation so he can go get off disability and off workmen's comp and go back to work. Like a man. That's all he wants. To get better and his pothole filler's job back."

Charles Pergola Jr. looked at Rory and swallowed hard.

"What can I do?"

"I figured maybe you could call your father, the Chairman," said Rory. "He cuts through red tape like Jim Brown running up the middle."

"My *father?*" Charles Pergola Jr. said, looking defeated. "I haven't spoken to my father in almost a dozen years. I'm a registered *Republican,* for goodness sakes. We don't exchange holiday cards. No communication. Not since we had a falling-out back in . . ."

"I know, nineteen fifty-two. Over politics. How stupid is that?"

The middle-aged man looked at the teenager and nodded. "It is pretty stupid, I admit. But, ya know, it's just one of those things. Both of us too stubborn to ever reach out. I have two children he's never even met."

"That's sad," Rory said. "And *mean.*"

Charles Pergola Jr. looked at Rory, a little annoyed at being lectured by a kid.

"You have no idea, son, how *mean* my father can be—"

"Oh, yes I do. He threw me out of his club the other day—"

"You mean you went there? You actually had the guts to walk in there and ask him? Congressmen and senators and presidents are afraid of him."

"Well, I kind of faked my way in. . . ."

"You must have the same onions as your dad. So, how'd my dad look? Healthwise?"

"Better than mine, put it that way."

Charles Pergola Jr. looked both ways, as Johnny Mathis sang "Winter Wonderland" over the speakers. And then the insurance executive looked at his watch, shuffled through the papers in his hands, and said, "Like I said, sorry, son, there's like nothing *I* can do. I sure would like to send your dad a small gift . . . loan . . . whatever."

"Believe me, he'd just send it back or tear it up."

The two of them stood in silence for another long, cold minute.

Then Charles Pergola Jr. said. "Tell Harry I said merry Christmas, will you?"

"Sure," Rory said. "But you know what?"

"What?"

"It just isn't right. It isn't right that you get a big shiny medal. A ceremony. A war hero's pension and medical coverage for life, which you deserve, don't get me wrong. I might still be a kid and I don't know as much as I should yet, but I do know it's wrong that you get all that and my pop, who saved your life and the lives of the other guys, doesn't get any of it. Doesn't get squat. That's just not right, man."

"Yeah, I agree with you, son. But one of the reasons I got out of politics is because I thought it was filled with double standards and hypocrisy and unfairness. I don't make the rules. I really wish there was something I could do but I have absolutely no influence on my father. In fact, I probably have less than anyone else alive."

"You know what, then?" Rory said. "I feel better that I came out here. Because maybe my family can't afford a Christmas tree or a portable record player, a Tiny Tears doll or a set of Fanner Fifties to put under it for my little brothers and sisters. But the Maguires have something the Pergolas don't have. We have a *family*. A little hard-up and screwed-up, sure, like a lot of others. But at least we *love* each other, man. No matter what. We'd never bust up over something stupid like *politics*. So when I think about it, I actually feel more sorry for you and your father than I do for my family. Like my father says, we might be broke, but we got each other and that makes us filthy rich with life."

Charles Pergola Jr. just stared at Rory, speechless, as Elvis Presley sang "Silent Night" from the outdoor speakers of the building. The lights on the big tree in front of Allstate reflected like emeralds and rubies in the businessman's eyes. The American flag whipped above them. Puffs of frozen vapor leaked from Charles Pergola Jr.'s nose and mouth as he twisted the sheaf of papers in his hands into a tight paper flute.

"I really am sorry, kid," Charles Pergola Jr. said.

"Merry Christmas," Rory said and walked off in the direction of the bus depot to head back home to New York.

When the sun went down Rory waited across the street from Mayflower Laundry, wearing his ski mask and his reversible ski jacket turned to the blue side and his work boots and gloves. He watched the washerwomen leave for the holiday. And then all the truckers left. Riley was the last one to leave, putting a padlock on the front gate.

As he walked to his new Plymouth parked in the parking lot, Rory walked up behind him. He tapped Riley on the shoulder. Riley turned, startled, and said, "Who is it?"

Rory never hit anyone harder in his life. He felt his right fist flatten Riley's nose like a bathtub stopper. The pile drive of the punch kept traveling until Rory was sure it took out at least three of Riley's front teeth. Riley fell to his knees, his face a bloody platter of terror. Then he collapsed onto his back, arms and legs spread like Ingemar Johanssen's after

Patterson knocked him out in the second fight. Rory took three steps back. And then he charged and booted the man who had tried to dishonor his mother square in the place that would make him think twice before he dishonored anyone else's mother again.

Riley cried like a girl.

"Please . . . don't hurt me no more," he said, whimpering and curling into a fetal ball. "I have a wife and kids . . . Please . . . *Who* are you? And *why* are you doing this to me? *Why . . . ?*"

Rory bent over the grown man, put his exposed lips close to Riley's ear, and whispered, "Incompatible, *mother*fucker."

29

Tuesday, Christmas Eve

On the morning of Christmas Eve, Tara sipped tea at the kitchen table with Harry and Rory. Dermot was already at work, bagging groceries, hoping to earn enough to buy a cheap tree.

Rory felt a gnawing guilt of wasting three dollars on the trip to New Jersey.

"A guy in Ryan's told me about an assembly-line job opening up right after the New Year," Harry said. "I'm gonna take it."

Rory asked, "What about the operations you need?"

"They'll have to wait," Harry said. "I promise you, I promise this family, here and now, there will never be another Christmas like this one again. I can stand now, walk a bit. And I still have two good hands and I intend to put them to work."

"Pop, this Christmas is gonna be okay," Rory said. "Remember what you told me the other night about how rich we really are?"

Harry nodded.

Rory finished his tea, pulled on his father's peacoat. The younger kids came into the kitchen to kiss Rory good-bye and he handed out three penny Tootsie Rolls he'd bought for them the day before in Mr. B's.

He rolled the ski mask up into a watch cap, pulled it on, and jammed his hands in his gloves and went to work. If the tips were any good today he figured he'd get his mother an Evening in Paris gift set and his father an Old Spice shaving set from Whalen's Drugs and cap pistols for Connor and a 45 single of "She's a Fool" by Leslie Gore for Caitlin, and some kind of made-in-Japan stuffed animal for Bridget in the last-minute Fifth Avenue sales.

He saw Dermot working the Bohack checkout counter, bagging groceries, and waved. Then Rory ground meat and washed platters, and sliced cold cuts, and delivered orders through the cold and overcast day. Ankles continued to tail him, like a motorized shadow. On one delivery he pulled Rory over to tell him that the kid in the Methodist had just died from his gunshot wound. And that ballistics proved that Lefty Hallahan's zip gun was the murder weapon. And so he wouldn't be seeing him again.

Rory felt grieved and sad for the dead kid's parents having to bury their son for Christmas. He wondered about Lefty, too, sitting in a cell. Maybe he'd never get out.

"If you have Sal's rod, now's the time to give it up before you wind up rooming with Lefty," Ankles said.

Rory told him for the thousandth time that he didn't have Sal's gun, and delivered the rest of his orders.

A little before dark the forecasted snow began to fall out of the big Brooklyn sky. Rory thought: *Everybody in New York must be singing "White Christmas" right now, sounding like Bing Crosby. Even the women. Except the parents of that kid who was shot to death. And the Kennedy family, who was having its first Christmas without Jack.*

Still, Rory loved watching the snow gather on the Christmas trees that were being hawked at half price along the avenue. He watched the snow collect on the shoulders and caps of a group of Methodist church carolers who strolled the avenue holding corny songbooks.

When Rory returned from his last orders of the day he passed Freedom Meats and slowed when he saw Sal and Tony behind the counter. Carol and her parents stood on the other side of the counter. Carol glanced out the window and saw Rory. She was dressed in the gorgeous brown velour outfit she'd shown him in the window of Saks. The outfit that Babe had bought for her. She half smiled at Rory. He pedaled off. The snow fell heavier, glazing the streets, glittering white polka dots against the deepening night.

As he parked and locked the bike outside of Bohack's, Rory heard a commotion at the front door. A woman screamed. Others gasped. A man yelled, "Stop him!"

Rory spun.

A man wearing a ski mask raced out of Bohack.

Clutching a big paper bag under his arm. A stack of bound bills fell from the bag.

In his other hand the masked man held a pistol.

The man wore heavy work boots and a hooded ski jacket.

He paused when he saw Rory. For just one moment. His eyes in the ski mask were dark and frightened.

And just then the Wells Fargo armored car rolled to the curb to collect the day's profits. As if the robber knew to rob the store just before the truck arrived.

"Holy crap," Rory said.

The masked gunman sprinted down the avenue. Just as Ankles, who had again been tailing Rory, skidded to the curb, leaving swerving ruts in the fresh snow. Ankles parked at a crazy angle, barking into his hand radio and flinging open his door. He jumped out. Gun drawn. And started chasing the robber down Seventh Avenue. Carolers sang. Snow fell. Shoppers lugged shopping carts and bags of gifts and Christmas trees.

The gunman kept slipping and sliding in the falling snow. Ankles gained on him in his ugly, round rubber ripple-soled shoes.

"Stop! Freeze, or I'll kill ya!"

The robber kept running. Ankles stopped to aim but two drunks staggered out of Fitzgerald's tavern, holding each other up and singing "Rudolph, da red-nosed reindeer." Rory duckwalked along the avenue, in the gutter, shielded by the parked cars at the curb. *I have to see the end of this,* he thought. *Like a newspaperman would. Like Jimmy Cannon would have done when he was fifteen. . . .*

When the armed robber zoomed across Eighth Street, Ankles had a clear aim. "I'll shoot if you don't stop!"

The robber kept running.

Ankles fired. The bullet hit the robber in the left thigh. Dropping him. He pushed himself to his feet and kept going, falling and limping, dragging his ruined leg that left a crimson trail in the linen-white snow.

"Drop that goddamned gun!"

The robber spun and lurched through the front door of Freedom Meats and collapsed face first onto the sawdust-covered floor. Blood ran from his wound.

Rory stood on the sidewalk outside, snow falling around him, looking for telling details like the ones Jimmy Cannon used to make his columns explode to life. He saw Carol scream and cover her mouth with a soft, black gloved hand. He saw Mrs. Sturgis fall into her astonished husband's arms. He saw Sal race around the showcase toward the fallen robber, his face a frozen howl.

He saw Ankles approach the robber with his gun aimed in two hands.

He saw Ankles step on the robber's gun hand. Saw him crush the bandit's thick hairy wrist with his slushy heel. Saw the big cop pry the gun out of the bad guy's gloved fingers. Saw Ankles wrap the pistol in his yellowed hankie. Then Rory saw Ankles handcuff the robber behind his back. Then he watched Ankles turn the robber onto his back and yank the mask off his face.

"I'm ... so ... sorry ... Dad ..." Babe said, sobbing.

Sal fell to his knees and cradled his son.

"Get away from him," Ankles said.

"He's my son."

"He's a turd," Ankles said.

Rory kept watching Babe, feeling sort of sorry for him, as he babbled to his father. "I knew you needed money, Pop, and I wanted to help but you wouldn't let me help. So I decided to go take the money Bohack was stealing from you ..."

Sal said, "Oh, Jesus ..." And sat on the floor next to his son, whose boots were covered in blood and sawdust.

An ambulance from Methodist hospital and a squad car pulled up, lights and sirens screaming and flaring. The uniformed cops and ambulance attendants tended to Babe.

Ankles walked to Rory.

"I owe you an apology, kid," Ankles said.

"It's okay."

"No," Ankles said. "No, it's not okay. First, your old man got jobbed and then I jobbed you. That ain't okay. I am very, very sorry. But sorry don't make it okay."

Carol stood with her parents listening to what Ankles said to Rory. She glanced down at Babe.

"I'm sorry, Carol," Babe said. "If you still love me, like you say, please forgive me. ..."

Carol said nothing. She turned away from Babe. Then she looked at Rory with pleading eyes. Rory stared her right in the eyes, this woman to whom he'd surrendered his boyhood, and then he walked off into the snow to go back to work.

* * *

Carol caught up with him at Seventh Street, clutching his arm in the falling snow. He saw his pals from Eleventh Street hurrying toward Freedom Meats to see the arrest. They paused to watch Carol and Rory.

Carol touched Rory's arm. "Rory . . ."

"I'm working."

"Listen, I just wanted to apologize. . . ."

He watched virgin snowflakes the size of Holy Communion land on her black beret and her long blond hair, watched them speckle and whiten her long black leather coat that covered the Saks suit that Babe had bought her. He stared deep into her big blue eyes that reflected bubbling Christmas lights, and watched those Ipana teeth broaden into a perfect smile.

Gorgeous.

She reached for his hand. He pulled it away and jammed it in his father's peacoat pocket. As his pals watched.

"Merry Christmas, Carol," Rory said and walked off to work, leaving her standing alone in the falling snow.

30

At home after work, Rory and Dermot took two quick baths and pooled their day's wages into a Christmas kitty—thirteen dollars and fifty cents.

They dressed, preparing to go down Fifth Avenue to buy some toys and the gift sets for their mother and father and a one-dollar tree to put the gifts under.

Tara had done wonders with the apartment, trimming it with garland from the basement boxes, setting up the wooden soldiers, illuminated angels, Frosty and Santas, giving the apartment a real feel of Christmas. Empty stockings hung from the living room mantel, bearing the stitched names of each Maguire kid. All the curtains between the rooms had been tied back so that Bing Crosby singing "White Christmas" on the old Philco radio could be heard throughout the apartment.

Tara had scoured the floors with ammonia and pine that would scare all the roaches away at least until the morning.

Harry sat at the kitchen table, face shaved clean, wearing a clean flannel shirt, trying his best to get into the Christmas spirit. He had just one crutch leaning against the table. But Rory noticed that Harry was gripping his baseball, which meant deep inside he was holding on for dear life to his crumbling world. Rory could see shame and failure clouding the squinty eyes, a good man hurt bad and done wrong at the worst time of year. But Rory knew Harry Maguire was a fighter. Rory knew that somehow, for his family, he'd find a way to get all the way back on his feet and rally back in the New Year. Bridget came to Harry and outstretched her arms. "Up, Daddy."

Rory knew how much pain was involved in just sitting his daughter on his knee. But he did it and sang along with Bing Crosby. After all, Harry Maguire had lived through much worse.

"C'mon, lamebrain, let's go," Rory said, tossing Dermot his jacket and pulling on his own peacoat. Now Perry Como was singing "It's Beginning to Look a Lot Like Christmas" on the radio.

"We're going to get a tree," Dermot announced.

The kids cheered.

Then a loud knock came on the door.

The Maguires looked at each other. The last time a knock came that heavy on the door it was Ankles accusing Rory or stealing Sal's gun.

"Anybody expecting anybody?" Rory asked.

"Santa Claus," said Bridget.

"He comes down a chimney, dummy," Connor said.

"Don't call your sister dummy, you," Tara said. "Or Santa will bring you a lump of coal and a bar of soap to wash out your trap."

"Answer the door, big guy," Harry said.

Rory pulled open the door. Just a crack. The four-inch space filled with pine needles. He stepped back and pulled it wider. The whole door was now filled with pine branches, dripping with freshly fallen snow. Dermot reached into the middle of the Christmas tree and yanked it through the door as the dumbstruck Maguires watched the big beautiful full spruce rise to the cracked ceiling.

Standing in the doorway was the Chairman.

He was dressed in a cashmere coat and trademark fedora, unlit cigar in his mouth, his arm slung over the shoulder of his son, Charles Pergola Jr., who held a big red sack in his right hand, lumpy with gifts.

Rory gaped at the two men in wordless bewilderment. Tara and Harry stared in disbelief.

"You gonna be as ungracious as I was to you, kid?" the Chairman said. "Or you gonna invite an old machine hack and his son in on Christmas Eve?"

"Come in, come in, come in," said Tara, lifting Bridget from Harry's lap. "Have a cup of tea."

"How about something a little stronger?" the Chairman said, plunking a bottle of John Jameson Irish whiskey on the Formica table.

Tara held up four glasses from the dish rack to the overhead light to be sure they were clean and placed the cleanest one in front of the Chairman. The boss of Brooklyn cracked the whiskey bottle and poured four shots.

Charlie Pergola Jr. leaned into Harry, and gripped each of his forearms. "Merry Christmas, Harry," he said. "It's been, what, twenty years?"

"Twenty-one, Charlie," Harry said, still confused, looking to a poker-faced Rory for explanation. "But who's counting? So, how ya doing?"

"Well, I'm alive—thanks to you," Charles Jr. said to Harry as the Chairman took a slug of whiskey and winked at a nervous Tara, who was holding Bridget on her hip.

"So what brings you here?" Harry asked, clinking his glass against the Chairman's and Charles Jr.'s, and Tara's. She splashed a touch of her Irish whiskey into her cup of tea, and sipped.

"Well," Charles Jr. said, grimacing after swallowing the

Irish. "I had a visitor yesterday. He brought me a stack of papers about a real unsung hero. . . ."

"Oh, *can* it, for Chrissakes, Charlie," Harry said, waving at him. "Load of crapola. What gives? Why you here?"

"Well, it isn't crapola in my eyes, Harry," Charles Jr. said, pulling out the sheaf of paperwork Rory had given him. "Or in the eyes of that son of yours over there. He showed me all this stuff you've gone through, Harry. I read all the paperwork. The medical reports. The fight with the bureaucracy. I read the essay that kid wrote about his old man called "You're Harry Maguire," and I knew that you were being shafted. I also knew, like your kid pointed out to me, that the only guy around who could get it straightened out was my old man . . ."

"Hey," Harry said, "we don't take handouts in this house. . . ."

"Shut up and listen, you stubborn old salt," the Chairman said. "And so then I got a knock on my door last night like the one you just got. It was this big lug. My only son I hadn't seen or spoken to in a dozen years. He had my two grandkids I'd never met in my life standing on either side of him. He walked in, told me I was an old fool. I told him he was a young dunce. We hugged. And I didn't let go of him for ten straight minutes. Then I sat my grandkids on my lap for the very first time and realized how much of my life I'd wasted living behind a curtain playing the Wizard of Oz, like your kid said, and so . . ."

" . . . and so I told him about the visit I had from Rory," Charles Jr. said.

Harry glared at Rory, tightened his lips, and shook a fist. Rory shrugged.

"Like the visit I had from this same little ballbuster a few days before that," the Chairman said. "Only I was too full of myself and old bitterness and you know what else to listen to the kid. . . ."

Charles Jr. said, "Then I showed him your paperwork, Harry . . . and the kid's essay, written Jimmy Cannon style . . ."

"You got screwed up and down and sideways and backward," the Chairman said. "Then I checked your work, medical, and war history, to make sure you were legit. My son told me all about what happened on the *Stephen O'Hara*. For years after he came home he would never talk about it. . . ."

"The memories were too—" Charles Jr. didn't finish the sentence.

"I never seen any man get so jobbed in my life, Democrat or Republican," said the Chairman.

"I'm neither," Harry said, swirling his whiskey.

"That's probably why," the Chairman said. "But anyway, I made a few phone calls to try to straighten out what everyone did you wrong. I got your disability and workmen's comp approved. . . ."

"Sweet mother of Jesus on the Holy Cross of Calvary," Tara said. "Please don't be telling us this if this is some sort of trick. After Jack Kennedy, Our Jack, my broken heart just won't stand it."

The Chairman reached into his inside coat pocket and took out a white envelope, thick with cash.

"There's about twenty-eight hundred bucks retroactive here," the Chairman said. "Buy the missus a hat. But get it straight, Maguire. This ain't a gift, a handout, or a favor. You're only getting to the dime what's coming to you. Plus, you'll be getting two checks a month until after you recuperate from your operations in a military hospital, all of which are all arranged. After that, as a disabled state worker, you'll also be getting full medical coverage for you and your family. You're also on top of the list for a four-bedroom in the new government-subsidized houses that are going up on Ninth Street and Fifth Avenue, just in case you think you could use a little more room. I think your condition requires an elevator building. And when you get back on your feet, Maguire, and you're up to it, drop down the Ben Franklin Club. I'm looking for a good honest man—even a damned unregistered one—to fill a foreman's job on the local DOT pothole crew. Last guy I had turned out to be a liar who maligned the reputation of a true American hero. A hero I'm gonna tell the Pentagon has a few medals coming to him. Oh, and seeing it's Christmas Eve, and the banks are closed, I hope you don't mind that I took the liberty of bringing you your retroactive money in cash."

He slapped the envelope into Harry's left hand. He held out his right hand to shake. Rory watched Harry look at the Chairman's hand and in that instant he saw the clouds of shame vanish from his father's eyes. He also saw his father let loose of the old scuffed baseball. Rory watched the ball drop and roll across the worn linoleum floor. Harry gripped the Chairman's hand.

"Merry Christmas, Harry," the Chairman said, leaning close to Harry's ear. "And thanks for saving the life of my son."

Harry just nodded.

Nobody asked me, but, Rory thought, *sometimes words are loudest when they're left unspoken.*

Harry riffled the cash, took a twenty dollar bill out for himself, and handed the envelope to Tara. She blessed herself first and then took the envelope in a trembling hand.

Rory looked at Charles Jr., who reached into the big red sack.

"Sorry, Santa got caught in the snowstorm and didn't have time to wrap this stuff, kids," Charles Jr. said, pulling a Tiny Tears for Bridget, who squealed a thank-you. He took out a portable record player and a stack of 45s for Caitlin and she accepted the gift as if she were receiving a Blessed Sacrament. Connor grabbed his Fanner Fifties from Charles Jr., thanked him, and then raced through the house firing red repeater caps.

Charles Jr. gave Dermot a $100 gift certificate to Belmont's and said, "I used to shop there once upon a time."

Dermot looked at Rory in disbelief, and tried to hide his hand where a bandage covered his punk test.

Then the Chairman stood up and reached into the bag and pulled out a bottle of Chanel No. 5 for Tara. He gave Harry a wallet to keep his money in. And then he reached all the way to the bottom and removed a brand-new, never-before-used Royal typewriter.

"Krauss tells me you wanna write for newspapers, kid," the Chairman said, handing it to Rory. "Here, go write me a Pulitzer Prize."

Rory ran his fingers over brass-edged keys that offset the gleaming baked-black-enamel finish. He clutched the type-writer like it was the passport to his future.

Tara gulped her whiskey tea, wiped one eye with the heel of her hand, and said, "How do we ever thank you, Mr. Pergola?"

Rory watched Harry Maguire and Charles Pergola Jr. sit off in a corner all alone. They shook hands and didn't let go as they whispered into one another's ears. The things they said, the memories they shared, didn't belong to anyone else but to those who had been to hell together and gotten out alive.

"Thank me?" the Chairman said to Rory's mother. "You nuts, lady? First your husband saved my son's life in World War II. Then when I was fool enough to lose him in an idiotic fight over politics, your son appears from the mist and brings my family back into my life. I'm the one who got the gift here, lady. Me, I'm the one who got the Christmas miracle. Thanks to the Maguire family. So thank you all, and merry Christmas. Now you'll have to excuse me, I'm going home to play with my grandkids until they pass out. And then I am going to get royally stewed with my son."

The Chairman and his son moved toward the door. On the way out the Chairman paused to straighten the photo of John Fitzgerald Kennedy that had been tilted by the Christmas tree.

And then as fast as they arrived, the Chairman and his son were gone, clattering down the tenement steps into the snowy night.

The three youngest Maguire kids played with their new gifts in the living room.

Rory, Dermot, and their mother and father sat at the kitchen table for a long silent time. From the living room Nat King Cole came on Caitlin's new record player singing "The Christmas Song."

Rory smiled. Dermot snickered. Tara gulped the last of her whiskey tea and let out a howl and said, "Thank you, St. Anthony!"

Then Harry Maguire stood up on his lone crutch.

Tara stood blinking, clutching the money, half-frozen in disbelief. Harry hopped around her on the crutch. Then he handed the crutch to Rory, who stood near the photos of Jack Kennedy, the Pope, and the Sacred Heart.

"Tara," Harry said, finding his balance, his voice low and modest. "Will you dance with me?"

And as the younger kids decorated the tree in the parlor and the snow fell outside the rattling kitchen windows, Harry Maguire grimaced in pain, and then took Tara Maguire by one hand and looped his other arm around her waist and as Nat Cole sang about chestnuts roasting on an open fire, Rory Maguire punched his kid brother Dermot in the arm as he watched his father dance with his mother on the night before Christmas of nineteen hundred and sixty-three. . . .

Visit
❖ **Pocket Books** ❖
online at

....

www.SimonSays.com

....

Keep up on the latest new
releases from your favorite
authors, as well as author
appearances, news, chats,
special offers and more.

SIMON & SCHUSTER
A **VIACOM** COMPANY
www.SimonSays.com

Pocket
Books

2381-01